CHARMING COLTON

SURRENDER, BOOK EIGHT

BECCA JAMESON

Cover Artist: Scott Carpenter

❀ Created with Vellum

ACKNOWLEDGMENTS

Once again I have to thank the people who spent so much time helping me brainstorm! Susan and Rebecca—you guys are the best! And to all the fans of this series who are enjoying it, I love you all! Your kind words mean the world to me.

CHAPTER 1

Colton

Need your help.

I stare at the text I just sent, hoping the recipient will realize who it's coming from.

Anything. Anytime. You know that.

I release the breath I've been holding and send another text.

Are you alone? Can you talk?

Less than a minute later, my phone rings and I connect to the call as I lean back against my sofa. "Hey, thanks for taking my call so quickly."

"You know you don't have to ask. I'm indebted to you for life." Davis chuckles.

"You are *not* indebted to me. Stop that nonsense."

Davis's voice is serious when he speaks again. "I'm glad you called anyway. I figured one day I would be able to repay you. I assume that day has come."

"Yes." It's been eight months since I last saw Davis, the day after helping him rescue his girlfriend, Britney, from a human trafficker. The day after *he* helped *me* catch the guy. Too bad even though that guy is dead, he wasn't the end of the line. "This is going to come straight out of left field, but do you know a woman named Evelyn Dean?"

Davis's breath hitches slightly. The average person wouldn't have noticed it, but I'm not average. I'm an undercover cop trained to notice a lot of things. And what I notice next is that Davis hasn't answered my question.

I smile. "Your silence speaks volumes, so no need to answer that question. Let me tell you why I know her." I close my eyes for a moment to remind myself that he doesn't need me to tell him she's damn sexy. That she has long wavy brown hair. Or that she's petite. Or that she looks a lot like Hudson's girlfriend Britney.

"Please tell me she's not the next human-trafficking victim."

I sigh and run a hand over my head. "I suspect she is. Yes."

"Fuck. Tell me what you know."

The only reason I would share information about this case with anyone alive is because I need Davis's help, and I trust him implicitly. He works for Black Blade Protection. Keeping people's secrets is part of his job. "We received an anonymous tip, so I've been keeping tabs on her. Today she went to lunch with a friend, someone you also know, no doubt. Her name is Leah. I sat in the booth next to them. If they hadn't happened to mention your name in conversation, I never would have made the connection. Seriously, I'm still unnerved by the coincidence."

"She was talking about me?" Davis's voice is strained.

"Don't worry. All good things."

"Do you know where I know her from then?"

"Yes." No sense pretending otherwise. This is why I'm calling. "A club called Surrender."

Davis says nothing.

I'm not surprised. I looked up the club. It's a private BDSM club. I'm certain the members do not kiss and tell. I hadn't known Davis was a member.

"Don't get the wrong idea. Evelyn and her friend were speaking in hushed voices. No one else would have heard them. I was working hard to catch as much of their conversation as I could. I'm trained to do so. They never mentioned the club by name. I already knew the name of the club because I've been keeping an eye on Evelyn for a few weeks. I've seen her come and go from Surrender."

"You're really worried about her."

"Of course. I'm also aware that she's dating another member of the club. Owen Karplus. Tall guy. Slender. Fortyish. Receding hairline, but he keeps it cut close to the scalp."

Davis groans. "I know him too. I didn't know his last name, but a guy by that description named Owen is a newer member of the club, and I've seen him with Eve. Do you think he's a suspect?"

"Not necessarily. I have no idea. I've been keeping tabs on him too though, just in case."

"Eve certainly looks a lot like Britney. Fits the profile." Davis's voice is stiff with concern.

"Exactly. I assume she fits it even more when she's not dressed for business in tight skirts, blouses, and heels, with perfect hair and makeup. Under all that, I bet she's young and innocent-looking."

Davis draws in a breath. "She is."

I hesitate. How the fuck does he know that? "Have you

dated her?" I ask before I can stop myself. "Shit. Don't answer that. It's none of my business. Sorry."

He chuckles. "No. It's fine. I have not dated her."

Okay... Then how do you know what she looks like without makeup? I don't ask. "Anyway, Owen owns a bar near the club. I've seen her come and go from there a few times, and she meets him for coffee."

"So you're trailing a man you think is the seller and a woman you think could be the victim."

"Perhaps. No particular reason to suspect Owen yet. Just because she's seeing him doesn't mean he plans to kidnap her. And..."

"What else?"

"I think someone is following her."

"Fuck."

"Yes."

"Can't your boss assign more guys to this? Sounds like you need more eyes." Davis asks.

"Not yet. I don't have enough evidence."

"Jesus. I'll talk to my boss, Blade. I'm sure he'll be willing to help out. Is that why you called?"

"No. I'm still collecting information. So far all I know is that Evelyn could be a target, someone might be following her, and she's been seeing Owen lately. He could be grooming her, or it could be a coincidence."

"Damn. I don't know Owen well enough to tell you anything about him."

"How well do you know Evelyn?"

"I've known her since I moved here a year ago. We're acquaintances. How much do you know about Surrender?"

I sigh. "Not enough. *That's* what I'm calling about. Hoping you can get me into the club. That would help me tremendously. It would also help if the owner was aware of my presence. Do you know the owner?"

Davis draws in a breath. "Yes. I can introduce you. That's not a problem. Like I said, I'll do anything. And Roman wouldn't want anything to be happening in his club that involved trafficking. In fact, I'll be calling him the very second we hang up."

"Could you arrange a meeting for me? Sometime when the club isn't open perhaps? It would make my job easier if I speak to Roman first."

"Yes."

I hear the hesitation in his voice. "Am I overstepping?"

"Not at all. I just need to speak to Britney about this, and a few other people. It's not simple. I'm not the only member you know. People are very private about their membership at Surrender. It helps that you're in law enforcement and I know you'll be discreet, but it's still a big deal. I wouldn't want anyone to be blindsided."

"Understood." I wonder who else he thinks I know from Surrender. Interesting. "How is Britney?" I should have asked that first. When I last saw the two of them, they were in a fresh relationship. I thought they fit together amazingly, but that was eight months ago. Anything could have happened since then. Apparently, they're still together.

"She's doing well."

"Did she go back to working at the animal shelter?" I hope she's recovered from the trauma of nearly being sold into human trafficking.

"Yes. She loves it there, and Cindy was glad to have her back."

I freeze for a moment as it occurs to me that Cindy and her husband, Hudson, are people I met through Davis and Britney. They are all close friends. I wonder if the two of them are the other members of Surrender I would know. Have to be.

A dog barks in the background, or maybe a puppy, making me smile. "I guess Britney conned you into getting a pet."

Davis's voice is muffled. "Sh sh sh. Come 'ere. That's a boy. You'll wake up your mama with that yelping." And then his voice is direct again. "Sorry about that. Charlie is a handful."

I glance at my watch and frown. It's the middle of the afternoon. "Britney's asleep? Is she sick?"

There's a slight hesitation before Davis responds. "Nope. She's fine." He gives me no other detail. "Listen, let me talk to Roman and get back to you. I'm sure time is of the essence, so I'll call him right now. Maybe I can arrange for you to meet with him in the morning. Would that work?"

"That would be perfect. Thank you."

"But wait. I have to ask. I'm confused. I still don't understand why Leah and Eve were discussing me."

I chuckle. "Mostly because they think you're...let's see... what did they say exactly?...one of the hottest Daddies at the club."

Davis sucks in a sharp breath.

I wonder if he's stressing over the fact that Evelyn and Leah weren't discreet enough to keep someone from hearing their conversation or if he's embarrassed that I know a bit more about him than he'd like.

"Let me quote the exact words that caused your name to come up. 'Owen's nice and handsome enough and all, but he's no Davis Marcum.' Those were Leah's words."

"Lord. I'm going to have a complex."

I chuckle. "Maybe don't let that go to your head."

"Too late," he responds, his voice lighter. "Okay, I'll call you as soon as I have something set up."

"Thanks, man. Talk to you later."

After ending the call, I continue to sit on the sofa, staring into the empty space that is my actual home. My condo. A place I sometimes see for a few weeks at a time before disappearing undercover somewhere. At the moment, I'm not in a deep cover. I'm still working my ass off trying to track down whoever Britney's true seller was. Her boss was killed in the sting, but he wasn't the end of the line. He'd been working for someone else. It's highly probable he hadn't even known who he worked for.

My job is to find out.

My mind is still reeling from today's pile of information. First, the shock of hearing Davis's name whispered from the lips of my suspected next victim. The coincidence still makes me shudder. I have done as much research on Surrender as I can, but it's a private club. Not much information is publicly available. That's why I called Davis.

I've never been to a BDSM club, but I'm not judgmental. I don't care a bit that Davis, and apparently Britney, belong to a fetish club. I don't care that Evelyn Dean does either. However, if I'm going to go undercover inside the club to observe Evelyn's interactions with the man she's been dating, I need to fit in.

I sigh and run a hand down my face. I've done a lot of things to prepare for an undercover job, but posing as a Dom has never been one of them.

Perhaps Davis isn't just a Dom. Evelyn called him a Daddy. I have no idea if she used the word as a simple term of endearment or if Davis is specifically the sort of Dom who takes on a Daddy role.

Before calling him, I did a bit of research on that topic too. Interesting kink. When I think back to his interactions with Britney, I can see where he might be a Dom. I can picture Britney as submissive. But is he her Daddy? And what the hell does that exactly mean?

CHAPTER 2

Evelyn

"What do you think?" I ask Leah as I spin around in a circle, admiring my newest dress in the full-length mirror behind my closet door. I'm grinning, so it's not like Leah has the option of telling me she hates it. Then again, this is Leah I'm talking about. She may be submissive, but she's not a little and refuses to even consider dabbling in that side of the fetish world no matter how many times I try to talk her into it.

Leah rolls her eyes and flops back onto my bed dramatically, her long brown curls fanning out all over the comforter. "No matter how many times you ask me how cute I think you are in your idea of fetish attire, you're not going to get me to understand the appeal of being a little, Eve," she teases as she rolls onto her side and props her cheek on one palm.

She glances up and down my body. "It's so short."

"It's supposed to be short." I flatten down the front of the lavender dress that got delivered earlier today. It fits perfectly.

Exactly what I'd hoped for. It looks like it belongs on someone who's about four, but sized for my thirty-year-old self. I trail my hands over the smocking across my chest and then the low-cut rounded neckline. The sleeves are puffed at my shoulders with elastic around my biceps. It spreads out full below the smocking, which means no one who hasn't seen me naked could discern what my body shape is underneath. And the best part, it flares out when I spin.

"It barely covers your ass, Eve. And not at all if you keep spinning around like that. Plus, you're going to get dizzy."

I tip my head to one side, plant my hands on my hips, and glare at her in fun. "Because that black skirt you wore last week at Surrender was so much longer."

She chuckles. "Okay, probably not, but that's different. I love that skirt. It's skin-tight. It makes me feel sexy, especially when I pair it with the red corset—the one that pushes my boobs up, making it look like I actually have boobs."

I shake my head. "You have more boobs than me."

"Seriously, Eve. You're not going to convince me of that. And why are we arguing about boob size?"

"We're not." I spin back around and look in the mirror again. "And it doesn't matter if you like this dress or not. I like it, and I can't wait to entice Owen to spank me in it."

When Leah doesn't respond, I glance over at her to find her picking on an imaginary piece of lint on my bed.

"What?" I've gotten the impression more than once that Leah isn't super fond of Owen.

She shrugs. "I don't know. The guy gives me a strange vibe is all."

"Well, he's been nothing but polite, and he's got a pretty strong Daddy tendency. It's been forever since I've played with a steady Daddy. Let me have some fun."

"Okay, but please don't go to his house or anything. Not alone. Not yet. Give it a bit more time."

I sigh. "I haven't been to his house yet. I promise." I have met him in public for coffee and twice for dinner, but Leah knows that.

"Worse, you've been to his bar. The place he works. Just… be careful."

I leap over toward the bed and jump onto it, making the mattress bounce next to her. "Maybe you're jealous."

She chuckles. "Of what?"

"Because I have a regular partner at the club finally. It's been a while since I had a Daddy I could count on." I shrug.

She laughs again. "I don't want a relationship with a Daddy, so no. Not jealous. Concerned."

I lift up the hem of my new dress. "We're not all that different, you know. We both like short skirts. I just like mine looser." I giggle.

She rolls her eyes and heaves herself off my bed. "Sure. Almost twins." She leans over and kisses my cheek. "Gotta go. I'll see you Friday night?"

"Yep. I'll be the naughty toddler getting spanked."

She groans with a smile. "You can get spanked without having a fake tantrum, you know. All you have to do is ask any Dom in the club."

I give an exaggerated pout. "What's the fun in that?" I shove off the bed and walk Leah to the door, seeing her out before returning to my bedroom. I stop in front of the mirror and spin around again.

I'm duplicitous. I know it. I work my ass off nine hours a day five days a week at Earnest and Heart. I'm a fantastic accountant. People pay me good money to save them as much as I can. I show up every day as the poster-woman for professionalism. Half my closet is filled with pencil skirts, blouses, jackets, and pumps. I can put my hair in the perfect bun in the dark without a mirror. I learned how to apply makeup from the best—my mother.

So what if my preferred method of relaxation after a long day or week is to pretend I'm a small child without a concern in the world? It's fun. It's freeing. Liberating, even. And even better when I have a partner who's willing to baby me and pamper me.

I flop on my bed and stare at the ceiling.

I've only been submitting to Owen for a month, but I think we click in the Dom/sub world. I find him charming. It's not like I'm planning to date him outside of the club. We're just friends. No big deal. I'm not sure why Leah finds him creepy. He's a perfectly nice man. He owns a bar nearby, which I found out by accident a few weeks ago when I went there for a drink after work.

Owen is a good match for me as a Daddy. He can be playful and fun but also stern and serious when called for. And when I'm in my little persona at the club, I always ensure the Daddy I'm subbing for ends up needing to discipline me.

I get a rush of endorphins when I scene with a Daddy. Usually, it's planned. I look cute, misbehave intentionally, and get my bottom spanked. It's not really different from what Leah enjoys. She gets spanked too. She just prefers not to have a tantrum first.

I giggle and roll to my side to grab my favorite stuffed animal, Jessie. She's a unicorn. Who doesn't love to curl up with a furry toy at the end of a long day and just breathe?

CHAPTER 3

Colton

When I step into Surrender the following morning, I have no idea what to expect. The receptionist area is perfectly normal. Desk, computer, bulletin board. The usual. I assume the door on the other side leads to the main club, and this makes sense because if anyone accidentally wanders in off the street, they won't have a clue what this place is from this room alone.

Davis is here, and he extends a hand. "Hey. Good to see you. It's been a while."

"You too." I shake his hand and then take a deep breath. "So, what am I getting myself into here?"

He nods behind him. "Follow me. I'll show you around. Roman Cortell is the owner. Julius Polk is the manager. They're both upstairs in Roman's office."

"Perfect." I follow Davis through the rear door and step into a large open space. The lights are on, so I can see everything clearly, but I imagine when the club is open, it's not usually this bright. The main room is painted entirely black, even the ceiling and floor. A wide variety of apparatus are spaced around the room, some even in the center.

"This is the main playroom," Davis tells me.

I nod slowly as I wander around a bit. I've done my research. I'm at least marginally familiar with most of what I'm seeing. St. Andrew's crosses. Spanking benches. An interesting chain structure that looks like a spider's web. There are leather-covered tables, sort of like what a masseuse would use. A variety of restraints hang from the ceiling. There's even a large cage.

Davis points to a hallway. "Down that way are private rooms and the daycare."

I lift a brow. "Daycare? People bring kids here?"

He chuckles. "God, no. It's for adults pretending to be young. Littles." He claps a hand on my back. "We'll tackle that room later. It's gonna take me a few days to educate you, my friend."

I nod. "Apparently." My mind wanders back to the possibility that Davis is a Daddy, and I wonder again what that might mean.

I follow Davis through a door on the far side of the room and then up a flight of stairs. We pass a few offices on the second floor before entering one.

Two men are inside, and they both stand as we arrive.

Davis steps to the side. "Roman. Julius. This is... Well, I have no idea what your name is or what you're going by this week." Davis chuckles. "You were totally undercover when we met as Gordon Shepherd."

I smile as I shake both men's hands. "My real name is Colton. You can call me Colt." I pull out my badge and flash it around. "Swear I'm legit." I also hand everyone in the room a business card. "This is my boss at the precinct. Captain Johansson. Call him. You should definitely verify I am who I say I am. He'll know who Colton is. I won't disclose my last name."

Both men are in their forties with dark hair. Roman has darker skin than Julius. He's also about an inch shorter, which is saying something. Both men are a few inches over six feet, as am I. I figure Davis to be six feet, and he's the shortest man in the room.

"Please, have a seat." Roman sweeps a hand to indicate a seating area with two armchairs and a loveseat. He and Julius take the loveseat. Davis and I take the armchairs.

Julius speaks next. "Davis has filled us in on a few of the details about how he met you last year and what went down. I understand two of our members are on your radar. This concerns us." His brow is furrowed.

"Concerns me too. That's why I'm here. It's always possible I'm barking up the wrong tree, so I don't want any of you to panic. I've been following Evelyn Dean for a few weeks based on a tip. I have no idea if Owen Karplus is involved in the case or not. Could be an innocent bystander. You never know. Unfortunately, Evelyn fits the profile of the sort of women that get picked up and sold into human trafficking by this particular organization I'm trying to infiltrate, so I'm being abundantly cautious."

Julius rubs his jaw while he listens. "Damn."

Roman sighs. "No shit."

I nod. "Exactly. Recent events have caused me to increase my attention on Evelyn. Ensuring her safety is more important than catching the buyer when it comes down to it."

Davis glances toward Julius and Roman. "He thinks someone else is following her."

Both men furrow their brows in discomfort.

Davis turns toward me. "I spoke to Blade, my boss. He'll do whatever he can to help. He's a member here too."

Wow. Okay. The world keeps shrinking. "Thank you. I'm

still early enough in the investigation that I don't want Owen to have a clue that I'm watching him. When I'm wrong about a suspect, it's best if they never find out I was surveilling them."

"I can understand that," Roman states, "but I'm not comfortable leaving Eve in the dark if you think someone is tracking her, no matter who that ends up being."

"I'm not either. I'd rather bring her into the inner circle. Besides, it's incredibly hard to protect someone when they aren't aware they need protection."

"She's done several scenes with Owen in the past month. They seem to have hit it off," Julius says. "Do you have any experience in the fetish community?"

I shake my head. "Admittedly none."

Julius nods. "Why don't you come with Davis as his guest, someone new to the scene? That way Davis can pretend to be educating you while you keep an eye on Eve and Owen."

I swallow the bad taste that idea leaves in my mouth. It's inappropriate that I'm attracted to Evelyn. Beyond inappropriate. And the thought of watching her do whatever she does here with other men brings bile to the back of my throat. But I must remain professional. "That'll work."

Roman nods. "We can give you a crash course in BDSM 101 so you don't end up looking suspicious as you wander around the club with your eyelids on the ceiling. Then we'll have you observe."

Davis leans back. "An evening at my house should bring him marginally up to speed. I'll talk to Britney. Make sure she's okay with it."

I glance at him, wondering what an evening at his house would entail. Maybe he's thinking he and Britney can do a demonstration of some sort so I won't be shocked. Very little shocks me, however.

"When do we bring Eve up to speed?" Julius asks.

"I'd prefer to be the one to confront her, if you don't mind.

I don't care who else is present. But sooner rather than later is best," I tell them.

"She's an accountant for a big firm," Julius states, "so I'm pretty sure she's not available during the day. How about if I try to get ahold of her and see if she can swing by here after work?"

I nod. "Perfect."

Roman stands. "Sorry to run, but I've got an appointment." He shoots a look at Julius and then Davis. "We've been tiptoeing around an important detail, but it seems like it would be better to wait until Eve is present to discuss her particular preferred kink."

Julius nods. "I agree."

I stare at them all, wondering what the hell I've gotten myself into. Not that I have a choice. My job is to protect Evelyn Dean.

I need to head back to the precinct and fill the captain in on all this. I already know what he's going to say though. I've been working for him for five years. He trusts me implicitly. He will defer to me on this matter. If I say my primary goal is Evelyn's safety, he will instruct me to see that she's protected. After all, if Evelyn is truly being stalked for the purpose of human trafficking, then sticking to her like white on rice will be imperative.

I just hope she doesn't balk at the fact that I'm about to become her new best friend.

Hell, more importantly, I hope I can remain professional when I'm in her presence. I've been following her for two weeks. Every time I see her, my breath hitches. Her smile melts me. Her laughter is even better.

Pull it together, Colton.

CHAPTER 4

Evelyn

I'm beyond curious as I enter Surrender. Julius called me in the middle of the day and asked if I could come by after work, so here I am, but why?

"Hey, Eve." I'm even more confused and surprised when the man waiting for me just inside the club is Davis Marcum.

"Hi." I glance around. No one else is here. The club isn't open tonight. It's only open Wednesday, Friday, and Saturday. Today is Monday. "What's going on?"

He nods over his shoulder. "It's complicated. We'll explain upstairs in Julius's office."

"Okay..." I follow him, but now I'm concerned. And who is "we"? "Should I be worried?"

Davis glances at me, hesitating. "Honestly, I'm not sure."

Well, shit. I keep up with him, my heels clacking on the hard floor as we cross the main room and head up the stairs. When we enter Julius's office, he stands. As does another man I've never met before.

I shake Julius's offered hand, but the other man takes my breath away. The only way to describe him is tall, dark, and handsome. I wonder if he's a member of the club I've never met before, or perhaps a new member. Either way, I'm intrigued as Julius releases my hand and motions toward the stranger.

"This is Colton."

Colton… He holds out a hand, and his firm handshake makes my heart race. Or maybe it's the way his gaze meets mine. Serious but friendly. "Evelyn."

"Please, call me Eve."

He smiles, and the initial flutter turns into something more like a tremble. Seriously. I need to get a grip. Then I melt a bit when he says, "Please, call me Colt."

My breath hitches at the way he repeats my words. He seems more like a Colton to me.

"Have a seat." Julius motions toward an armchair as he resumes his spot across from me. Colt returns to his spot on the loveseat. Davis pulls up a chair from the small table.

"Who's going to tell me what's going on?" I ask.

"I am," Colt says.

I shift my attention more fully toward him. This is the oddest assembly of people. Colt is a stranger. Julius, I've known for years since he's the manager. And Davis is a member of the club, but I've never scened with him. We only know each other in passing. He has a serious girlfriend and doesn't scene with other members anymore.

Colt clears his throat. His brow is furrowed. "I'm an undercover agent with the local police."

I flinch.

"Don't worry. You're not in any trouble." He offers a small smile to emphasize his words. "I'm investigating a human trafficking ring in the area, and I'm concerned that you're on their radar."

I gasp. My hand comes to my chest. "What? Why?"

"I wish I knew."

"So, you think someone is planning to...what? Snag me off the street and sell me?"

"Essentially, yes. That's my concern. There's no way to sugarcoat it."

My hands are shaking now and I fist them in my lap as I tuck my crossed legs closer to the chair. I suddenly feel vulnerable and scared. It's not a feeling I relish. When I'm at Surrender, I'm usually in my little space, but I just left work. I'm totally out of sorts in my adult persona with a hint of my little peeking through. Adult Evelyn does not panic or cower. I lick my lips. "What the hell am I supposed to do with this information?"

"Let me protect you, basically. I've been watching you for a few weeks."

I flinch again. "Seriously? I've never seen you."

He smiles. "I'm good at my job. You weren't supposed to see me."

I narrow my gaze. "Wait. How closely do you follow me?" I flatten my palms on my thighs but grip them with my fingers. The thought of someone spying on me for two weeks is unnerving.

"Don't worry. I've never been inside your apartment or anything. I've just kept an eye on you from a distance so far."

"And now? Did something change?"

"Another man is also following you. I've spotted him several times. It concerns me. I'm worried he's watching for a weakness in your routine. Right now, it's too early in the investigation to be certain. I can't be certain any lead I'm following is legit."

"But you're concerned enough to confront me," I point out.

"Yes. It's safer for you if you're informed, and I'd rather not remain in the shadows anymore."

I stare at him. "Do you know who's following me?"

He shakes his head. "Not a clue. He wears a ballcap. I haven't gotten a look at his face, but I will catch him eventually." His voice is confident. So is his stance. This is not a man who fails.

I lean back in the chair, my breathing quick and shallow. "This is crazy."

Davis speaks next. "Colt is going to start coming to the club on the nights you're here."

I glance at this undercover cop who had me clenching my legs together just five minutes ago and try to picture him in the club. "Do you have any experience with fetish clubs?"

He shakes his head. "No."

I groan and lean back. "What a disaster."

Davis speaks again. "I was thinking the two of you could come over to my place for dinner tomorrow night. Britney has agreed to help Colt understand our particular type of fetish so he isn't blindsided."

I rub my temples. I'm not embarrassed about my age play. Not when I'm around like-minded people. Not when I'm at the club or alone at home. But the thought of exposing that vulnerability to a stranger is unnerving. "How about I just don't come to the club at all for a while?" I wince. "Except, shit. I have plans to meet Owen here Friday night. What am I supposed to tell him?"

Julius nods sympathetically. "You need to keep your routine the same, Eve. You should come to the club because it was already planned."

I sit up straighter. "Why? So I can lure some madman in? Am I bait?" I jerk my attention to Colt, the man I'm now deciding maybe isn't so sexy after all. Or, I tell myself that at least.

He shakes his head. "No. I would never use you as bait. But if someone is watching you, they might be inclined to move up their timetable if they think you've gotten suspicious. Like Julius said, you need to keep your routine the same for now."

My head is starting to pound. I look toward Davis again. "What have you told him about me?"

Davis shakes his head. "Nothing yet. I wouldn't break anyone's confidence like that."

"How did you get involved at all?"

Colt answers before Davis has a chance. "I met Davis last year when Britney was targeted for human trafficking."

I jerk my attention back to Davis. "God, I never knew that."

He nods. "It was over before Britney started coming to the club. She doesn't like to talk about it."

"I'm so sorry," I tell him. How horrifying. I'm still confused though.

"Colton is good at his job, Eve. He helped save Britney's life."

I jerk my gaze back to the man who has put himself in charge of…keeping me alive?

Before I can ask another question, Colt speaks again. "I was in the booth next to you yesterday when you had lunch with your friend Leah."

I think back. "Jesus. You listened to my conversation with Leah?"

"Yes."

As my memory floods, my face heats. "We mentioned Davis."

"Yes. Pure luck on my part that I happen to know Davis. I didn't know he was a member of a club, but once you spoke of him, I knew I could ask him to help me out."

My head is spinning and I cringe and shift my attention to Davis. "I'm so sorry. We never should have been talking about you."

Davis waves me off. "Don't worry about it. You weren't badmouthing me." He smiles.

I groan. "No. That's for sure. Could I be more mortified?"

"Please. It's not a big deal. If anything, you've boosted my ego."

I drop my head into my hands and groan.

After a moment, Colt interrupts my pity party. "I have to ask. What specific kink are you all tiptoeing around here?"

Yep, I *can* be more mortified.

I glance at Davis as if he's going to save me.

Luckily, he does. In a way. "Eve is a little."

Colt lifts a brow. "You mentioned littles earlier. What's a little?"

"Someone who enjoys age play, spending time roleplaying as if they were much younger."

Colt nods slowly. "What age?"

Davis shrugs. "Littles come in all ages. Everyone's kink is different."

I stare at Colt while he absorbs this information. Ordinarily, I do not get embarrassed about my kink. I own it. But it's not something I share with outsiders. My vanilla colleagues and friends are unaware of my preferences.

"Okay," Colt murmurs. "I've heard of age play, but I didn't realize it was so prevalent."

I shudder. "There's no way I can share that side of me with someone I don't know."

Colt shifts his weight, leaning forward. "I promise I'm not a judgmental person. I don't want to disrupt your life in any way."

I plant my hands firmly on my thighs, my voice rising. "You don't want to disrupt my *life*? You've just told me that some unknown group of people might be planning to kidnap me and sell me into sex slavery, and you're not sure who is following me, and you don't want to disrupt my life?" I'm panicking.

Colt's face tightens. "You're right. I'm sorry. My primary goal is to protect you."

Another thought comes to mind. "Why isn't someone still after Britney?" I ask.

Davis opens his mouth and then hesitates. "She... Well, to be honest, that's incredibly personal. I'll let her tell you if she's comfortable sharing."

I blink at him in complete confusion. What a clusterfuck. I know Britney. We've spent time together. We're both littles. We've colored and played games and any number of things in the daycare room. I had no idea she'd been the target of human trafficking, and I can't fathom what her personal secret might be.

I rub my forehead with two fingers. I'm shaking. "Now what? I'm just supposed to go home and hope no one kidnaps me?"

"I'll be watching you."

I jerk my gaze to Colt. "From where? Jesus. How the fuck am I going to sleep? Unless you're planning to watch me from my bed, I don't see how I'm going to relax until you catch these fuckers."

Colt draws in a slow breath. "Obviously, I'm not going to sleep in your bed, but I'll be happy to sleep on your couch. It would be ideal, actually. I would never insist on so deeply infiltrating your life, but we'll both sleep better if I do."

I cringe and flatten my entire hand over my face now, swiping it downward. I can't believe this is happening. I stare at the floor for a long time, thinking through my options. When I consider going home alone, I feel panic rising. But this cop is...too sexy for his own good. On top of that, he may not know a damn thing about age play, but he puts off serious

Dom vibes that could have Daddy characteristics, which is a dangerous thing for me to think.

The way he stares at me with such intensity makes me squirm, and this is not a sensation I'm used to. I've never mixed my kink with sex. I don't sleep with the Daddies I submit to. I come to the club, arrange for a specific scene, pretend to be naughty, get my butt spanked, and return home where I sleep like the dead.

Getting disciplined is a stress reliever for me. Like I've explained to Leah, we both like to get spanked. It's invigorating. I just choose to set the scene in such a way that I pretend that my spanking is a necessary punishment. Whereas, Leah just flat-out asks someone to spank her, bends over, and pulls up her skirt.

I don't know why I like the game I play, but I do. It's not that I'm a brat... Okay, maybe I am. Or I could be if I had a deeper relationship with someone. It's just never happened. My scenes are for the evening. An hour or two. We both go home. I don't have sex with them.

My heart is beating too fast. This cop has the power to bring me to my knees. If I met him in a bar, I'd go home with him for a one-night stand. He'd never know about my little side. It's another persona altogether. The lines don't usually blur.

But now? I'd like this man to spank me so hard I cry and then fuck me clear into tomorrow.

I shudder, shaking off the ridiculous thoughts. I'm in serious trouble here. I need to make a decision. I glance at Colt and lick my lips. "I don't even know you," I point out, stalling.

Julius interrupts. "I can verify he is who he says he is. I spoke to his boss at the precinct. He is indeed an undercover cop working on this case."

I'm breathing hard. "Fine. Okay. Let's say you stay in my

apartment, what happens when whoever is following me finds out?"

"He won't. Not for now. We'll worry about that later. Tonight, I'll arrive after you and make sure no one knows what unit I enter when I get there."

I nod slowly. That will work. Not forever, but for today. "Okay." My shoulders drop.

Davis stands and comes to me, setting a hand on my shoulder. "I'm so sorry this is happening. I've been there, or rather Britney has been in your shoes. Come to our house tomorrow for dinner. We can help Colt understand age play and you can take some time to speak to Britney. She survived this. You can too."

"Did someone move into her damn house and guard her?" I'm angry. I can't help it. It's so violating. I don't want anyone in my home. I like to be alone. It's my haven where I can be my little self and unwind in the evening. No way I can do that with Colt there.

"Yes," Davis responds. "I did."

I flinch. "Oh. Shit. Sorry. That makes sense."

"It's how we met. She was in trouble. I brought her home with me. She never left." He smiles. "I can't imagine my life without her now."

"Was she...little?"

He shakes his head, his next words contradicting the head shake. "Well...yes, but she didn't know it yet." He gives my shoulder a squeeze. "You can do this, and if it helps, I would trust Colt with my life. I have trusted him with Britney's life."

I nod. "Okay." I glance back at Colt. "I guess we're doing this then."

CHAPTER 5

Evelyn

My foundation is cracked. I drop my keys on the floor while trying to unlock the door to my apartment. I'm shaking as I glance up and down the hallway, worried someone is going to jump out and grab me. Worried one of my neighbors might step out of their apartment and want to make small talk.

I jump out of my skin when I hear the door at the end of the hall open, knowing someone is stepping out of the stairwell. I'm in such a state that I nearly cry out even though the man I find coming toward me is Colt.

He has a bag over his shoulder, and he moves efficiently toward me, somehow looking calm but determined at the same time. He also moves swiftly without appearing to be in a hurry.

When he reaches me, he eases the keys from my shaking hands and unlocks my door, a hand at my back ushering me inside.

I don't breathe until the door is shut, realizing that I have been holding my breath for a while. Suddenly, I switch from scared to furious. I yank the keys out of Colt's hand, stuff them back in my purse, and drop my purse on the coffee table as I rush past it.

This is not me. I'm solid as a rock when I'm my adult self. Nothing gets to me. I can face a room full of middle-aged men and turn them into putty while I explain to them why their business can't claim daily alcohol consumption as a deduction.

It's not surprising that I'm raw right now. This is *my* time. I left the office three hours ago. I should have been here in my home a long time ago, dressed in my footed pajamas, sipping a juice box, eating animal crackers in front of one of my favorite animated movies.

I'm shaking because I haven't gotten my fix. Some people may do drugs or drink. I unwind by turning off my adult. It works for me. I had a hard day. I'd promised myself a bubble bath, chicken nuggets, and mac and cheese.

Now? I have a permanent house guest who doesn't know the first thing about my fetish and is going to put a cramp in my style.

"Evelyn?"

I spin around on my way to the kitchen. I'm hangry. "Eve."

He nods. "Sorry. Eve. I've been thinking of you as Evelyn for two weeks."

"Well, stop it."

"Do you dislike your name? I think it's lovely. Sophisticated. Like the owner." He's offering me a slight smile.

I set a hand on one hip and rub my temples with my other hand. "I don't dislike my name. It's just that…" I spin around before finishing. "You wouldn't understand, and I don't feel like explaining."

"Okay. Fair enough. I'll try to remember to call you Eve."

"Good." I head for the kitchen. Seriously, my blood sugar

has taken a dive from not eating for so many hours combined with the rush of adrenaline I've been managing poorly.

"How about if I order us something to eat?" he offers.

I grab a glass and fill it with tap water, downing it before answering. At least I won't be dehydrated.

"Do you like pizza?" he continues.

I set the glass down a bit hard, the sound reverberating through the room, and meet his gaze. "I'm sorry I'm completely rattled. I realize it's not your fault. Pizza would be perfect. Thank you." My little would love to have pizza. She'd also love to come out and play now. If I could just change into her, I might be able to put the past few hours out of my head for a while and buy myself some time to regroup.

Alas, not an option. At least I can have pizza.

"What would you like on it?" he asks as he pulls out his phone.

"Just cheese." I don't look at him as I brush past him, intent on at least changing out of my skirt, heels, and blouse. I aim directly for my bedroom, shut the door, and turn the lock.

Finally, I can breathe. I rush over to the window and close the blinds, shuddering at the thought that someone outside might be watching me. Maybe they have seen me changing or in my bra. *Ugh.*

Two seconds later, I'm in my closet, stripping off my adult self, including my bra and lace thong. Surely I can find something comfortable to put on that won't make me appear too little. The footie PJs will have to wait another day. If I walked out to my living room wearing them, I would be embarrassed, and Colt would be uncomfortable.

I choose a pair of pink panties with a princess on the front. He'll never see those. Next, I dig to the bottom of my pile of leggings to pull out the black pair I rarely wear. Lastly, I shuffle through my sweatshirts and find the only one that doesn't have an emblem on it. It's lavender, my favorite color.

In the bathroom, I tug out my bun and let my hair fall down my back. I sigh as the tension ebbs from my head. I brush it out, intending to put two braids in, but then stop myself. Jesus. This is fucked-up. I want to wash off my makeup but opt to leave it instead.

I can't hide in here forever. I'm hungry. No, I was right before. Hangry. And I need to be polite to the cop who is going to shadow me for God knows how long.

When I emerge from the bedroom, I'm marginally less pissy.

Colton is wandering slowly around my space, which unnerves me. He spins around as I enter. "Hey. I hope you don't mind, I surveyed your beverage selection in the fridge and added a two-liter of soda to the pizza order."

I wince inwardly. "Okay."

"Do you not drink soda?" he asks tentatively.

"Not at home." My little doesn't drink it. She doesn't drink caffeine. She wouldn't be able to sleep if she drank it anyway.

"And coffee? I notice you don't have a coffee pot."

I force myself to breathe. "I do. It's just not out. There's a Keurig in the cabinet next to the stove."

"You don't drink coffee either?"

This inquisition needs to stop. "I do. Just not…here. Listen," I rub my forehead. "Can you just not…ask me so many questions right now?"

He nods. "I'm sorry. You're right." He points at the sofa. "Sit. You're exhausted. I'm cramping your style. The pizza will be here soon. We'll eat and go over some things."

I'm certainly happy to sit, so I choose my usual spot in the corner of the sofa and tuck my legs under me.

Luckily, a knock at the door prevents further chit-chat. I flinch, but then force myself to calm down. It's the pizza for God's sake.

Colt looks through the peephole, opens the door, and pays

the delivery kid. He somehow manages to shut the door and lock it in two places while balancing the pizza box in one hand and the two-liter under his arm.

Colt sets both things on the coffee table. "Are you okay with eating in here? I can grab plates and get you a drink if you tell me where they are."

I lick my lips and glance at my kitchen. He's safe from shock if he only opens the top cabinets. "Glasses are up and to the right of the sink. Plates to the left."

He heads that way and returns moments later with a glass of ice for himself and ice water for me. "This okay?"

Marginally. "Thank you."

The plates are under his arm, and he opens the pizza box next.

I smile as I see half is cheese and half is supreme.

"I wasn't sure if you were vegetarian or something. I hope you don't mind if some meat touched your half." He eases two slices of cheese onto a plate.

"I'm not vegetarian. It's fine." I take the plate from him and settle back in my corner, not hesitating to eat the first bite.

Colt fills his plate with several slices and pours himself a soda before sitting at an angle from me in the armchair.

For several minutes, we eat in silence, and I start to feel more human. Slightly.

"I'm sorry," Colt says when he's done. He leans back. "I know I'm imposing. It sucks. You didn't intend to have a houseguest. I can see if there are any units available in your building tomorrow and rent one."

I flinch and shake my head. "No. Don't do that." I look at my lap. Seriously, it would be worse if he weren't here. When I meet his gaze again, he's leaning forward, his elbows on his knees. He's so comfortable in his skin. His sleeves are pushed up his arms a bit, revealing hard muscles. His thighs are straining against his jeans.

No matter how I slice it, the man is smoking hot. If I spotted him out at a bar or something, I would hit on him. Perhaps I would even go home with him. I bet he knows what to do between the sheets.

I shudder, shaking the unwelcome thought away. "I'd rather you stay here, if you don't mind. How long do you think it will take to catch these people?"

"I don't know. I don't want to make promises."

I rub my forehead again. There is a dull throb behind my left temple.

"Headache?"

I nod.

"I'll run through a few things with you, then give you your space. Maybe a bath and some aspirin."

I stare at him. Does he know he's a bit dominant? Hell, he sounds like a Daddy. It's not intentional, of course. But it's oddly unnerving. "I'll do that."

"So, tomorrow. What time do you normally leave?"

"Eight."

"Okay. I'll discreetly see that you get to your car and then follow you. Once you're safely in your building, I'll head to work myself. If you'd do me the favor of not leaving your office without telling me—"

"I won't," I interject. "I'll bring my lunch or order in for now."

"Good. We can exchange phone numbers. Just text me when you want to leave and I'll follow you back here."

"I'll get you a guest pass so you can park your car in the parking garage here."

He nods. "That will help. We can probably go a few days without anyone noticing me staying here. I know that's hard to explain. Eventually, we might need to tell your neighbors I'm a cousin visiting from out of town or something."

I smile for the first time all evening. "Sure. That doesn't

sound at all like a lie. The eighty-year-old man across the hall will buy that for sure," I add sarcastically.

My breath hitches when he returns the smile. Damn, he's even more attractive when the dimples come out. I'd like to feel that five-o'clock shadow rubbing against the inside of my thighs.

Great. Now I'm flushed.

Colt chuckles. "Okay, well, I'm more worried about imposing on your personal life. I know you're dating Owen Karplus and—"

I cut him off again. "Dating is a strong word. We're friends. We...scene together at the club. We've had coffee and a few drinks outside of the club."

"Oh." He looks a bit shocked.

I smirk. "You don't think men and women can be friends?" I joke.

He chuckles again. "You really want my opinion on that issue?"

I pull my legs up and wrap my arms around my shins, leaning my chin on my knees. I feel less angry now that I've eaten. "Sure. Why not?"

His smile melts me as he stares at me before answering. "I think women *think* they have male friends. But most men are not on the same page. They just play along. But even if you're right, even if some men can be friends with women, Owen doesn't think you're a friend."

I wince. "It's unnerving enough to realize you've kept such close tabs on me that you know who I spend my time with, but how the hell have you been close enough to know what Owen thinks about me?"

He shrugs. "I can't know for sure, obviously. Just a hunch."

"But your hunches tend to save lives," I point out and then stiffen as I drop my knees and plant my feet on the floor. "Is Owen a suspect?"

He cringes a bit. "Suspect is a strong word." He uses my own words.

I roll my eyes. "Jesus. You think Owen might be planning to kidnap me?" I shake my head. "No way. He's a super nice guy. I don't believe it for a minute." I glance away, remembering that Leah doesn't really care for Owen. *Shit.*

"Look, I have no idea. I'm not ruling anyone out."

"What about the guy you think is following me? Is it Owen?"

"No. This guy is larger. Built. Stocky."

No way he can mistake the stalker for Owen then. Owen is slender.

"I do think it's possible whoever is keeping tabs on you has infiltrated the club. It's logical. Maybe he or she isn't the kidnapper, but someone positioned to watch you. I can't know for sure."

I can't process all this. It's overwhelming.

"I'm just saying, I don't want to disrupt your life. I'll try to stay out of your way. If you want to have coffee with Owen, go ahead."

"And you'll what? Sit with us like a bodyguard?"

He shakes his head. "No. I'd stand discreetly outside."

I groan. "And after you visit the club Friday night, you think he's not going to recognize you?"

Colt rubs his hands on his thighs. "I can be as discreet as you need me to be, Eve. I can even be disguised. Owen won't know I'm around."

I sigh. "I don't like lying to people. I'd rather not go anywhere until this is over anyway. I'm freaked out. Work. The club. That's it. And honestly, I'm leery about the club."

"I promise you'll be safe there."

I glare at him. "Safety isn't my concern inside the club."

"Okay. What is?"

"There's not a chance in hell I can relax and be myself with a bodyguard lurking around." I'm really starting to hate this arrangement. This man is going to put the kibosh on every aspect of my little space.

"Let's see how it goes with Davis and Britney tomorrow night. Maybe you'll feel more comfortable after I have some exposure to BDSM."

I shake my head. "You have no idea what you're about to experience, Colt. Not even close. Whatever porn you've watched that makes you think you know everything about the fetish world has seriously misled you. Trust me."

"Okay. I won't deny you have a right to be apprehensive, but give me a chance. I don't want you to change your routine. If there's a possibility Owen is involved or even whoever is following you, they might act sooner than planned if they think you're behaving out of the ordinary."

"Fine." I push to standing. "Are we done here? I need some time alone."

"Yes."

"Guest room is the first door on the right. Guest bath is on the left. There are clean sheets and towels. Do you need anything else?"

"Nope. I'll be fine."

"Good. I'll see you in the morning then." I flee the room without another word. The man confuses me. I don't want to talk to him anymore. He's charming and funny and endearing and sexy and so very much not a Daddy. Right?

CHAPTER 6

Colton

I watch Evelyn, Eve, leave the room as though it were on fire.

She's an enigma. That's for sure.

The Eve I've been following does not give off any vibe that she likes to pretend to be a child. She's professional, well-dressed, and completely put together from head to toe.

The Eve who spent the last hour with me was transformed. I get the feeling she hasn't let her hair down quite as much as she would have liked to if she were alone, but she did make me do a double take.

I can't totally fathom what it means to be a little, but I'm trying. Does she slide into that role here at home when she's alone or is it something she does only at the club?

Shocking me further, the thought of that gorgeous woman fully relaxing, even if it's to pretend to be younger, is oddly appealing. I'd like to see it. I got a glimpse, but it wasn't enough.

I actually feel kind of empty now that she's left the room. As I head for the guest room to drop my bag on the bed, I hear the bath running in the master bathroom. Good, she's taking a bath. That will relax her. And I'll try not to wonder what she looks like when she's leaning back under the bubbles.

I hate that I wanted to fist pump when she told me she and Owen were just friends. I wasn't kidding about Owen. No way does he agree with her. Either that or he's incredibly good at grooming the women he lures in before selling them.

In all honesty, Owen is not an incredibly likely suspect for several reasons. One, he has been openly carrying on a relationship with Eve—romantic or otherwise. He would be questioned if she ever disappeared. A lot of people know he's been seeing her. Everyone at the club.

Two, if this was his usual MO, other disappearances would be associated with him too. They aren't. I've pulled every detail about Owen Karplus. Graduated from the University of Seattle, bought this bar from the previous owner five years ago, up to his eyeballs in debt. That's just the tip of the iceberg. But I don't want to spend much time dwelling on him. He's that unlikely.

I also don't want Eve to change her plans from seeing him because, like I told her, I'd rather she not break from her usual routine.

Eventually, we will have a problem on our hands. I get that. She'll need to explain my presence in her life. She might even need to pretend she's dating me at some point, but we'll cross that bridge later. She's not going to like the idea.

I grab my toiletry kit and head to the guest bath to brush my teeth and use the toilet. Back in the guest room, I only shut the door long enough to change into flannel pants. I consider putting on a T-shirt just in case I run into Eve in the hallway but decide against it. Even the pants are more than I prefer to wear to bed.

I open the door before pulling the covers back and dropping onto the bed with a heavy sigh. This is one of the weirder assignments I've been on in a long while. I've done some crazy things undercover, but I don't usually move in with women to protect them.

I cringe as I remember Eve's frustration about being used as bait. To an extent, she was right. If I really wanted to keep her as safe as possible, I could put her in protective custody. I need her to be safe, but I also need to catch the assholes who are trafficking women.

The apartment goes silent after a while, and I close my eyes, though sleep is not going to come quickly. My mind is racing. I want to know more about the mysterious woman in the other room. I'm drawn to her.

I hate that she's embarrassed to share her kink. I don't fully understand it, but I will *not* let myself flinch or judge her in any way. Everyone deserves to enjoy life to the fullest, no matter what that might look like for them.

The concept of pretending to be little eludes me. I can't wrap my head around it. Does she dress young? Talk in baby talk? Play with toys?

Based on the contents of her fridge, I know she eats strange things. I tried not to dwell on what I saw or stare very long, but the woman has juice boxes, cheese sticks, and sliced apples in her fridge. To name a few things. What stands out more is what she doesn't have.

What on earth does she mean that she drinks soda and coffee but not at home? Though she told me where the coffee maker is, I wonder if she has actual coffee to put in it. Guess I'll find out when I rummage in the morning.

Tomorrow I will watch her like a hawk when she leaves for work. I really want to know who is also watching her. It makes my skin crawl. Is there any chance I'm mistaken? Doubt it. My gut tells me the larger man in the ballcap who walks away from the curb when she leaves the parking garage is stalking her.

I need to catch him. Hell, I need to get a picture and have my boss run him through facial recognition software. That's going to be my primary goal for a while.

It takes forever for me to fall asleep, and seems to last only five minutes before a scream yanks me fully awake. I jump to my feet, yank my weapon from the outside pocket of my bag, and rush toward Eve's bedroom. I doubt I'm going to need to shoot anyone, but instinct forces me to be prepared.

I don't even knock before I yank her door open, keeping my gun at my side. A glance around tells me she's alone. My heart is racing as I realize she's probably had a nightmare.

She's breathing heavily as her gaze comes to me. The bathroom light is on, the door ajar, bathing the room in enough light to see clearly.

"You okay?" I ask as I approach. I try to keep the weapon out of sight, but she sees it and her breath hitches.

"You have a gun."

I set it on the bedside table as far away from her as possible. "Yeah, it's part of the job description." I try to sound light. I'm unable to resist stroking her cheek as she tips her head back and looks up at me with her doe eyes. Her hair is a tousled wavy mess that looks sexy as hell. I force myself not to smooth it from her face. That would be far too intimate. "Bad dream?"

She shrugs. "I don't remember."

The blankets have dropped to her waist, and my gaze wanders to the tight pink tank top she's wearing. The outline of her breasts is obvious, her pert nipples standing out. They're just the right size. Not huge, but not small either.

When I realize I'm still cupping her cheek, I release her. "I'll let you get back to sleep." I start to reach for my weapon, but she grabs my wrist, making me look back at her.

She licks her lips. "Remember when I joked about you sleeping in my bed?"

I nod slowly. *No. No no no no no.*

"Would you? Please? I can't relax. I'm scared."

I nod again because what the hell else am I going to do. Without a word, I snag the gun, take it with me to the other side of her bed, and drop it on *that* nightstand instead. Afterward, I lower myself onto the bed, on top of the covers, not touching her. I'm flat on my back when I turn my gaze her way. "Better?"

"Yes. Thank you." She slides back under the covers, curling onto her side, facing me. When she reaches out a hand to rummage under the blankets, I stiffen, uncertain what she's doing. But a moment later, her hand lands on the slight bulge under the covers between us, and she tugs something to her chest.

I catch a glimpse of white fur and something colorful. A rainbow? Oh, yeah. A unicorn horn. I can't help but smile as Eve settles down next to me. Her eyes are closed and she burrows deeper. She smells like vanilla, which must have been her soap or lotion.

I want to reach over, drag her into my arms, turn her to her other side, and spoon her. She wants to be comforted. I could do that. But I won't. Good God. Of course not. I'm not here to hold this woman while she sleeps. I'm here to protect her.

Suddenly, I remember what Davis said yesterday when I spoke to him. About Eve looking much younger and innocent under the professional façade. Now I know what he meant and why he's seen her like this. If she attends the club as a little, everyone at Surrender sees her as innocent and young.

I swipe a hand over my face and sigh louder than I mean to.

"I'm sorry," she murmurs without looking at me. "You

don't have to stay if you don't want. I'm being ridiculous. It's improper of me to ask you to stay in my bed."

I roll onto my side, facing her, and reach for her to follow my earlier instinct, easing a lock of hair from her forehead. "It's fine," I whisper, my voice sounding more gravelly than I expected. "I'll be right here. Sleep, Evelyn."

Her breath hitches.

"Shit. Sorry. I forgot. Eve."

She shakes her head, still not tipping back to look at me. Her face is halfway under the covers anyway. "I don't mind," she murmurs.

I'm not sure what to make of her response. She'd been so adamant earlier.

I can't stop touching her, mostly because it's calming her. Her breathing slows down as I stroke her forehead and then slide my hand down to her shoulder. An odd protective instinct rises in me. She's not like any woman I've ever dated. In fact, she's not even like the woman I met earlier this evening in the club, nor is she like the woman I've been following for two weeks. The one who looks like nothing would ever rile her up. The professional version of Eve in the pencil skirts and heels. The one who must make everyone she encounters at work nervous.

This is another Eve. Her little? Seems reasonable. In which case, I know I'm cramping her style for sure. She obviously likes to drop her adult self at the door when she gets home and unwind in a different kind of mindset.

It's...cute. In no way am I taken aback. In fact, she's bringing out a protective instinct in me. I vow once again to be open-minded no matter what I learn about her in the coming days. The last thing I want to do is hurt her feelings or insinuate she's not exactly perfect the way she is.

I don't know when I fall asleep, but the next thing I know,

I'm on my back and my arm is around Eve's shoulders. She is snuggled up against me, her cheek in the crook of my arm. She's dead asleep and I don't have the heart to dislodge her.

I'm smiling as I fall back into slumber.

CHAPTER 7

Colton

I awake slowly to the smell of coffee, wondering how that's possible since I obviously am not up yet to make it. It's not until I open my eyes that I remember where I am and startle.

Eve is sitting on the edge of the bed on my side. She's dressed for the day in another high-power, chew-them-up-and-spit-them-out outfit. And bless her, but she's holding a mug of coffee.

I push myself to sitting and glance at the clock on her side of the bed. "Shit," I mutter, wondering how the hell I slept this late, including through her getting ready which surely happened all around me. "Sorry. I never sleep this late."

She smiles and hands me the coffee. "I figured."

I take the warm mug and blow on the edge before taking a sip. "Mmm. Bless you. I wasn't sure you even had coffee in the apartment."

"I do. It's in a drawer next to the stove."

"But you don't drink coffee..." I'm trying to remember her exact words from last night.

"I drink coffee. Two cups every morning. After I get to the office."

"I'd never make it to the office, or the shower for that matter, until I've had at least half of the first one."

She shrugs.

"Give me ten minutes to shower and get ready?"

"You have plenty of time. No rush. Oh, and you might want to use my bathroom. The shower head in the guest bathroom is so low you'll have to duck. Mine is higher, more powerful, and larger."

"Okay. Thank you."

She stands and heads across the room, talking over her shoulder. "I'll just grab my lipstick and get out of your way."

Damn, she is totally ready. Makeup. Hair in that bun again. Fucking legs that go on for days in those heels. Her ass makes my cock hard, tenting the front of my flannel pants. I jerk my gaze back to the coffee, willing my dick to stand down.

Who the hell is this woman and who was the woman who slept with a stuffed unicorn and snuggled up against me?

Eve leaves the room, shutting the door behind her. When I tug back the covers, I find the unicorn deep under them. I smile. It's indeed a fluffy white ball of soft fur with a rainbow horn. If I found this in any other woman's bed, I'd be concerned, but the version of Eve who slept with that stuffed animal was adorable, so I'm not going to judge her.

I'm ready as promised in ten minutes, having used Eve's shower then switched to the other bathroom to shave and brush my teeth. Standing at her vanity and spreading my things out in her space seems too intimate.

Eve bustles around the apartment doing I have no idea what until the moment it's time to leave. That's when she takes a deep breath and meets my gaze. "Kinda freaking-out here," she declares.

I slide my hand up her arm to her shoulder—knowing every second that I shouldn't have touched her. "You'll be fine. I'll walk you all the way to your car and make sure you are in safe and the doors are locked before I go get mine. When you pull out of the garage, I'll be on your heels."

She nods. "Okay."

"When we get to your office, I'll wait in my car until I see you go safely inside. Got it?"

"Yes." She nods definitively. "I'll be fine." She repeats my words.

"You will." *God, I hope so.*

I do exactly as I've explained and follow her in my car until she's safely at work. Only then do I breathe easier. I don't pull away just yet. Instead, I scan the area for a while, watching for the man I've seen outside her apartment. So far, I've only seen him on foot. I'm hoping to catch him in a vehicle eventually.

No one is loitering around her building this morning, so I head to the precinct, taking the most roundabout way imaginable, just in case.

That evening, ten minutes before we are supposed to leave to go to Davis and Britney's house, I'm leaning against the kitchen counter, wondering what Eve is doing in her bedroom. She went in there the moment we got back home and shut the door, mumbling about needing to change.

I glance at my watch again and shove off the counter, angling for her door. I knock softly. "Eve?"

Moments later, she opens the door. She's wearing a soft pink robe, which she's clutching around herself. Her hair is down, and I'm quickly learning I love it when it's loose like this.

She's been in here for over an hour, and she's still not dressed for dinner?

"You okay?"

She sighs. "Not really." She tucks a lock of wavy hair behind her ear.

I glance past her. The closet is open and a lot of clothes are lying on the bed, still on their hangers. I'm not sure what to say. I don't have a clue what's going on here. Eve does not strike me as an undecided woman who can't throw some clothes on.

She clears her throat. "I'm not ready to be little in front of you."

I nod. "Okay."

"If you weren't going to be with us, I would be myself in front of Britney. In her home. She'll be little tonight. She's little every night."

"And what does it mean to be little exactly?"

She shrugs. "It's complicated, but right now I'm just trying to decide what to wear, and frankly every time I pick something else up, my stomach ties into knots."

"I don't want you to feel stressed like that around me."

"Can't help it."

I inhale slowly, hating that I'm causing her to panic. This is way outside my realm of understanding. "How about you just dress in something comfortable. I'm sure everyone will understand."

"Yeah, I'm working on it. Give me five more minutes." She shuts the door in my face.

I grin. I can't help it. As much as I loathe disrupting her life, she is adorable when she's flustered. It's another side of her.

I wait in the living room, not bothering her again. She

knows we're late. I doubt anyone will say a word. This entire situation is awkward.

When she finally emerges, I'm surprised to see her in jeans and a white sweater. There's nothing unusual about her attire. She has on dressy leather tennis shoes too. Her hair is hanging full down her back. A small white purse with a gold chain strap hangs from her shoulder. She opens the coat closet and grabs a puffy white ski jacket. As she puts it on, she meets my gaze. "Okay. I'm ready."

I pull on my coat at the same time. "Can we go in my car?"

She nods. "No one will notice me leaving with you since your car is in the parking garage now."

I open the door and let her pass through first. When she pulls the keys from her purse, I gently take them from her hand and lock the door. She doesn't say a word about my highhandedness. I'm not even sure why I would do something like that. I rationalize that for one thing, she's clearly shaking with nerves. For another, I want to ensure her door is indeed locked for my peace of mind.

She doesn't say a word as we head down the stairs and approach my SUV. I open her door for her and wait for her to get settled before closing it. I'm perplexed by her many facets. Every time I've seen her in her professional work attire, she's been strong and confident. It's like she changes into another personality when she takes off her daytime clothes.

When we arrive at Davis and Britney's house, I park out front and turn toward Eve. "We don't have to do this." She has been wringing her hands the entire drive.

"Yeah, we kinda do." She says those heavy words as if she's announcing that we have no choice but to attend a funeral. And she opens her door to jump down from my SUV before I can round the hood.

Davis opens the front door as we step onto the porch. I've never felt so unnerved with a woman. My instinct is to set a hand on the small of her back or thread my fingers with hers. I want her to relax, and I imagine I could accomplish that if I were touching her. But it wouldn't be appropriate.

Eve is not my date. She's a woman I'm protecting. The majority of my thoughts about her are completely inappropriate and I need to rein them in. I have no idea why I'm so drawn to her. I mean, other than the obvious. But looks aren't everything. It's not that. It's something inside me that wants to protect her. Comfort her. I want to pull her into my arms, tip her head back, and reassure her that everything is going to be okay. Even though I have no proof that is true.

I suspect I'm about to have the strangest night of my life.

"You made it," Davis states as he steps back to open the door wider. "Come on in."

I let Eve enter in front of me and follow her.

It's not until we're inside that I realize Britney is hovering out of sight pressed against Davis's side almost behind the open door. When Davis shuts the door, I force myself not to react.

Britney grips Davis's waist and does her best to squish even closer to him. Her gaze is down, but she can't exactly hide behind her hair because it's braided behind her ears. She has on a soft pink knit sweater dress with long sleeves. It fits slightly loose on her and hangs only a few inches below her butt. It's winter, so she's also wearing knit white tights. Pink ballet slippers that match the color of her dress round out the outfit.

I'm starting to understand.

Davis holds out a hand to shake mine. "Good to see you." He tips his head down to Britney. "Are you going to say hello?"

"Hi," she whispers, lifting one hand to give a little wave without looking at either of us directly.

"Hey," Eve says quietly as she removes her coat. "I love your dress."

"Thanks," Britney murmurs.

Davis meets my gaze. "She's not usually this shy, but it's hard meeting new people. Or...exposing your kink to people you already know."

"I get it. It's good to see you, Britney. Please don't let me make you nervous. Just be yourself." I have enough nerves for both of us.

She gives a slight nod, but that's all I get.

After shrugging out of my own coat, I take Eve's from her and hook them on the coat rack next to the front door.

Davis waves a hand in the direction of the living room. "Please, have a seat. Can I get you anything to drink?"

"I'm fine." I could use a shot of something strong, but I need to be completely level-headed for this evening. I stroll over to the couch and sit on one end.

Davis leads Britney to an armchair. He sits and then lifts her onto his lap, settling her sideways as she leans her head on his shoulder. His hand comes to her thighs.

Eve sits cautiously on the other end of the sofa, a good distance between us.

A rattling noise, followed by the clear sound of a dog whimpering, makes me turn around to see a cage in the kitchen area. "Ah, the puppy. Charlie?"

Davis nods. "Yep. The little rascal would jump all over everyone. He's going to stay in the kennel until after dinner."

Britney gives a humph and crosses her arms. Obviously, the idea of keeping Charlie in the kennel is not one she approves of.

Davis frowns. "What did I say about Charlie?"

She sighs. "That it's not polite to let him jump all over the guests."

"That's right. We'll let him out after dinner."

I can't help but smile. The dynamic between Davis and Britney is fascinating. I'm intrigued. I was worried about this all day. Concerned about how I might react to this lifestyle. But somehow I'm not as unsettled as I expected. I'm not sure I have it in me to be the kind of Dom Davis is, but I do know I'd give my left arm to have a woman look at me the way Britney looks at him.

I glance at Eve, wondering if she wants what Britney has. Wondering if she's ever had a relationship like this. She's so timid right now, sliding her palms under her thighs and pursing her lips. Her gorgeous hair creates a bit of a curtain, letting her hide her expression when she leans forward.

I thought the professional take-charge version of Eve was hot. This side is also grabbing my attention. I flatten my palms on my thighs and rub them against my jeans. I don't want her to feel uncomfortable. I want to reach over and haul her into my side, onto my lap even. I want her to be able to relax, not have to worry about what I'm thinking. Because there's no mistaking that her discomfort is directly related to the fact that she's too nervous to be herself in front of me.

I jerk my attention back to Davis. I have no business thinking of either the adult version of Eve or the little version. I'm here to protect her, not hold her in my damn lap. Jesus.

"How was your day? Anything new?" Davis asks me. He's talking about the investigation, of course.

I shake my wandering thoughts away. "No. It went smoothly." If you don't count the stress of learning the multiple sides of Eve. I lean back and glance at Eve again to point out the obvious. "I'm certain I'm upsetting Eve's usual routine though."

She shifts her weight, sitting awkwardly, her hands crossed on her lap now. "It's fine."

Davis nods. "I'm sure it's hard." He rubs Britney's thighs. "It'll get easier." He's speaking to Eve.

She doesn't respond though.

Davis turns his attention back to me. "Let me tell you a bit about our lifestyle. It will help if you understand better."

I sit back, trying to appear as calm and collected as possible.

"Britney and I have a nearly full-time Daddy/little arrangement when we're in the house. When she goes to work or we have some sort of engagement outside the home with vanilla folks, she leaves her little at home. But when we're here or at Surrender, Britney is my little."

She squirms on his lap, and he steadies her with a firm grip on her thighs. It's captivating.

"Essentially I'm a Dom who prefers a nurturing role. Britney is a submissive who enjoys being taken care of. I make most decisions for her at home. She obeys me or finds herself over my knees."

Britney wiggles on his lap again and tucks her face into his neck.

I've only seen her as a strong independent woman, so this side of her is mind-boggling.

I lick my lips, aware of the woman next to me who is fidgeting. I realize this is the kind of person she is too. Like Britney, she'd rather be little right now. That's why she took so long getting ready. She's chosen an outfit that's somewhere in between—appropriate in public, but comforting at the same time. I wonder how she normally lives since she doesn't have a full-time Daddy figure living with her.

"It's not confusing? Flipping a switch like that?" I don't even know who I'm asking.

Britney shakes her head. "Nope."

Davis lifts her chin to meet his gaze. His expression is serious. "I know you're nervous, but I expect you to speak respectfully to Colt. Understood?"

"Yes, Sir." When he releases her chin, she faces me. "It's not confusing, Sir. It's just who I am."

I turn toward Eve. "It's who you are too."

She nods, not meeting my gaze.

"It's freeing," Britney murmurs. I hope she's growing more comfortable in my presence. I wish I could say the same for Eve.

I look toward Britney again.

She shrugs. "Some people like to have a drink when they get home from work. Some watch sports. Some sit in a hot tub. I like to leave my adult self at the door and slide into a youthful persona. Kids don't have any worries or responsibilities. I leave them at the door and shake them from my mind."

"Makes sense."

Davis speaks again. "Littles come in all ages. Older ones are called middles. Britney gravitates to about four, which means I do nearly everything for her when she's in her little space. I'm strict because she likes it that way. We have an agreed-upon dynamic and we take a pause every once in a while to make sure we're meeting each other's needs. Usually, I can tell when we need to stop and reevaluate even before Britney realizes it. She tends to get defiant and break the rules when she's frustrated."

I'm curious to know how sex fits into this arrangement, but I'm not going to ask.

Davis slides his hand higher up Britney's thigh, under her short skirt and gives another squeeze. "Sit still, sweetie. If you don't stop squirming, I'm going to spank you before we've had dinner."

She freezes. "Sorry, Daddy."

He kisses her forehead. "I know you're nervous, but I trust Colt to keep our secret, and I'm asking to extend the same courtesy."

"Yes, Sir."

One thing is for sure, I would never in a million years break this confidence. "He's right, Britney. I'm humbled that you've allowed me to come into your home to see this side of you. I would never break that confidence. Same goes for the club. I appreciate you preparing me for what I'm going to see at Surrender. It means a lot to me. I don't want to stand out and embarrass myself. This is a tremendous help."

She meets my gaze. "You're welcome, Sir."

It feels odd when she addresses me like that, but I'm gathering it's expected from her.

I glance at Eve, addressing Britney still. "My goal is to keep your friend Eve safe just like Davis did for you. I can do my job better if I understand her better."

"I don't want those bad men to get Eve," Britney says. "Thank you for keeping her safe."

"You're welcome."

Eve has been sitting stiffly this entire time. She finally scoots back into the corner of the sofa and pulls her knees up to her chest in the same position I saw her take last night at her apartment. I assume she feels calmer when she's curled into a ball. I hate that I'm the reason for her stress.

The odd urge to reach out and hold her consumes me again. It's unnerving. I can't act on it. Of course not. On a few occasions in the past, I've slept with women when I was undercover and turning them down would have looked suspicious. But this is not that kind of job. Eve knows I'm a cop. I don't need to convince her. She needs me to keep her alive, not fuck her.

She's just so...vulnerable. Especially tonight. And though I might not have any knowledge of this aspect of the fetish world, I am a rather alpha sort of man. My inclination right now is to do anything I can to help her relax, including pulling her closer.

It's not outside of the scope of my job to ensure Eve is comfortable around me. It's necessary. I'm rationalizing this when Davis speaks again.

"I need to finish dinner." He pats Britney's thigh. "Why don't you take Eve to your room? You can play for a while. I'll let you know when dinner's ready."

"Yes, Sir." She slides off of his lap and shuffles over to Eve. "You want to go to my room?"

Eve unfolds, nodding, and I watch, my chest tight, as she follows her friend out of the living room. At least I no longer need to make the immediate decision about whether or not to touch her.

CHAPTER 8

Colton

I run a hand through my hair and draw in deep breaths, hoping Davis doesn't notice my plight as I follow him into the attached kitchen. My shoulders are tense, and nothing is going to relax me anytime soon.

Davis looks over his shoulder. "You can help me get dinner on the table."

I nod. "Sure."

"I know you're overwhelmed, but damn, Colt, I'm impressed with your open-mindedness."

I glance at the hallway. Faint noises are coming from deeper in the house. "I'm trying. It's outside of my comfort zone, mind you, but I want to understand. More importantly, I want Eve to be safe. That's my job."

"I've never seen her this stressed," Davis admits as he grabs a salad bowl from the fridge and sets it on the table which is already set for dinner. "This is hard on her."

"I hate that."

He smiles at me. "You're a good man, Colt. That is actually your name? Colton?"

"Yes." I chuckle. "If I'm deep undercover, I assume totally different names, but I'm not so deep right now. I don't flaunt that I'm a cop, but I will if I need to. I wouldn't give out my last name to just anyone. I make one up on the spot when needed."

Davis pulls something from the oven, and the room immediately smells divine. My stomach grumbles. "Lasagna. Dude, you are a God."

He chuckles again. "I'm not the best cook in the world, but I can make a mean lasagna. My grandmother taught me because it was my favorite food growing up, and she insisted a man should know how to cook some key meals to impress the ladies."

I smile. "Well, I'm not a lady, but it's working for me. I'm impressed."

He adds a basket of French bread to the table, then reaches for the two glasses and fills them with ice. "What would you like to drink? Water, tea, soda?"

"Tea would be great. Thank you."

I watch in fascination as he pulls two sippy cups from the cabinet next and fills them with a splash of apple juice and the rest of the way with water. He screws on the lids and sets them on the table.

Davis leans a hip against the counter when he's done. "I can see Eve straddling both worlds. She's not comfortable being little in front of you, and I totally understand. I think she'll accept my gentle guidance though. She knows me, and she would ordinarily accept the direction from any Daddy at the club."

I nod, wondering if there might come a day when I have to step up to the plate and fill this role for her, in order to keep up the ruse. If there's even the slightest chance the seller or one of his men is a member or guest at surrender, I need to be on alert at all times there. I also need Eve to be herself in front of me so that no one suspects I'm a cop. That's going to be challenging.

"Thank you for doing this," Davis says, his voice serious. "I mean it. Roman and Julius are grateful too. They don't want anyone at the club to be in danger. If there's even the smallest possibility a member is involved in human trafficking, we all want to do whatever it takes to catch him or her."

I nod. "That's the plan."

"I've spoken to my boss too, Blade. He'll be at Surrender Friday night. An extra set of eyes all around can't hurt."

"Thank you." I remember Blade. I met him eight months ago. Extra eyes are in everyone's best interest. "Do you have any other friends I know that I'm going to see at Surrender?"

Davis glances at me. "If you go often enough, yes. I was going to mention that to you. Cindy and Hudson are members. Cindy owns the animal shelter. They won't be there this Friday, however."

I nod. I had guessed those two might be members.

Davis looks at me again, not saying anything.

I lick my lips. "Please be assured I will keep everyone's identity confidential. I have no intention of upsetting anyone's lives. My concern is ensuring Evelyn is safe."

Davis chuckles.

"What?"

"Evelyn?"

"Eve. I'm still getting used to thinking of her by the nickname."

He cocks his head to one side, a slight smirk on his lips. "You sure you're not into age play?"

I narrow my gaze. "Why?"

He shrugs. "She lets Daddies call her Evelyn. No one else."

I swallow. Or perhaps gulp.

He laughs again. "Shall we eat?" He turns toward the hallway, his voice rising slightly as he continues speaking. "Britney. Eve. Time for dinner."

Moments later, the two women enter the kitchen. Britney bounces over to what I assume is her usual spot at the table. "Can Eve sit next to me, Daddy?"

"Sure, sweetie." Davis moves the second sippy cup and plate and silverware to the other side of the table next to Britney.

I wait for the two women...*girls?*...to sit, then I settle into the chair meant for me. "This smells and looks amazing."

Davis is still standing. He picks up the spatula and cuts into the lasagna. "We aren't super formal here, Colt. Help yourself. I'll just serve the girls."

He's just answered my question. He does refer to them as girls. Again, I'm curious how this translates to a sexual relationship.

He scoops out a steaming serving of lasagna onto Eve's and Britney's plates. After handing me the spatula, he serves them each from the salad bowl too.

Britney leans forward to peer at the plate. "Did you put carrots on it, Daddy?"

He taps her nose. "No, sweetie. I did not put carrots on the salad, just for you." He grips her chin. "So, no excuses. You'll eat every bite. And wait a moment for the lasagna to cool so you don't burn your mouth."

"Yes, Sir."

I watch, mesmerized as he cuts her food and then sets a slice of bread on her plate.

"Would you like me to cut yours too, Eve?" he asks.

She shakes her head. "No, Sir." Her voice is soft. She's not meeting anyone's gaze.

My chest is tight. I hate that I'm stifling her.

Once we're all served, Davis sits, and we all start eating.

"Damn, this is delicious," I state as I swallow my first bite.

Britney giggles and covers her mouth.

I glance at her and realize she's reacting to my language. "Oops. Sorry. I guess you don't cuss in this house."

Davis chuckles. "You can cuss all you want. Britney may *not*. She knows she won't be able to sit for a week if I hear her using naughty words."

I can't help smiling as she squirms on her chair, no longer giggling.

This entire dynamic is intriguing, but Davis and Britney are clearly happy, and it's endearing in a way. I will never judge another human being for their life choices in my life. That's for sure.

Eve is quiet as she eats. She's been quiet the entire time we've been here.

I wish I could make some sort of small talk with her, but I'm afraid to make things worse. My inclination is to ask her about her day, but I get the feeling her workday is so far removed from her evenings that she would be even more unnerved if I suggested she mix the two.

Davis dotes on Britney. He refills her juice when it's empty, gets her another helping of lasagna, even hands her a napkin when she gets sauce on her face. He loves her to pieces.

When we're done, everyone takes their dishes to the sink, and I help Davis put things in the fridge while Britney and Eve wander toward the kennel where the puppy is whimpering.

"Can I let Charlie out yet, Daddy?"

"In a minute, sweetie."

"But he wants to come out now, Daddy," she whines.

"And what will he need to do the moment you let him out?" Davis asks.

"Go potty," she responds.

"Where is he going to do that?" Davis asks.

It's like ping pong watching them. I can't help but smile.

"In the backyard," Britney murmurs dejectedly.

I'm missing something here, and I imagine I'm about to find out what.

"Are you permitted to go out back without Daddy?" He keeps loading the dishwasher.

Ahhh. I see where this is going.

"No, Sir."

"Then exercise some patience, sweetie."

"Yes, Sir." She sticks her fingers through the cage to stroke the puppy's fur. "Just a few minutes, Charlie," she tells him.

I struggle not to chuckle as I wrap tinfoil over the lasagna and put it in the fridge.

I'm pretty sure Davis takes his time finishing in the kitchen before turning back to the girls. "Okay. You can open the kennel now, sweetie. Careful not to pinch your fingers."

Britney jumps to her feet and opens the little cage. Eve stands next to her.

A very rambunctious puppy scrambles out of the confined space, jumping up on Eve the moment he can.

Eve giggles and threads her fingers in his fur. "Aren't you the cutest puppy ever?" It's the first time she's cracked a smile since we got here. I like seeing her more relaxed. The puppy has caused her to forget her plight.

"Come on, girls. Quickly. Outside. Before he pees on the floor." Davis opens the sliding door, and Charlie runs past everyone into the yard.

We all follow, but it's too cold to stay outside long.

Eve wraps her arms around her middle and shivers.

Again, I want to hold her. I really need to stop thinking of her like this.

Luckily, Charlie pees quickly, and we all go back inside.

The little dog runs like crazy all over the great room, while

Britney chases after him and finally manages to catch him. She plops onto her butt on the floor and pulls him into her lap, giggling at his puppy kisses.

Eve sits next to her, legs crossed. She looks eager but waits patiently until Britney hands her the puppy so she can have a turn petting him.

Davis and I return to our spots from earlier, me on the couch near him, him in the armchair.

Britney tips her head back. "Can we watch a movie, Daddy?"

"What did I tell you before they arrived?"

She sighs. "That it would be too late and past my bedtime."

He narrows his gaze. "You didn't have a nap today. Don't fall apart on me."

"Yes, Sir."

I smile, remembering that on Sunday she'd been napping when I called. Now I understand why.

"Put Charlie back in his kennel and come here," Davis commands.

Britney scoops up the puppy and carries the wiggling little guy back to his cage. He goes in and settles down almost immediately, a testament to how hard they must be working to train him.

When Britney returns to stand in front of Davis, he grips her chin.

"You're being intentionally naughty, aren't you, sweetie?"

She squirms and looks down. "Maybe."

He chuckles and looks at me. "Britney isn't usually disobedient, but we spoke earlier about me spanking her in front of you so you can witness the dynamic. It's a little out of our norm to perform intentionally. It's not a game for us. It's a lifestyle. I spank her when she's disobedient. Setting up a time to intentionally spank Britney isn't our regular routine. Lots of couples do though. It's not uncommon for littles and Daddies to set aside a specific time when they intend to play and then include certain elements that fulfill their needs."

My brow is furrowed as I try to grasp his meaning.

Eve surprises me by coming to my side and sitting next to me on the couch. "It's what I usually do," she tells me. "I arrange to do a scene with a Daddy at Surrender at a specific time. I misbehave on purpose. He spanks me. Then he cuddles me, and we're done. We go our separate ways."

I look toward her and nod. "I get it." I don't stop myself from touching her this time. She's so close, and I can't resist. Plus, I think she needs it. So, I brush a lock of hair away from her forehead and tuck it behind her ear.

She tips her head into my hand, melting me. What happens next makes my heart pound. Eve scoots slightly closer and wraps her arm around mine before leaning her cheek against my biceps. She did something similar in the middle of the night, but I'm surprised by her doing so in front of others.

I'm also not sorry. And I don't want her to pull away. So, I reach across with my other hand and hold her free hand in my lap. It's like she thinks I might need comforting for what's about to happen.

I turn back to Davis who's watching us closely, almost smiling. "I don't want you to do something unnatural and out of the ordinary on my account," I tell him.

Britney steps between Davis's legs, but turns to face me as he wraps his arms around her middle. "Spanking is a key element of age play," she tells me. "It's important for you to understand it if you're going to fit in at Surrender. You'll probably end up needing to spank Eve if you come very many times. Plus, there are several nuances. You'll need to understand them."

Davis gives her a squeeze. "She's right. Not everyone enjoys exactly the same dynamic, but some basic aspects hold true for nearly everyone. Namely what your intentions are when you spank someone. Pleasure or discipline or both."

I nod, listening closely, trying not to let Eve sense my nervous tension through my body language. I stroke the back of her hand with my thumb where I'm holding her fingers against my thigh.

Davis continues, "Those aspects are true for all submissives, not just littles. Some subs get a tremendous release from a hard spanking by itself. It's freeing. Other subs get very aroused from spankings and like to finish with an amazing orgasm."

I lick my lips. Christ, this is complicated.

"A lot of the subtle difference stems from where you spank a submissive. It tends to hurt more and not lead to arousal when you spank higher on their bottom. When you swat at the junction of the butt with the thighs, many women can feel the vibrations clear to their clit."

I've never in my life had such a frank discussion about orgasms and body parts. I have to force myself to breathe. No one else in the room is as unnerved as me. Not even Eve.

Davis's expression grows devious. "Some Doms like to make their sub squirm, with or without giving them relief. When I spank Britney, I don't avoid the sweet spot. I can read her well enough to know when she's aroused. But, if I'm spanking her for discipline, I don't let her come afterward. Leaving her wanting adds to the punishment."

No way to keep my eyes from growing wide.

Eve finally shifts uncomfortably next to me.

I glance at her. "You okay?"

She nods, but her grip is harder on my arm. "I…uh… I don't mix sex with my punishments."

I stare at her. I'm taking in so much information that I can't even process what she's insinuating, so I simply squeeze her hand.

Davis responds. "Like I said. Everyone is different. Just like there are some subs who get what they need from a spanking alone, there are also littles who do too."

All my questions about where sex comes into age play are running through my head. I'm not remotely sure anyone has made it clear either.

Davis moves Britney from between his legs to one side. He cups her face and meets her gaze. "You still okay with this?"

"Yes, Sir."

"You don't have to be. I won't be mad if you don't want to perform for Colt."

Part of me wants to interject and stop them, but I don't. Mostly because there's more going on here than just how I feel. I sense that this is a line Britney needs to cross for some reason too.

"I want you to spank me, Daddy."

He strokes her cheek and kisses her gently on the lips. "Good girl." He doesn't look back at us as he lowers her over his lap.

I don't move a muscle, praying to God I don't gasp or react in any way. It seems like Eve is intentionally grounding me, as if she knows I need someone to help me through this.

I've watched porn. I've seen spankings. On my computer.

This is *not* my computer.

I hold my breath while Davis pushes Britney's dress up her back, higher than necessary, and my pulse races when he lowers her tights and panties down to her knees.

I'm sitting at an angle to them, close to her feet. Close enough to see everything.

Davis pulls her hands to the small of her back and clasps her wrists together. He palms her bottom before nudging her thighs. "Spread your knees wider, sweetie."

She obliges him, stretching her panties and tights.

I don't look away, because that would defeat the purpose

here, but holy shit, I can see her pussy. It's shaved bare and glistening with arousal. She's squirming too. This gets her off.

Eve pulls her hand from my grip and sets it on top of mine instead. I was probably squeezing too tight. She snuggles closer. "He's not going to injure her," she whispers. "No one gets hurt. Just hard enough to sting for a few hours. In her case, it's meant to remind her not to repeat whatever disobedient thing she did to end up over his knee."

I nod, about half-understanding.

Davis lifts his hand and lands the first swat, making me flinch. Britney doesn't move much.

Eve holds on to me. Damn, she's amazing. She's comforting me after I've spent the entire evening wishing I could comfort her.

Davis starts out slow and picks up the pressure and speed, spanking one cheek then the other, making sure to cover every inch of her skin which is turning bright pink. When he strikes her at the juncture of her cheeks with her thighs, she lifts her head and moans. "Daddy..."

He smooths his palm over her heated skin. "You're doing well, sweetie. Keep your knees apart. You don't have permission to come."

She whimpers. Her pussy is so wet.

My cock is fucking hard. That in and of itself is unnerving.

"Five more, sweetie."

"Yes, Sir." Her voice is wobbly.

He lands three more swats on her upper cheeks and the last two in that sweet spot again, one on each side.

She stiffens as he finishes, panting.

"That's my good girl." He rubs her bottom again. It's bright pink now and admittedly sexy.

"Please, Daddy..." she begs, though I'm not sure what for.

He stands her on wobbly feet and pulls her panties and tights back up before tugging her between his legs.

She must have some tears because he wipes her cheeks with his thumbs.

I can't see her face from this angle.

"Deep breaths."

She draws in a huge breath.

"Good girl. I'm proud of you for accepting a spanking in front of our guests, and we both know you didn't really do anything to deserve it, so I will reward you for being such a sweet girl. Let's wait until after our guests leave, okay?"

She nods and wraps her arms around his neck. "Thank you, Daddy."

He pats her bottom gently.

She wiggles free of him. "I need to go potty, Daddy."

As she pulls away from him, he grabs her hand and hauls her back, his fingers on her chin again. "Take your tights and panties off. Don't put them back on. After you use the potty, come back to say goodbye to our guests."

"Yes, Sir." She steps away again, but he tugs her right back.

"Do not touch your pussy more than necessary, sweetie. If you do, I'll change my mind about letting you orgasm and spank you again."

She shudders. "Yes, Sir."

He releases her, and she skips from the room.

Eve releases me at the same time, seemingly embarrassed all of a sudden as she scrambles to put some distance between us.

"Welcome to the world of spanking." Davis smiles.

I pull in a deep breath and rub the back of my neck. There are so many thoughts running through my mind. I'm stunned by my reaction to all of this. My cock is stiff. My hands would probably be shaking if I didn't rub them on my thighs next.

How the hell am I aroused from watching my friend spank his girlfriend? It wasn't just that though. They exchanged dirty talk that made me stop breathing.

I'm starting to understand the appeal. Not sure it's my cup of tea, but I can see why others would enjoy the dynamic. I glance at Eve. She's withdrawn again, hands under her thighs, knees squeezed together. Did she find it arousing too? "You ready to go, Eve?"

"Yes, Sir." She flinches. "I mean, yes."

Yep. My cock jumped when she called me Sir. *Holy shit.*

We all stand, but Davis addresses Eve. "Go check on Britney, honey. Give us a minute."

She nods and rushes out of the room as if she's beyond grateful.

"You okay?" Davis asks.

I rub my hands together in front of me. "I think so. That was intense."

He smiles. "But you aren't running from the house, and you didn't freak out. Maybe you even enjoyed it?"

I roll my shoulders and look at the ceiling.

"I know it's confusing. No reason to be embarrassed. It can be mesmerizing to watch someone get spanked. Even if they aren't little. The members of Surrender practice many types of BDSM. It happens to be a club that is extremely friendly to the Daddy/little dynamic, so many of the members are into age play, but you'll see other fetishes too. Hopefully, you won't be as stunned now that you've had a glimpse."

"Maybe." I'm hesitant.

Davis claps me on the shoulder. "You'll be fine. We'll go to the club together separate from Eve Friday night. It will be like you're my guest. I'll show you around. It will get easier. I promise. Eve will do a scene with Owen. You'll watch. It will help you understand better, and maybe you can work up to doing a scene with her yourself."

I lift both brows. "We'll see."

He smiles. "You've got this. The best way to protect her is to keep an eye on her at all times. The best way to do that is to appear to be interested in her and start spending time with her." He tips his head to one side, a question on his face. "I don't think it's going to be a hardship." One brow goes up.

I smirk. "No. You're right."

He leads me to the front door. "Girls," he calls out.

Eve and Britney emerge from the hallway. Britney is no longer wearing the tights as instructed, and it's incredibly awkward to know she isn't wearing panties either.

She gives Eve a hug. "Call me if you need to talk."

Eve nods. "Thank you."

Davis chuckles and gives one of Britney's braids a tug. "Care to rephrase, sweetie? You suddenly have open cell phone privileges?"

She swallows and looks at Eve. "Text or call my Daddy to see if I can talk."

"I will. Thank you."

Britney looks at me, far more confident than she was when I arrived a few hours ago. She doesn't even seem embarrassed to be standing here with nothing on under her dress after letting me watch her get spanked and aroused. "Thank you for coming and for bringing Eve."

"You're welcome. Thank you for having me and for letting me get a glimpse into your life." It was far far far more than a glimpse, but what else am I supposed to say?

Davis hands us both our coats and waits for us to put them on before opening the door. "Call me if you have any questions. Otherwise, we'll see you Friday night."

CHAPTER 9

Evelyn

"Go ahead. Ask me all the questions," I tell Colt as soon as we're in the car. It will be easier to discuss whatever he's thinking in the dark in a moving vehicle so he can't look me in the eye while we talk. Easier for *me* anyway.

He glances at me. "I have a hundred or so."

I smile. "That's okay. I want you to be comfortable."

"Like how you've been so comfortable all evening?" he teases.

I sit on my hands. It's a habit I picked up that keeps me from fidgeting when I'm nervous.

"Sorry. I shouldn't make light of this."

"It's okay. You're right. It's hard for me to be comfortable with a stranger, especially one who's totally green. It makes me feel exposed."

He grips the steering wheel. "I'm sorry. If there were another way..."

"I know. It'll get easier." I reach over and touch his arm

instinctively before pulling away again. "You're a dominant man even though you've never exactly been to a club. You have tendencies that would lead anyone to believe you have at least some experience. No one will stare at you. That's helpful. You'd never be able to pull off pretending to be a Dom if it wasn't dormant inside you."

He glances at me again. "Thank you? I think?"

I chuckle. This entire situation is surreal and beyond awkward. I feel like I need to sort of teach Colt about the fetish world and my kink in particular. It wouldn't be fair to say nothing because it doesn't help if he's in the dark. But it's hard for me. I'm not a top. I don't have the instinct to train someone to be a Daddy.

"Well, if you're open to helping me understand, I'll be grateful, but if it makes you uncomfortable, that's okay too."

I shake my head. "I'm good. Better than I was earlier. I can help you. I want to. I want you to fit in. It could be the difference between life and death for me." I shudder at the thought.

He reaches over and grabs my hand, not letting it go. "I'm not going to let anything happen to you, Eve. It's my job."

I swallow, hating that he had to add that last sentence. I'm a job. He's here to protect me. I'm emotional and confused about him. I find myself having all sorts of inappropriate thoughts about him. Partly because I react to him unlike I react to any other man and partly because this is all a ruse. It's not real. I'm not supposed to have any thoughts about Colt. He's not mine. Or rather, I'm not his.

Colt draws in a breath. "Okay, here goes nothing. So, this spanking. How is it actually a deterrent at all? I mean, Britney was...you know..."

"Aroused." I can't help but smile.

"Yes, aroused."

"Well, for her yes. It's a deterrent despite the arousal. Or at least it's meant to be. Britney likes boundaries. It's their dynamic. Davis is strict with her because she craves it. He makes the rules, and she follows them because it comforts her. It also arouses her to do as she's told. Not every little is like that."

He glances at me again at a red light. "But she likes it when he spanks her?"

"Yes and no. She likes that he demonstrates she cannot control him. So, she tests him every once in a while to make sure he hasn't gone soft, so to speak. Davis doesn't let her get away with any naughty behavior, so Britney knows she can expect to get punished if she misbehaves. She won't like it because he also ensures that she gets aroused, and then he won't follow through and let her come."

Colt stares at me, the light still red.

"I'm not that kind of little," I inform him.

He looks back at the road and continues driving. "Can you explain that to me?" he asks gently.

I take a deep breath.

"You don't have to if you're not comfortable. I'm just trying to understand so I don't fuck this up."

I shake my head. "No problem. It's just hard to talk about it. But you need to know, so I'm working on it."

"Okay." He gives my hand another squeeze. I love how he does that. It's reassuring. Everything about my life is awkward right now, but when Colt touches me… It calms me. That fact alone should freak me out.

"So, I've never had my own Daddy, someone I saw regularly or lived with. There are a lot of littles like that. We play at the club with other littles and do scenes with Daddies."

"You schedule them?"

"Yes. Often ahead of time or that night." I turn toward him a bit. "I schedule a time slot with someone and then we negotiate what we're going to do, either ahead of time or right then."

He nods, his brow furrowed in concentration. It's intense, and sexy.

"Usually we agree that I'm going to do something naughty or that I previously did it. Totally pretend. It warrants me getting spanked, so he spanks me. Afterward, just like any scene in a club, the sub needs aftercare."

"What's that?"

"The Dom who just did the spanking, flogging, caning, or whatever, looks after the sub, or in this case the little, holding her and giving her water and praise. A spanking gives me a sort of high and I separate from myself a bit. It leaves me shaking and raw. Woozy. I need a blanket and cuddling."

He pulls up to my apartment building and looks around.

I don't say anything else while he concentrates on our surroundings. I'm looking around too, hoping no one is lurking in the dark. Finally, he enters the parking garage, and we remain quiet while he parks and leads me into the building.

We don't speak again until we're inside my apartment. He helps me out of my coat, then removes his before leading me to the sofa. When he sits, he pats the spot next to him. "Are you too tired to continue?"

"No." I shake my head as I lower myself awkwardly beside him. I'd rather finish this odd conversation than leave it for later. At least right now I'm not currently in a panic.

"You were telling me about aftercare. I think I get it. Like the act of getting spanked draws you into a state of relaxation that leaves you depleted."

"Exactly." I blow out a breath. He gets it.

"So, do the uh...Daddies spank you for pain or pleasure? You, in particular, I mean."

I lick my lips. "Doesn't matter. I don't sleep with them. It's not what I need."

"Oh." He looks surprised. "You never have sex with them?"

I shake my head. "Nope. I want the release I get from a spanking. I enjoy spending time in my little space relaxing. It's not sexual for me." Or it never has been. I'm startled by my reaction to Colt. I think it's because the lines are blurred between us. I've been attracted to him as a man from the moment I met him. The sort of guy I definitely want to enjoy a night between the sheets with.

I shouldn't be interested in him at all. It's not rational. But I can't help that I'm attracted to him physically, nor can I help that his job is going to entail him pretending to dominate me at the club for the sake of keeping me safe.

"But it's sexual for Britney?"

"For sure. For her the entire dynamic is sexual. Submitting to Davis makes her horny. It's not uncommon. But neither is my way."

"Okay. So, you go to the club, meet up with a Daddy. He spanks you. He snuggles with you. Then you leave and go home alone."

"Yes."

"And this is the sort of relationship you have with Owen?"

She nods. "Yes."

"But you see him outside of the club too," He points out, his voice lifting as if he's asking me a question. My dynamic with Owen is confusing to him.

I shrug. "Only because I ran into him at his bar one night. I didn't know he owned it. I talked to him for a while, and then we started meeting sometimes for coffee. We're just friends." I glance at him and roll my eyes at his incredulous expression. "Even though you don't believe in that possibility."

He holds up both hands in surrender. "I'm not the one who has to believe you," I tease.

I chuckle. "Owen gets me."

"Okay, okay. Now… Don't answer this question if you don't want to, but do you date other people who are vanilla and have sex with them?"

I smile. "Yes."

He swallows as if this makes him a bit unnerved. It's cute. Him thinking about me having sex with other men and it disturbing him. I feel kind of powerful right now.

Nothing can happen between us, and I'm certain he agrees, but the thought that he's attracted to me is enough to bolster my ego.

"Are you dating such a man right now?"

I smile again. "Nope. And before you ask, it's a complicated arrangement. Believe me, I know. I don't share my little space with anyone ever outside of Surrender. It takes far too much trust to get to that level of comfort. It opens up vulnerability that I can't deal with, so usually, my sex involves a one-night stand after a night out with coworkers or something. Always at his place. I don't bring men here."

He stares at me.

I roll my eyes again. "Oh, don't get all righteous on me. Men have one-night stands all the time. Why can't women? And, let me point out, for every man on a one-night stand, there's a woman beneath him. Or…on top of him." I grin.

Colt chuckles. "Okay. You're right. I just can't really picture *you* doing it."

"Well, I'm not a robot. I like sex." I shrug.

"But you never mix it with your little space."

"Right. Maybe I could if I found the right Daddy and entered into an actual relationship with him. I don't know. Maybe not." It's kind of sad when I hear myself tell this. My life consists of scenes with men I don't sleep with, and sex with men I don't share my life with. Pitiful.

I guess I've dreamed of having a Daddy in my life like

Davis or Roman or any number of other Daddies I've met, but I've never even come close to having a relationship like that, so I've convinced myself I don't even want or need a permanent Daddy. Being little is something I can do all alone without a Daddy. Just like no one needs a man to have sex. I've got vibrators. They work too.

"You're thinking awfully hard," Colt points out.

I shake the thoughts from my head. "This arrangement is beyond awkward."

He nods and reaches for my hand again, staring at it and stroking my knuckles while he speaks. "I know it is, and I'm also certain I shouldn't reach out and touch you like this. It's just that..."

"It calms me."

He lifts his gaze. "Yes. When you get agitated, I've noticed I can relax you with a touch. I'm blurring the lines between us though and that's dangerous and unfair. You're an attractive woman. Fun. Witty. Smart. If I met you randomly somewhere, I would be interested. But it's inappropriate to get involved with you. I'm here to do a job."

My heart rate picks up. This is the first time he's voicing the elephant in the room. "I'm attracted to you too. If I met you randomly somewhere, I'd pursue the one-night stand I mentioned." I grin.

He returns the smile. "I'd take you up on it in a heartbeat. But let me just say something to squelch that idea."

I swallow. I'm not super fond of squelching the idea. Part of me would like this man to fuck me into the middle of tomorrow, damn the consequences.

"I like you a bit too much."

I scrunch up my face. "That's the most absurd line I've ever heard. Ranks up there with 'it's not you, it's me.'"

He chuckles. "True. What I mean is that I'd never walk away from you after one night. It wouldn't be enough. And one night is all I have to offer. I don't have the kind of job that's conducive to maintaining relationships. I work too much. Sometimes I go deep undercover for months at a time. That's not fair to a woman, so I don't get into relationships. When I meet someone I find myself craving for more than one night, I turn and run in the opposite direction."

I cringe. "That's so sad."

He shrugs. "It is what it is."

"Well, we're even then, because I don't do relationships either. What I'd want doesn't exist in any sort of world, so I've arranged my life so that it works for me. I get what I need from a Daddy at the club. I get what I need from vanilla men on the side without much discussion. In between, I take care of myself."

He frowns. "That seems kind of lonely."

I lift a brow. "Less lonely than your life?"

"Touché." He glanced down at our combined hands. "Do you mind if I continue to touch you like this?"

"No." My voice is soft. I don't mind at all. I like it. I wish I could have more, but I can't. So I'll take what I can get. "Do you mind sleeping in my bed like we did last night?"

"No." He smiles at me. God, I love his smile.

"Good. I'm afraid I won't sleep without you close to me." I shiver.

He releases my hand to stroke my cheek. "I'll sleep better close to you too. It reassures me you're safe."

I take a deep breath. "Okay. I'll go get ready for bed." I ease away from him and stand, fidgeting.

He reaches for my hand once more, giving it a reassuring squeeze. "I'll use the hall bathroom and meet you there in a few."

"'K." I step back until our hands disconnect, then I flee. I don't look back as I rush through my bedroom and into the bathroom, closing the door behind me. I'm a mess. I need my little. She would calm me, even more than his touch. But he's not ready to see me fully in my little persona, and I'm not willing to share anyway. I'd never be able to relax. If this goes on very long, I'm going to have withdrawal symptoms. *Ugh.*

I quickly brush my teeth and change into a soft pink tank top and cotton shorts. They're white with bunnies on them. Babyish, but I think that ship has sailed. He won't judge me.

I climb into bed and burrow deep with Jessie, surprised to find myself drifting off even before I feel the bed dip next to me. I'm half asleep, but I exhale deeply after Colt joins me.

CHAPTER 10

Colton

I'm in over my head. I've known this since the moment I laid eyes on Evelyn Dean. The woman has me wrapped around her finger. Both the woman and the little that she's barely permitted me to glimpse.

She's scared. I don't blame her. I hate that I'm the reason she can't be herself in her own home. I wish I could do something to alleviate her nervous tension. But it's out of my hands. Maybe after Friday night she'll feel more comfortable around me. After I've seen her fully in her little space at the club. After I've watched her scene with another man.

I cringe at the thought, which is not fair. She can do whatever she wants. I don't own her. Not even close. I couldn't if I wanted to. Nor could I ever give her what she deserves and needs. I'm not cut out to be a Daddy. I can get over the shock and play the role she needs, but full-time? Not a chance.

She's adorable all curled up next to me in her bed. I'm kind of surprised she fell asleep so easily, but the last several hours have been difficult. I'm sure she's exhausted.

She's left the bathroom light on again. I wonder if that's something she always does or if it's because of the threat or because I'm here. In any case, I can see her clearly, and I can't stop watching her as she settles deeper into sleep.

Finally, she sighs heavily and rolls fully toward me. It's completely subconscious on her part, but I lift my arm above her head, making it easier for her to burrow into my side. Her head rests perfectly in the crook of my arm, and I set my palm on her hip.

The covers have fallen down to her thighs, so I have a view of far too much of her now. The tiny pink tank top she's wearing hides nothing. Her breast is high and pert. Not very large, but perfect. Her nipple is a hard point that I'm itching to stroke—either with my fingers or my lips.

I swallow as my gaze roams down to her small cotton shorts and then smile. They suit her. Her little anyway. I wonder what else her wardrobe consists of. I only got a glimpse inside her closet earlier. I'd like to see more.

I stroke her hip with my fingers and she snuggles closer.

Yeah. I'm in trouble with a capital T.

When my gaze wanders back to her amazing tit and that hard little nub, I force myself to stop staring at her. I jerk my gaze to the ceiling and take deep breaths. I need to find the asshole who's trafficking women and fast. The longer I'm guarding Eve, the harder it's going to be to extricate myself from her life.

Already it feels too late, and that's not acceptable. I wasn't kidding when I told her why I don't have relationships. It's not fair to date anyone seriously since I never know when I might get called away at a moment's notice. Hell, sometimes it's even more complicated than that. Sometimes I end up in women's beds during a case. I would never be able to do that if I were in a relationship.

I groan inside. There's no reason to ponder this. It's not going to happen. Eve made it clear she isn't looking for someone either. She likes her life compartmentalized like it is. I can see why. It would be very difficult for her to combine the parts. Perhaps impossible.

I suspect she likes to spend time at home in her little space, and I'm cramping her style. If she doesn't have sex with the Daddies who discipline her but she does like to have sex with other men... Good grief. What a mess.

It takes me forever to fall asleep, and I'm once again stunned to awaken in the same manner as yesterday. Eve is sitting next to me, coffee in hand. Dressed to kill at the office. Her adult is fully in place. Makeup. Hair in a bun. Jewelry. Navy blouse today. Black skirt. I bet I'll choke when I see her heels.

I push to sitting and accept the coffee. "Thank you. I have no idea how I keep sleeping so late. It's embarrassing."

She smiles. "I bet you lie awake half the night before dozing off. It's no wonder."

I flinch. "Do I keep you awake?"

She shakes her head. "Not at all. I was out like a light last night. The night before too after you joined me. I never noticed anything. I'm just speculating that a man with a job like yours probably has trouble sleeping."

I take another sip of coffee. "You're right." I glance at her clock. "How much time do I have?"

"Thirty minutes. You're good." She pats my chest. "I won't let you oversleep." Her smile... Just damn.

I watch as she stands and walks toward the door. "You could move your toiletries into my bathroom. If you want, I mean. Whatever."

My gaze is on her legs as she leaves. Those heels. *Fuck. Me.*

I close my eyes and inhale slowly before shoving off her bed and heading to the master bath. Fifteen minutes later, I'm ready to go and find her in the kitchen. She hands me a second cup of coffee. "Bagel or toast or something?"

"Thank you." I reach for the bagels and pop one in the toaster. "I don't want you to feel like you have to…" I don't know how to finish that sentence.

She chuckles. "No worries. You're here for the time being. You have to eat. Help yourself to whatever." She lifts a brow. "However…"

I hesitate and meet her gaze. "Yeah?"

"Now that you know me better, don't be surprised at what you might find in my kitchen or anywhere else in my apartment. Like I said, I don't bring men here. Not ever. This is my getaway. My safe space. If a stranger came in and rummaged through my things, they would think I have a small child living here." She smiles. She's far less uncomfortable today. I'm glad.

I shouldn't keep touching her, but I do. I cup her face. My voice comes out gravelly. "No worries. I won't judge you. This is your home. Please, be yourself. Pretend I'm not here if you need to."

She chuckles, not sounding amused. "Like that's possible."

I drop my hand to grab the bagel and slather it with cream cheese. "Do you think I could drive you to work and pick you up? We could be discreet about it."

She giggles, a sound that goes straight to my cock. "Because you don't trust me to stay where you leave me?"

I flinch and turn toward her. "That's not it at all. And you're not a prisoner. You can go anywhere you want. I'm just asking you to let me know so that I don't have to worry. I can't keep you safe if you go places without my knowledge."

Her eyes are dancing with mirth. "And you think you don't have a Daddy inside you?"

My eyes go wide, and I nearly choke on my bagel.

She laughs again and changes the subject. "Actually, now that you mention it, I do have a lunch meeting today. It's at the Woodfire Grill two blocks south of the office. About ten of us will be there. We have a reservation." She bites her lip and, for a moment, looks hesitant. "Do you think it's safe?"

I nod. "Absolutely. What time is your lunch? I'll go there at the same time, just in case. I'll sit at the bar and keep an eye on you. You won't have to mention me to a single person. Just pretend you've never seen me before."

She stares at me. "You'd do that?"

I grin. "What part has you flummoxed?"

She licks those full lips now, distracting me. "All of it. Do you have time in the middle of the day to waste watching me eat with my coworkers?"

I frown. "It's my job, Eve. I go where you go. Even if I need to remain in the background. Keep your phone in your pocket in case I need to message you. Otherwise, ignore me. Enjoy your lunch."

She hesitates. "Okay. You're sure? I could make an excuse and stay back in the office."

I shake my head. "No. Eve. I don't want your life disrupted. Not any more than it already is, I mean."

I can say with absolute certainty that nothing could have prepared me for seeing Eve in action in her work environment. She may be small in stature, but she's a force to be reckoned with when she puts on her power suits and those damn heels.

I follow her from her office to the restaurant and enter after her party of ten. As I take a seat at the bar, she glances at me briefly and smiles. Her face flushes, making my cock hard. Dammit.

For several minutes, she stands around with her coworkers, all of them talking in small groups while they wait for their table to be ready. I know immediately that she's well-respected and well-liked. Everyone finds a way to get in front of her and secure a moment of her time.

She sits near the head of the table next to her boss, and I'm struck by how different she looks dining with her coworkers as opposed to last night at Davis's. She sits tall, spine extended, legs crossed at the ankles as if she's been trained by royalty. Confidence wafts off of her. She sips her iced tea and daintily eats her salad. All the while, she keeps up with no fewer than four conversations.

I can't hear much from my distance, but I catch a word here and there, enough to inform me that they're discussing numbers and tax laws. These people carry on animated conversations about loopholes as if they could orgasm on the details.

It's interesting, and I have to force myself to keep a straight face while I eat. I'd look like a doofus if I sat here grinning.

I can't stare at her because that would look suspicious too, but I rationalize even if the bartender catches me looking, he'll just think I've got my eyes on a hot woman. He'd be right. But I'm here to watch other people, not Eve.

I glance around at everyone in the restaurant discreetly every few moments. I look outside the wall-to-wall windows too. After a while, I realize I'm going to need to draw out my meal because the luncheon isn't going to end quickly.

I'm nursing a cup of coffee and pretending to scroll through my emails when I spot my suspect outside, the man who has been following her. My chest tightens. I calmly pay my bill and leave a nice tip while sending a text to Eve.

Do not panic. Do not change anything you're doing. The man I've seen watching you is outside. I'm going to follow him. Please, stay with your group at all times. Go straight back to your office. Do not leave again until you've heard from me.

I keep one eye on the stalker and one eye on Eve as I remain seated. I see her flinch when her phone buzzes in her pocket, and I watch her closely as she reads the text in her lap.

She stiffens, and I doubt she's breathing, but she manages to pull herself together, put the phone back in her pocket, and glance my way. Her fucking amazing brown eyes are freaking out. The rest of her remains outwardly calm.

I lift a brow.

She bites into her bottom lip and returns to the conversation on her left, but her hands are shaking and she tucks them in her lap.

I rise and exit through a side door, hating that I've left her unprotected. She'll be fine. No one's going to snag her from a group of people in broad daylight. That's not how these people operate.

Her stalker is leaning against the building across the street, casual as can be, his phone in his hand while he pretends to peruse it. This is my first time getting a solid beat on him. He's just over six feet, about my height. Built like a linebacker. Khaki slacks. White shirt. Leather jacket. Brown ball cap.

I've seen the leather jacket and brown ball cap several times. It's definitely the same guy. Now, I just need to get a look at his face. I snap several pictures while I pull out a pack of cigarettes and light up. I hate this part of the job. I hate smoking. It's disgusting. But it comes in handy when I need to stand around and keep tabs on someone, especially since no building allows smoking inside anymore.

I pace casually while I inhale from the cigarette as infrequently as possible and keep an eye on both my suspect and Eve. Finally, her party finishes. They gather their coats and exit through the main door. I ignore them and keep my eye on my suspect.

As soon as they begin to stroll back toward the office, he moves with them across the street. I move also, keeping a distance behind them. Luckily, the guy does not enter her office building. If he had, I'd have freaked the fuck out. Instead, he stops again as she enters. He sends a text, then lifts his gaze to her building as if he could see her wherever she is inside.

That's the moment I get a good picture of him. Not great, but at least what I can see of his face.

He puts his phone away and starts walking. I keep up with him, following on the other side of the street still. Three streets away, he gets in a car parallel-parked. At least I get several pictures of his vehicle. If I'm lucky, the plates will trace to him and the entire mess will be that much closer to over.

I'm five blocks from my own car now, so there's not a damn thing I can do to follow him. *Fuck*. As he drives away, I head toward my SUV, fuming. Who the fuck is this asshole, and what does he intend to do with Eve?

CHAPTER 11

Colton

I pick Eve up at six. She waits inside until I pull up and then rushes out to get in my SUV.

It's cold out, and she rubs her hands together as I pull away from the curb. I'd rather take her pulse first, but I know she doesn't want anyone from her office to see her coming and going with me. Not yet. How is she going to explain me without sending the entire office into a panic?

"What happened?" she asks the moment we start moving.

"Nothing. I got some better pictures of him, but I'm not sure it will be sufficient for facial recognition. Followed him to his car though and got the plates, for all the good that did. They were stolen. Shocker. There was no way for me to follow him. I was parked too far away." I grip the steering wheel, still pissed.

"Well, fuck." She's fidgeting, rubbing her hands on her skirt, but when I squeeze and release my tight grip on the steering wheel, she finally reaches across and sets her hand over mine. "Sorry. I didn't mean that the way it sounded. It's not your fault."

I turn toward her, grateful I'm at a light. I thread my fingers with hers and hold them in my lap. "I'm sorry too. I'm just frustrated. I get this way when I can't solve a crime fast enough for my liking."

My anxiety has caused her to relax to balance things. She grins at me. "Maybe you should slow down the investigation. I kind of like having you around," she teases.

I lift her hand to my cheek, though I should not. "Maybe you shouldn't use words like *fuck*. I might go all Daddy on you and wash your mouth out with soap."

She sucks in a breath and doesn't move.

"Shit. Sorry. That was uncalled for. It slipped out before I could filter myself." I release her hand, kicking myself mentally.

When I glance at her, she's staring at me, part of her bottom lip between her teeth. She's breathing heavily, and she slowly turns to face the front.

The light turns green. I keep driving. *What the fuck is wrong with me?* I couldn't have said anything more inappropriate if I had tried.

When we arrive at her apartment, we still haven't spoken another word. I help her down from the SUV and follow her inside and up to her floor. I take her keys from her hand and open the door. This has become a thing with us. I also lock the door in both places.

I turn around to find her hurrying across the room, heading for the hallway. I know she probably wants to change, but I feel like a fucking asshole. "Eve."

She doesn't stop or glance back.

I hurry to follow her. She's in her doorway when I speak again. "Eve, I'm sorry."

She shuts the door, and I hear the lock turn.

"Fuck." I pace the hallway, needing to talk to her. Needing to make this right. Five minutes go by, then ten. Not a single sound is coming from her bedroom. Finally, I lean against the door and knock. "Can we please talk?"

Nothing.

"Eve. Please." I'll happily beg for as long as it takes. I hate that I've crossed a line with her and possibly hurt her feelings or triggered her in some way. Or worse. I wouldn't want her to think I was making fun of her fetish. "I shouldn't have said what I did. It was insensitive. I didn't mean to make light of your kink. It was rude and uncalled for. Please forgive me."

She yanks the door open so fast I nearly fall into the room. Thank God I have a hold of the frame.

She's no longer dressed for the office. She's not dressed at all actually. She's in that soft pink robe. She turns around and starts pacing. "It's fine. Don't worry about it."

"It's *not* fine. I've obviously hurt your feelings."

"You didn't hurt my feelings, Colt. Stop it. You have it all mixed up, and how could I expect you to understand? You were thrown into this lifestyle two days ago. You hardly know what the fuck to think about much of anything." She stops pacing and draws in a deep breath.

I consider interjecting but it doesn't seem wise. I hold my spot, my grip still on the doorframe.

Her words rush out. "The truth is that I'm stressed. I'm stressed because you're in my private space where I come to unwind and be who I want to be at the end of a long day. And I can't do that with you here."

I swallow. I suspected this was a problem. "I'm so sorry. I don't want to infringe on your space."

She rubs her brow. "You can't help it. And I don't blame you. But I'm used to a certain routine that I'm not getting. So, forgive me for freaking out."

"There's nothing to forgive. What can I do to make this

better? Would you like me to go into the guest room and shut the door so you can have your space? I can do that."

She shakes her head. "Of course not. That's not fair to you."

I search her face, trying to come up with something. Anything. "You're used to being in your little space at home."

She nods, her teeth clamping down on her lip now. A tear slides down her face.

Fuck.

I release the doorframe, watching her closely as I slowly approach. I want to touch her, but I won't if she doesn't want me to.

She drops her gaze to the floor, her head dipping. I pull her into my arms, grateful when she lets me and slumps against me. Her small hands go around my waist and she holds on tight.

I thread my hands in her hair and cup the back of her head. "I'm so sorry," I repeat.

After a few moments, she tips her head back and looks up at me.

I stare into her eyes, searching for answers. I don't get them, but when she licks her lips, my gaze slides to her mouth. We're so close that I can smell the breath mint she must have eaten after lunch.

She shudders in my arms, and that's the last straw. I can't stop myself from lowering my lips to hers. I kiss her gently at first, then deeper, angling my head to one side while I direct hers at the same time.

When she moans into my mouth, I growl back, stroking her tongue with mine, then sucking it just enough to make her tremble. I walk her backward until she hits the wall, and then I press against her as I continue to devour her.

She's heaven, and I'm the devil.

When I finally break the kiss and look into her eyes, she's panting. "Oh, God."

"Yeah…"

She looks away.

I grip her chin and force her to look at me. "I need to know something."

She swallows.

"Who was I just kissing? Which Eve?"

She stares at me, her chest rising and falling. Finally, she responds quietly, "I don't know." She starts trembling again.

I set my forehead against hers and stroke the sides of her face with my thumbs. "It's okay, Eve."

"It's not really."

I draw back a few inches to give her room to breathe. "Here's what we're going to do. I want you to spend the next two hours in your little space. Dress how you would if I weren't here. Do all the things that help you relax at the end of the day. Let me make you dinner. Let me pamper you for two hours."

"I don't know, Colt. That's huge. I'm not sure I'm ready for something like that."

"Do it anyway. Do it for me. I know I'm asking you to take a risk, but I'm also asking you to trust me that I won't let you down. That I won't freak out. I can do this. I can stay out of your way and give you the space you need."

She hesitates.

I lift a brow. "See, now, you're just being defiant. I think you've known me long enough to realize I would never do anything intentionally to hurt your feelings. Do you still think I'm the sort of guy who would make fun of you for living your truth?"

She shakes her head. I see her little peeking through.

I lift a brow.

She licks her lips. "No, Sir."

My cock jumps to attention, and I pray she doesn't notice. In fact, I take a step back, grip her chin, and meet her gaze dead on again. "You have ten minutes to put some clothes on and meet me in the kitchen. I'll find something and start dinner."

"Yes, Sir," She mumbles, her doe eyes wide now.

I release her and turn to leave the room, not stopping until I've shut the door behind me. I run a hand through my hair. What the fuck have I just started?

There are so many reasons why this is a bad idea, but I started it, and I intend to see it through. I head to the kitchen and start opening cabinets, the pantry, the freezer, the fridge. In the end, I choose frozen dinosaur chicken nuggets and mac and cheese from a box. These are things she has a lot of, so I assume she enjoys eating them.

My brain is running at full speed as I pop the nuggets in the oven and set a pan on the stove to boil water. I kissed Eve. Jesus, I kissed her. And I liked it. I'm not sure she was her adult self at the time. And I suspect she isn't sure either. She doesn't mix sex with her kink. I might have crossed a line. It won't happen again. For the next two hours, I will show her that she can be herself in her own home.

The smallest sound behind me makes me turn around to find her leaning in the doorway, peeking around the corner really. I glance at my watch. "One minute to spare. Good job." I'm out of my element, and yet, I'm also not. This isn't as hard as I suspected.

I don't comment on her appearance. I try not to look too hard either. She's wearing a tight white T-shirt with a pink bear on it and a pink skirt that matches the bear. It's short. Really really short. Her feet are bare. Her hair is in pigtails.

"Why don't you pick out a movie while I finish dinner? We can eat in the living room."

Her eyes go wide. She starts to speak then stops herself,

glancing away. "Okay," she murmurs as she shuffles toward the couch. She turns on the tv and scans through the channels, settling on a cartoon station.

I keep half an eye on her while I cook the macaroni and pour us both a drink. Mine is a glass of soda. I take my cues from Davis and the contents of Eve's refrigerator and cabinets and decide to fix her a sippy cup of part apple juice, part water.

When I take it to her ahead of the meal, she tips her head back and stares up at me. "Thank you," she finally murmurs.

I know her mind is wired for more though. She proved that in the bedroom. And it's so easy to get her to shift deeper into her role. The one I know she craves. All I have to do is lift a brow.

She bites that lower lip again and then rephrases, "Thank you, Sir."

I pat her head instinctively and return to the kitchen. Damn, this is odd. Beyond odd. But not in a bad way. Just... different. Outside of my wheelhouse. Eve is more relaxed already though, so this is what we're going to do.

I finish cooking and prepare two plates. I bring her a pink plastic plate and a short chubby plastic fork, things I found in her cabinets. The shock on her face makes my chest tighten. She takes the plate from me carefully. "I can eat on the sofa?" she asks, her voice incredulous.

"Uh, sure. Just this once." I try to sound stern.

She smiles. "Thank you, Sir."

I can't stop watching her as she digs into the food.

"Do you want catsup or something to dip your nuggets in?"

She makes a pained face. "Bleh. Gross."

I chuckle as I return to the kitchen and grab my plate. Can't say I've eaten chicken nuggets or mac and cheese from a box in a long time, but I don't mind. It's actually better than fast food.

I sit on the other end of the sofa, balancing my plate in my lap while I eat. The tv is in the middle of an animated movie about some animals, and I find myself sucked in.

This entire thing may be completely from the upside-down, but it's what Eve needs, so I'll do this for her. Every night I'm here. I hope that will work.

When she's done eating, she carries her plate to the sink and sets it inside. She returns to the sofa, picks up her sippy cup, then crawls across the cushion toward me. Her gaze never leaves the tv as she settles on her side, her cheek on my thigh.

I set my plate on the end table so as not to disturb her and smooth my hand down her pigtail, resting it on her hip in the end.

She sighs, relaxing further by the minute. It's mesmerizing to watch, and eventually, her eyes grow heavy and she falls asleep curled up next to me.

There are so many problems with this picture I can't even enumerate them. First and foremost, I'm fucking infatuated with this woman. I can't begin to explain how or why, but I am. Not just her adult. Her little is adorable too. My mouth is dry. My cock is hard again.

I continue stroking her hip because I have been doing so for an hour. The swell of her small breast is impossible to ignore. The tip of her nipple is tempting. Apparently, she doesn't wear a bra when she's little. Her skirt is so short that it has risen up enough for me to catch the edge of pink cotton panties.

I force myself to stop staring, tip my head back against the cushions, and close my eyes. I try to rationalize this situation and why I find it sexy and smoking hot. I've never been in a situation like this, but I'm a dude. I watch porn. I've masturbated more than once to the vision of a woman pretending to be a schoolgirl, pigtails and all. It's no wonder I'm turned on.

There are differences. Eve isn't pretending. This is her. Or one side of her. It's not a game. It's not a role she's performing to turn me on. She does this alone most of the time for relaxation. She made it clear to me that she doesn't mix sex with her little.

I have to clean up my thoughts ASAP. I'm definitely mixing sex with her little. Hell, I'm mixing sex with her everything. And I can't do that. I'm not here to fuck her. Jesus. I keep having to remind myself of this fact. Not only would it be highly inappropriate, but she hasn't asked me to do anything of the sort.

Sleeping with her would fuck with both our minds.

Nope. It can't happen. I'm here to keep her safe. I need to do that, catch the fucking people who are after her, and move on to my next assignment. Maybe the captain will agree to send me deep into a drug bust in another part of town. Something that will purge my mind of my currently inappropriate thoughts about the amazingly complex woman asleep next to me.

It's not very late, but I know Eve hasn't gotten enough sleep this week. She's dead to the world. I decide to put her to bed.

She whimpers when I lift her into my arms and carry her from the room. Her arms go around my neck. "Where are we going, Daddy?"

My breath hitches. I rein myself in. "To bed, baby. You're tired."

"Okay." She hugs me tighter.

I pull back the covers on her side of the bed and lower her onto the sheets. Then I consider her clothes. Her shirt is soft enough to sleep in, and she's wearing panties, but the skirt is bunched up and looks uncomfortable. When she rolls to her side, I find the zipper, lower it, and pull the skirt over her hips and down her legs.

Before I lose my mind at seeing the fucking hot swell of her bottom encased in pink cotton panties, I find her unicorn, tuck it in her arms, and pull the covers over her sweet body. "Thank you, Daddy," she murmurs as she snuggles deeper.

I stare at her for a while, mesmerized again by her duality. Finally, I turn the bathroom light on, pull the door almost closed, and pad from the room. I won't join her for a while. I need to open my computer and check my email anyway. I pray to God that my boss gets a positive ID on her stalker ASAP. The sooner the better. The longer I stay here, the more of my heart I will lose to the gorgeous multifaceted woman in the other room.

I hold my breath while I open the captain's email, and I don't release it until I read that the system has been unable to readily identify the face, which means he's not in the system. Interesting. My boss will send it to another department to dig deeper.

I groan and consider punching something. Not because he didn't find a match, but because I'm glad he didn't find a match yet.

Fuck. Me.

CHAPTER 12

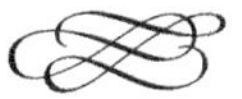

Evelyn

I'll never understand how this man can sleep so hard in the morning while I get ready for work all around him. Alas, for the third morning in a row, I'm waking him up with coffee in my hands. I like doing this for him. It might be a bit out of my usual persona to take care of a man instead of the other way around, but it feels nice.

I also like waking him. The way he slowly realizes where he is and who he's with. The smile that spreads across his face as he takes the steaming mug from me. His tousled hair and unshaven face. Sexy with a capital S.

I'm feeling shyer this morning than usual. I allowed myself to be vulnerable with him last night. It was way out of my comfort zone, but it was impossible to turn down the offer. Hell, it was more like a demand from him. Also sexy with a capital S.

Once I was finally able to relax and be myself, I know I fell asleep with my head on his lap. I was exhausted. I don't remember too much about going to bed, but I'm pretty sure he carried me. I'm pretty sure I called him Daddy. And I'm pretty sure he took off my skirt because I woke up in just my panties and T-shirt.

And then there was that kiss. Before. Before I let myself be vulnerable and little with him. Before I dressed in toddler clothes and put my hair in pigtails. I bite my lip as I stare at his lips. He's an amazing kisser. Gentle and firm at the same time.

No one has ever quite made my panties melt with a kiss the way he did. It's unnerving to think about. I can't believe we did that. Crossed into dangerous territory. Way outside of my usual norm. I don't kiss men I submit to and I don't submit to men I kiss.

But I did. And it felt right. Good. Now it's just scary. I need to stuff it to the back of my head.

I'm still staring at him, sitting on the edge of the bed. It's a good thing I put the coffee down on the bedside table because I would be spilling it now as his hand suddenly slides down from his chest to cover mine a moment before he opens his eyes.

I'm flustered as he threads his fingers with mine and pulls them to his lips, kissing my knuckles before muttering, "Good morning."

"Good morning," I return, almost tacking on the word Sir. *Jesus.*

"Thirty minutes?" he asks.

I nod and ease my hand free before slipping out of the room.

We do our morning dance in the kitchen fifteen minutes later, me trying to stay out of his way, him fixing a bagel and another cup of coffee. It's not until we're in the car that he turns to me and asks, "Tell me about this caffeine quirk of yours."

I glance at him. "It's no big deal. It's just that my little doesn't drink caffeine."

"Ahhh. So when you get to work, you are your adult self and you caffeinate for the day."

"Yes."

"Do you drink alcohol? You don't have that in the apartment either."

"Yes. When I'm out as a vanilla person."

"Got it."

"Told you I'm not quite like other people. This is why I don't get too serious with anyone. I'm complex."

He reaches over to take my hand. He's getting bolder about holding my hand as the hours tick by in our strange arrangement. I'm not sorry. "Complex is not a bad thing. It's who you are. Is there any other aspect of you that you've kept hidden from me?"

I think for a second and shake my head. "Nope. You pretty much know all my secrets." I shudder. There are very few people who know as much as Colt does about my life.

"Then how about you stop tiptoeing around and worrying all the time. I've seen it all. I'm not going to judge you. From now on, when we get home, I want you to go directly to your room and change into whatever makes you comfortable. While you do that, I'll get dinner ready, and you can spend two hours in your little space. If you're exhausted and you fall asleep like last night, that's fine. I'll put you to bed. If you're still awake or need to take care of anything adult, you can switch personas and manage whatever needs to be seen to."

Besides how damn appealing his offer is, one thing stands out above all else. No. Two things. First of all, he hasn't asked me a question. It wasn't a suggestion. He just laid down the law. And secondly, holy mother of God, it was hot. I'm fighting the need to squirm.

It's not like me to react this way to demands from any

Dom. I don't have many interactions with Doms who aren't Daddies of course, so I can't be sure how I would react to other types of commands, but Colt is not my Daddy.

Except that he kind of is. He certainly took care of me like a Daddy would last night. Never batted an eye either. It's not really shocking for him to go alpha on me. He's probably on the bossy side at all times. I have no doubt he's a dominant lover. But he's known about my world for less than a week, and somehow he's managed to fill a role I desperately need filled.

He's rubbing my knuckles with his thumb casual as can be, but when we arrive at my office, he gives my hand a tug to get my attention before I open the door. His brows are raised in that way that makes my panties melt. My heart is pounding and my nipples are tight. He lifts his brows higher, and I finally lick my lips. I realize I never responded to his proclamation. He's waiting for me to comply. My entire body trembles as I speak. "Yes, Sir."

Colton dictating how our evenings will be conducted from now on was extremely dominating, but the way he lifted his brow, waiting for me to respond is off-the-charts controlling. Full Dom. Full Daddy. Does he know it?

"Good girl. Have a nice day. Text me if you leave the building." He lets my hand go, and I exit the car on wobbly legs. I'm confused and bewildered. Colt has gotten under my skin. I'm in a strange gray zone as I walk to the front of my building.

I'm dressed for success, but my mind is in little space. I need to shake myself out of it, and fast. It's hard. Colt is so dominant. He just issued a command and silently insisted I verbally agree with the most respectful language commonly used in the fetish community. *Yes, Sir.*

Perhaps there could have been some doubt about his domination from the demand alone. I could have misunderstood his tone or the meaning behind his words. But the second he lifted that brow and held my gaze... Holy Christ. I melted, and I'm not sure when I'll recover.

It was the hottest interaction of my life. And it was with a man who's never seen me naked. Hasn't had sex with me. Hasn't spanked me.

He doesn't fit in any of my worlds really. He's not my Daddy or my boyfriend. I don't get to keep him after the threat to my life is over. I'll probably never see him again. I don't know his last name. He's a house guest. A house guest who has managed to cause my two distinct worlds to collide on more than one occasion.

He takes control and forces my little to come out in my adult space. It's disconcerting on so many levels. I never in my wildest dreams expected to meet someone who could be my everything. I may sleep with a stuffed unicorn but I don't believe they exist in real life.

I'm still struggling as I reach my floor. After I drop off my purse, I head straight for the break room and make a cup of coffee. While I watch the machine, the scent of adult liquid filling the air, the sounds of it percolating, I slowly pull myself together.

Thank God I don't drink coffee at home. Before Colt, I often dallied in the morning. I would get up earlier than necessary and stay in my little space for a while. I sometimes eat sugary cereal or pop-tarts. I tend to drag my feet as I shed my little and transform into my adult self. I don't leave her completely until I step out my front door.

Today, that line blurred badly, but the coffee is going to help me seal the transition. And I'm right. The moment I take the first sip, my brain shifts gears. It's right on time too, because one of my coworkers steps into the breakroom. "Hey, Eve. You have time to go over the numbers for the Smyth account? I feel like something is off."

"Sure. Meet me in my office in five." I lift the mug, indicating I need a few moments to let the caffeine enter my blood flow.

Lacy smiles. "You got it. See you then."

I'm deep in my morning meeting when my phone vibrates in my jacket pocket. I pull it out absentmindedly. Not many people text me during the day. I don't have a lot of friends outside of work and Surrender. When would I have time?

Leah is my closest friend at the club, and I have casual relationships with a few ladies at work—including Lacy—but that's about it. Leah doesn't text me at work.

I can't help but smile when I see it's from Colt, but then I remember that any text from him is probably not something I want to see. Either he's spotted a threat or he's solved the case. I shouldn't be wishing he wouldn't wrap things up quickly of course. That's insane. I need him to find out who's following me and put an end to the threat. But that also means an end to our strange relationship.

I take a moment to brace myself before opening the text, glancing around to make sure no one is looking at me.

> *Just want to make sure you're okay. You were flustered when you got out of the car. I hope I didn't push you too far.*

My hands are shaking as I put the phone back in my pocket. I can't possibly respond to him right now.

The meeting ends ten minutes later, and I wait until I'm back in my office alone before I consider my response.

> *I'm fine. I wasn't flustered. And you didn't push me too far. Don't you have bad guys to catch? Why are you texting me?*

I grin as I send it.

Seconds later, I'm watching the three little dots that indicate he's responding already.

Amazing how you can manage to both lie and sass me in so few words. What shall I do about that? Get back to work. I'll see you at six.

I gasp as I set the phone on my desk. *Holy shit*. My legs are bouncing under the desk. It feels too warm in here. And for the first time in my career, I'm aroused at work. I might have lied about being flustered when I got out of the car, but I'm ten times more flustered now.

Lacy pokes her head into my office, making me jump in my seat. She frowns. "You okay?"

"Yep. Yes. Sorry. You startled me. What's up?"

"I just wanted to see if you'd like to grab lunch? I'm in the mood for a salad."

I ponder how to respond. "Sounds great. Can we order it to be delivered? I'm not sure I have the time to go out today. But I could take thirty when it gets here. Will that work?"

"Perfect. I'll place our order. The usual?"

"Yes, and add a large iced tea."

"Got it. See you when it arrives." Lacy wanders away.

I stare at the door. Iced tea? Do I think that's going to shake me out of my hazy gray zone like the coffee? Good grief.

CHAPTER 13

Colton

I slide into the booth at the greasy burger joint I love moments before Davis arrives to join me.

"How's it going?" he asks as he sits across from me. "I keep thinking you'll need some backup help from Black Blade, but I haven't heard a peep out of you."

I smirk. "You think I can't handle my job on my own?" I joke.

He chuckles. "I have no doubt you can."

A waiter comes by to take our orders. Davis meets my gaze again. "Seriously though. Have you made any headway?"

I sigh. "Not much. I'm paying close attention to Owen Karplus and the mysterious stalker. That asshole was waiting in front of Eve's building again today, but he hasn't cottoned on to the fact that she's been leaving in my car yet. I wonder how he thinks she gets to work or if he believes himself to be slipping."

"Shit, though. I can't stand the idea of someone watching her. Does she know it?"

"I don't always tell her. Had to yesterday while she was at lunch outside of her office building, but I don't mention it in the mornings or when we come home."

"And Owen? What's he been up to?"

"Nothing. Seems clean so far. Goes to work. Goes home mostly. I've dug deeper into his finances though. His bar is upside down. He's hurting for cash flow."

"That could mean something. Or it could mean nothing." Davis sighs. "Plenty of people lose their businesses every day without deciding to sell a human being to save themselves."

"Exactly." I sit back. "Hopefully I'll get a better read on Owen tomorrow night at the club. Otherwise, I'm spinning my tires right now. I finally got a picture of the stalker, but he's not in the system."

"Damn. That sucks."

"My boss sent it for deeper analysis, but that's going to take some time. He hasn't done anything. He's no real threat to anyone as far as the law is concerned. Maybe he just finds Eve attractive and he's building up the courage to ask her out."

Davis smirks. "You don't believe that."

"Fuck no. Neither does anyone else. But that's where the rule of law stands right now."

Davis sighs. "Send me the picture and I'll ask Roman and Julius if they recognize the man on the off chance he's a member of Surrender or has ever visited. I'll give a copy to Blade too. You never know what he might come up with."

I nod. "Good idea." I have no doubt Davis's boss has a database that would rival anything at the police station. Black Blade Protection is the equivalent of a privatized police agency.

The waiter drops off our drinks, and then Davis meets my

gaze when we're alone again. "That's not why you asked me to lunch."

I shake my head. "No."

He smiles. "How did it go with Eve after you left the other night? It was intense. I hope you don't feel like I tossed you to the wolves."

"Not at all. I needed the education. I'll be far more prepared tomorrow night. I appreciate it. And please, thank Britney for me. I know that wasn't easy on her either."

"She's fine. I rewarded her well after you left." His grin is big.

I roll my eyes. "Please, spare me the details."

He sobers and sets his elbows on the table. "How's Eve?"

I draw in a slow breath. "Confused. And I'm not helping out any." I play with the napkin in front of me, picking off small chunks absently as I stare at it.

"You're into her."

I roll my shoulders back and groan. "Yes. And I can't be. It's so unprofessional. Plus, there are a dozen or more other reasons I need to keep my pants on."

He chuckles. "Life gets messy sometimes when we least expect it. Maybe you should just follow your instincts."

"I have and they're leading us both into dangerous territory." I groan again. "I've gone all Dom on her. I didn't even know I had such a dominant side. It just comes out of me from somewhere. Or she brings it out of me. Mostly because she's been lost without it. She needs it. It calms her. So does my touch."

"I noticed that the other night. Has she let you see her little?"

I nod. "She was very hesitant at first. I don't blame her. I'm sure she feels vulnerable. But it was stressing her out. She's used to coming home and relaxing in her little space. With me there, she's been stifled. So, last night, I insisted she let it go. I think we had a breakthrough."

"That's good. So, what's the problem?" He's smirking again.

Our food arrives and we begin to assemble and doctor our burgers as we continue speaking. "Besides the fact that I cannot mess with this woman?"

"Why not? You're entitled to a life, Colton. No one can be expected to devote their entire lives to their job and never settle down."

"It's the nature of my job, and you know it."

He waves a hand through the air. "Let's cross that bridge later. Stop worrying about the future and deal with the present. Are you surprised to find you have dominant tendencies?"

I shrug. "I don't know. Never really thought about it. I guess I would have described myself as a fairly alpha sort of guy, but the shift in my mindset to someone bossy and demanding is unexpected."

"But it's what Eve needs."

I nod. "Yes. So it just sort of comes out of me."

"That's not a bad thing."

I set my burger down and meet him eye-to-eye. "I dominated her hard this morning. She needed it. It was hotter than hell. But I also know I overstepped in doing so. On top of that, I piled onto that domination by text two hours later. She's either throwing stuff at the wall in her office or squirming in her seat. I'm not sure which is worse."

Davis chuckles. "Could be both. And good for you. Eve is incredibly submissive. She needs a strong Dom in her life. Someone who can help her see things through a new lens."

"The woman maintains two personas like they're a lifeline. She doesn't let them cross, nor does she let the lines blur. I'm messing with her tidy plan."

"Britney knows her better than I do, but from what I've heard, you're right. She's been kind of rigid and it keeps her from letting anyone get close."

"It took her a long time to explain her preferences after we left your house. I could see that Britney gets off on the submission and every aspect of her life. Eve made it clear that she does not."

Davis nods and finishes his bite before responding. "That's not unusual. Lots of littles keep sex out of it. They want to escape and find it refreshing to color or play with toys to block out the real world for a while. Nothing wrong with that, nor is it peculiar for them to enjoy getting disciplined without getting aroused. They prefer to keep the two sides separate."

"That's exactly how Eve described things to me, and I get it. It makes sense. But either she's been lying to herself and others or it's different with me."

Davis cocks his head to one side. "How so?"

I meet his gaze. "This doesn't leave this table, right?"

"Never. Hard rule in the BDSM community. I would never break a confidence. You have my word."

"Eve likes me. Both of her personas like me. I know it. It's as clear as the sun in the sky." I glance at the window. This is Seattle. The sky is not clear most days, including today. "At the equator."

Davis laughs. "Okay, so that's great. She likes you. What's the problem? And don't tell me again about your job." He waves his hand dismissively again. "Pretend that issue doesn't exist for now. What other roadblocks are there?"

"Eve. She has it set in her mind that she doesn't sleep with Daddies and she doesn't tell her vanilla boyfriends about her little side."

"I figured. So, she never gets close to anyone."

"Right."

"And now you're in her space and it's confusing."

"Exactly. There's no way for her to compartmentalize like she's used to. The lines are blurring. I can see it. She shares both sides of herself with me, and that's not something she does normally." I hesitate but then tell him more because damn, I need his advice. Who the hell else am I going to ask? "She sleeps with me. And by that I mean, I sleep in her bed. I have from the first night when she woke up scared. She's little in her bed, and she subconsciously gravitates to my side and curls up against me. It's fucking adorable."

Davis grins. "How cute."

I groan yet again. "That's not helpful."

"Look, just because she can sleep next to you doesn't mean she would be willing to have sex in her little space. Even if she responds sexually while she's little doesn't mean she wouldn't prefer to get out of that headspace and be an adult while having sex. It's possible, but not mandatory. Everyone is different."

I nod. "That makes sense."

"That being said, I have no idea what Eve is thinking. Britney is never out of her little space with me. We marginally set her little aside when we have sex, but it's subtle at best. Not everyone is the same, and it's possible Eve is staring at new possibilities. The woman deserves to find a man who can be everything to her. Let her be little when she needs it but also step aside while she achieves world domination."

I laugh. "I have no doubt she's capable of that. She's a force of nature at work."

"I believe you. I've seen her come into the club from work. She's a different person when she heads into the locker room to change. The girl who comes out hardly resembles the woman who goes in."

I can totally picture what he's describing. "I feel bad that I toyed with her today. She has made it clear that her adult persona doesn't submit, and I blurred that line. She's probably pissed."

"I doubt it, but if she is, she'll tell you, and you'll deal."

"I'm scared out of my mind about tomorrow night. I don't care what she's told me about how she doesn't find her scenes sexual. I do. I find all of her sides sexual. It's going to be very hard to stay out of her way and watch her submit to another man."

Davis nods. "I understand, but you have to do it. At least this once. You can talk to her about how it made you feel afterward, but let her do her thing tomorrow. If she feels as much for you as you do for her, she won't enjoy submitting to another man, especially if the lines between you two have blurred as much as you think."

I play with a fry, dragging it through the catsup even though I have no intention of eating it. "I'm in way over my head."

Davis leans forward. "You're not. Take it one day at a time. One hour if you need to. Take your cues from Eve. All you can do is say and act on whatever feels natural to you and watch how she reacts. I know she has a prearranged scene with Owen tomorrow night, but keep in mind, she has told you that things with him are strictly platonic. Don't doubt her or accuse her otherwise. Let her work this out in her own way. I'm confident you won't be sorry."

I lean back and stare at Davis before saying one more thing. "I kissed her."

Davis gives me a slow smile. "I figured."

"I don't even know if I kissed her little or her adult. She doesn't know either."

"That's okay. She'll figure it out. You'll figure it out together. It's not like there are rules and you broke them. You make the rules. Both of you. Together. I get that she'd compartmentalized her two sides up until now, but maybe it's time to break down that barrier and combine them."

He might be right, but what if I'm doing irreparable damage to her? I'm not going to stick around to see this through. I'm messing with her life and it makes me fucking nervous.

CHAPTER 14

Evelyn

"I owe you an apology." Those are the first words out of Colt's mouth as I close the door to the SUV at six o'clock.

"Why?" I ask as I fasten my seatbelt. I can guess why but I don't need him to apologize. We're in uncharted territory, and we're in it together. "Please don't apologize for how you feel."

He glances at me as he pulls away from the curb. "I shouldn't have spoken to you like that this morning, nor should I have texted you while you were at work. It was inappropriate, and I'm sorry."

I turn my head toward the passenger side window and stare out, seeing nothing. I've been in his presence for ten seconds, and already I'm under his thumb. I can't stop it from happening. The man is dominant even when he doesn't mean to be, and my submissive side has slid under his control even though I don't want it to. Mostly because I'm not ready. I just stepped out of work. I'm in my professional body right now.

I can feel the power and authority radiating off him inside the SUV. Somehow he's able to apologize from a position of authority that maintains his obvious domination over me while humbling me at the same time.

I'm shredded. I never ever leave my adult persona until I get home and change clothes. Never. But he undoes me in seconds. He would have even if he hadn't spoken. "You shouldn't apologize," I murmur. "You weren't wrong. I did lie and I did sass you." I don't turn my head toward him as I speak.

At the next intersection, he takes a right even though he should have gone straight. I glance at him and then back at the road as he pulls into a parking lot. He puts the car in park in a random spot. He twists his body to face me. He searches my eyes for several seconds. He's breathing heavily.

I can't keep from fidgeting at the intensity. We're on a weird precipice here. I'm not sure how this is going to teeter, but it's about to tip one way or the other. I'm not even sure which way I prefer. One is safer and will cause me less anxiety and prevent me from getting hurt in the long run. The other is dangerous territory that will probably break my heart and leave me curled up in a ball. The second option is more appealing though. The risk is attractive. He's making me feel something I've never felt before.

The longer we sit in silence, the more nervous I get. Agitated. I sit on my hands. That usually works. I'm completely out of my element. Not home. Dressed for the office. Feeling very very little.

He swallows. "Eve..."

I make a decision. "Sir?"

He runs a hand over his head. "My instinct tells me to take control here. Dominate you. Give you everything you crave and many things you didn't know you desired. Things I never imagined myself. My head tells me to back up, keep our relationship strictly professional. My head is not winning because my mouth keeps getting in the way." He smiles slightly.

I stare at him. I won't interrupt. I won't make this decision for him or for us. I can't. I want him to dominate me so badly that I don't have the power to stop him. Damn the consequences. I know this can't last. I know he's not really mine. I know our time together is probably only days, not weeks. But I won't deny myself this odd experience, no matter how scared I am.

It's not really a decision. I can't stop this train. It already left the station. I'm already his for however long he stays. I don't have a clear picture of what this looks like, but we'll figure it out together.

"There's nothing to decide, Sir. The choice has already been made. The line has already been crossed. There's no turning back. I suspect we'll both get hurt in the end, but we'll cross that bridge when we come to it."

"I suppose you're right."

"I usually am, Sir." I smile at him.

"Are you always this sassy?"

I shrug. "It gets me what I want."

"Well, it's not going to work on me."

I pout. Full on. Cross my arms, lift my shoulder, push out my bottom lip, and blow out a breathy pout.

He chuckles. "You're cute when you pout, but that isn't going to work on me either. I know you're used to negotiating an arranged scene at the club, and I'm anxious to witness it in person tomorrow night, but I'm staying in your home. I'm going to be with you every moment you're not at work for the foreseeable future. Nothing between us at your apartment is a scene. It's just life in whatever fashion we make it."

He's rocking the very basis of my foundation. So many

firsts for me. I don't submit in my adult persona. I'm never little except when I'm dressed for it at home or at the club. I don't mix my vanilla life with my fetish preference. My head is spinning.

"I'm going to lure you out of your comfort zone, Eve. Starting now. I'm going to do it because it's what we both want. I'm not going to spank you tonight because I have no experience doing so yet. I'll watch closely tomorrow night and take some pointers from Davis before I lay a hand on you. But that doesn't mean I'm not going to be in charge."

"Yes, Sir." My voice is low. I'm shocked and intrigued and aroused and unnerved. So many emotions.

"Are we in agreement then?"

"Yes, Sir."

"Repeat what we've agreed to, Eve."

I lick my lips. "I'm going to submit to you starting now. I won't question your decisions."

He finally reaches across the void and takes my hand, giving it a squeeze before brushing my knuckles over his cheek. "Good girl. Shall we go home?"

"Yes, Sir."

I can't believe this is happening. I knew from the moment he took control this morning that the tide had changed between us. I knew from his texts that I was no longer in charge. It was only a matter of spelling it out, and he has done so.

When we get to my apartment building, he circles it twice, his gaze darting all around. Finally, he pulls into the garage and drives to the third-floor level before parking.

I wait for him to come to my side of the car and let me out because I know it's what he prefers. He holds my hand as we enter the building and head for my unit. Damn the consequences. If my neighbors see me, they do.

I hand him my keys and wait while he lets me inside. My

heart is racing. There's going to be a permanent shift in our reality the moment the door is closed.

Sure enough, Colt locks us inside and then turns to me. He helps me take my coat off, then points toward the hallway. "You have fifteen minutes to change and meet me in the kitchen."

"Yes, Sir." I turn and rush from the room. For the first time in my life, I'm excited. I'm not going to be little alone tonight. Colt is going to be my Daddy. It's weird and scary, but I can't wait. Sure, we sort of did this last night, but it wasn't negotiated or planned. We were testing the waters.

After shutting my bedroom door, I hurry into my closet, already kicking off my heels. I quickly remove everything and put on lavender panties with little red hearts on them. Next, I tug a dress from the hanger. It's pink with white sheep scattered on it. It's also cotton with a scoop neck, three-quarter length sleeves, and a full skirt that reaches a few inches below my panties.

I skip to the bathroom and take off my makeup before unpinning my bun and putting my hair up in pigtails high on my head. I even add pink bows. Deciding to go barefoot, I head to the kitchen.

I hesitate at the entrance to the kitchen. Colt has his back to me. He has never once judged me, so I don't expect him to now, but I'm nervous anyway. This is new. The look on his face when he sees me could destroy me.

He finally turns around, and my heart leaps when he grins. "You look adorable."

I breathe again and smooth my hands down the front. "Do you like my dress?"

"Love it."

"I call it a twirl dress," I inform him.

"What does that mean?"

"It's the ones that flare out wide when I spin around in circles."

He chuckles. "Show me."

I hesitate. He's going to see my panties if I do so. The blurred line between us has turned into a very wide chasm. The thought of him seeing my panties makes my tummy feel funny. I know he's seen them at night, but this is daytime. I try to ignore my hesitation as I lift onto one foot and push off, spinning around and around in circles as fast as I can. The skirt flares out wide and my pigtails do too.

When I stop, I'm dizzy and breathing heavily.

Colt reaches out to grab my shoulder and steady me. "I see why you call it a twirl dress. Warn me when you're going to do that so I can make sure you don't fall, okay?"

I nod, my chest pounding. Not just from the activity. I'm aroused. My panties are wet. The way he's looking at me combined with his words is making me feel things I'm not used to. Not in my little. "Yes, Sir," I mumble inaudibly.

He lifts my chin. That eyebrow rises.

Fuck me. It's so intense when he does that. My nipples are tingling and stiff. I'm sure he can see them through the thin cotton. "Yes, Sir," I state louder.

"Good girl." He pats my bottom. "Go sit at the table. I found your coloring books and crayons. You can color while I make dinner."

I bite into my lower lip as I shuffle toward the table, shocked. He's everything I ever dreamed of in a Daddy. And every moment we spend together is going to make it that much harder when it's over between us.

"I went to the store today while you were at work. I'm going to make myself a pork chop. Would you like one too, or would you rather have Spaghetti-O's?"

I smile and swing my legs as I glance at him. "Spaghetti-O's."

"Coming right up."

I color him a picture while he cooks, and I'm just finishing it when he sets a plate down in front of me. It's one of my partitioned plates with princesses on it. He's put the canned pasta swimming in red sauce in one section, apple sauce in another, and steamed broccoli in the last section.

I jerk my gaze up to him. "I don't like broccoli."

He frowns at me, his brows furrowed. "Hmm. I don't think I believe you, Eve."

He shouldn't believe me. After all, he found it in my freezer. Obviously, I do eat broccoli. But my little doesn't. I look back down at my coloring. "I'm not eating it."

He sets a hand on the table and lifts my chin with the other. That damn brow is lifted again. "You'll eat everything on your plate, or no television after dinner."

I groan. "But..."

"No buts. Every bite. You can't live off of Spaghetti-O's. They have no nutritional value."

I'm testing him. I know it. My blood is pumping. I've never once had a Daddy figure in my home like this. I'd give almost anything to get Colt to spank me, but he's right. It's too soon. This odd dynamic is new to us, and he has no experience spanking littles. "Yes, Sir."

"Put the crayons away while you eat. You can finish coloring after dinner."

I obey him, mostly because I'm hungry, but also because I've pushed him far enough for tonight. I don't want to alienate him with my naughty ways.

He sits at the end of the table with his plate. Pork chop, broccoli, baked potato.

I start eating too quickly, and he stops me with a hand over mine. "Slow down. You'll choke."

"Yes, Sir." I finish my meal and resume coloring while he cleans the kitchen. I feel kind of bad about this arrangement, but it was his idea. I assume if he didn't want to take care of me, he wouldn't have suggested it.

When I'm done with my picture, he hangs it on the fridge and leads me to the living room. He sits in the corner of the couch where he sat last night, and I snuggle up next to him as he turns on the television. "You have half an hour, time for one show."

"This one," I declare as he surfs slowly through the cartoon channels. I set my cheek on his thigh and let myself get absorbed in the silliness of the cartoon. When it ends, he turns off the tv, and I groan. "Can't I watch one more?"

"Nope." He nudges me to sit up and lifts me to my feet. He holds me by my hips and meets my gaze. "Your two hours are up. Go change into whatever you want to sleep in and let your hair down, okay?"

I nod, and then I throw myself at him, wrapping my arms around his neck and hugging him close. "Thank you."

He returns the hug, his large palms sliding up my back. "My pleasure."

I skip from the room. Part of me would rather stay in my little space. I often do until I go to bed. But I've agreed to two hours in this space, and it would be unfair to renege. It was incredibly generous of Colt to do this for me. He's gone above and beyond my wildest expectation. I owe him the respect of spending the rest of the evening in my adult persona.

Granted, I don't really have many bedclothes that would be considered adult, so I can't help that part, but I can take my hair down and brush it out. I study my sleeping options for a few moments before choosing a white tank top. I leave my panties on and cover this up with my usual pink robe. It's not really childish.

When I return to the living room, Colt is staring at his phone. He doesn't look up, but he reaches for me with one hand, and I sit next to him.

"Everything okay?" I ask in my adult voice. "Anything new?"

He sighs as he drops the phone onto the end table. "No. Nothing. It's frustrating." He turns toward me and slowly smiles. "Just out of curiosity, do you eat that shit food every night?"

I chuckle. "Not every night, but often. I eat like a champ at lunch. I promise."

"I hope so. I'm not sure how you can manage to stay so toned eating Spaghetti-O's and processed mac and cheese."

I shrug. "Good genes, I guess." I glance down at my lap and back at him. "Colt, thank you. I know it's hard for you to indulge me like that, and I want you to know I appreciate it."

He slides his hand up to my shoulder. Then he surprises me by twisting my direction and lifting me onto his lap. He cups my face. "You're kind of irresistible. Both of your personas."

I flush and bite my bottom lip.

He tugs the lip free with his thumb. "I'd like to kiss you. Did you leave your little in the other room?"

I smile. I get what he's saying. He'd like to kiss an adult. "Yes. She's gone for the night."

He smirks. "Until you fall asleep. She comes back when you climb into bed."

"Yeah, I guess she does. Does it bother you?"

"Not at all. She's growing on me. I'm fond of her. But I'd rather kiss the adult inside you right now."

"I'm right here," I murmur, anxious to feel his lips on mine again. The only time he's kissed me so far was our heated exchange against the wall last night. He made me forget the world with that kiss. Was it a coincidence?

His hand comes to my hip, making me wiggle closer. I can feel his erection against my hip and it emboldens me. I want more than the kiss he's about to give me. I want to have sex with him. Both of me do. I know I told him I'm my adult self right now, mostly because it's what he needed to hear. Probably what I needed to believe also. But the truth is I'm always straddling the line when I'm with him. I have a foot in both worlds. When I'm fully little, I'm still sexually attracted to him, which isn't like me and unnerves me.

What about when I'm fully adult? The truth is I haven't been fully my adult self in his presence since I met him. Not from that exact second I laid eyes on him. He had a power over me even then, and it's done nothing but grow in its intensity.

He's Dominant. At least with me. Even though he had no actual experience in the BDSM community, he's still dominant. Alpha. He brings me to my knees with just a look. My adult persona is automatically submissive when I'm with him.

I managed to stuff my little into the back corner of my mind this morning after he left me at work, but it took me a while. I was completely shaking when I got out of the car, unsteady on my feet as I entered the building. His demand was still ringing in my ear for long moments, over and over again.

From now on, when we get home, I want you to go directly to your room and change into whatever makes you comfortable...

His declaration had shocked me, mostly because he wasn't asking me; he was telling me. Then there are his texts... When he speaks to me or texts me, I lose my firm grip on my adult self.

One thing is for sure; I'd never be able to take him to a work function. I'd end up spilling something down the front of me. Or inadvertently call him Daddy in front of people. I'd be confused as fuck. He scrambles my brain cells.

This time when he lowers his lips to mine, he's not in a rush. This time he holds my gaze. He starts out gently and then angles to one side and deepens the kiss.

My toes curl and I can't help but lean into him.

When he angles his head to one side to deepen the kiss, I squirm against him, my hands flattening on his chest. Would it be too bold to reposition myself so that I'm straddling him? My little would never do something like that. My little would be way too shy. Then again, my little has never kissed a man. Why is she interrupting my thoughts now?

I think it's because my adult would never take orders from anyone. My adult gives orders. And yet…adult Eve does in fact take orders from Colt.

He flattens a hand on my thighs, both thighs at once encompassed with his large palm. His mouth releases mine. We're both panting, but his expression is jovial. "Sit still, little imp."

I pout. It's instinctive. It's not like me. It's confusing.

He lifts that brow. He's not angry. There's laughter in the corners of his eyes. "Are you sure I just kissed Eve the adult?" His voice is teasing. Thank God.

I bite my lip. I'm sure of nothing. I'm not even sure the sky is blue anymore. I start to panic. I can't do this. I don't know who I am when I'm with him. When he's touching me.

I scramble off his lap and nearly trip and fall as I take a step away from him.

"Eve?"

I turn and rush from the room. I run down the hallway and into my bedroom. I need to be alone, so I shut the door. Should I lock it?

I don't. I'm not sure why. I think because no matter how confused I am, I still feel his pull. He's in charge. I'm not. If I lock this door, he might get mad. Or maybe I want him to come after me.

Nope. I need to think. I spin around and head for the bathroom. That door I can lock. It's not as defiant as the bedroom door. I shut the door, lock it, and slide down to the floor, pulling my knees up to my chest and wrapping my arms around them.

What the hell is going on with me? I'm completely unnerved. Not only is my damn little sexually aroused by Colt, but I can't even get her to go away. Colt doesn't want to have sex with my little. He wants me to be her for two hours and put her away. I can't do it. She keeps peeking back through. My little wants to be with Colt.

I groan. I can't handle this confusion. It's too much. I can't get a grip on Eve the adult. She's there, near the surface, but she isn't interested. Maybe because I'm not used to maintaining that side of me in my apartment. Maybe it's because now that I no longer need to worry about Colt judging me, I feel comfortable enough to be myself.

Those might be factors, but they don't explain why I feel submissive even in the car with him. On my way to and from work. I can't transition that quickly. I'm going to need to drive myself tomorrow. If I don't, I'll end up just as confused as I was today.

If I take my own car to work, I'll be able to make the switch to my adult self before I get there and decompress on the way home. That's what I'll do. Problem solved. One of them anyway.

What about the fact that I desperately would like to have sex with him? I don't even know what that looks like if I'm little, and it's not what he wants either.

A knock sounds on the door. "Eve. Will you come out, please?"

I sigh. His voice instantly controls me. Shit.

"Eve, open the door, baby. Talk to me."

Great. That was even more dominating than the first request.

"Here's the thing. In twenty-four hours, I'm going to get schooled on every nuance of spanking, then I'm going to pepper your little bottom until it's so pink you won't soon forget. I don't care if you scene with three other Daddies tomorrow at the club. I'm going to be the last one to spank you. The number of swats I intend to use is increasing by the minute, so I suggest you open the door."

I inhale sharply. A moment later I scramble to my feet, facing the door. My hand is over my chest. My robe has fallen open. I don't think I've ever been this horny in my entire life. I also don't want to risk him spanking me any more than he already intends. I yank open the door.

"That's better." He seems ten times larger filling the doorframe with his hands on both sides. "Eve, I get that you're confused. Hell, I am too. But don't shut me out. I want you to talk to me."

I look at the floor, wrapping my arms around me, but not bothering to close my robe. He can see my panties and my tiny tank top. I don't care. "You're incredibly dominant, Colt."

"Can't say I was aware of that before this week, but you seem to bring it out in me. Does it scare you?"

"Yes."

"Why?"

"Because when I'm with you, your intensity brings out my submission." It's all suddenly much clearer to me, and I lift my gaze. "My adult is never around dominant men. Or she puts them in their place. She's strong and determined and in charge. You're topping her. And when you do that, she fades, leaving me mostly little."

He nods slowly. I can see him processing. "No one else has dominated you outside of the club?"

I shake my head. "I guess not. I don't let them. If they tried,

I'd put a stop to it. I only do vanilla relationships outside of the club."

"You must be exhausted."

I nod. He's right. I am.

He releases the doorframe and steps further into the bathroom, holding out a hand. "Come here, baby."

I melt when he calls me *baby*. That's twice tonight and once last night. I'm keeping track.

He pulls me into his arms and rocks me back and forth, smoothing his hand down my hair. After a few moments, he turns us toward the sink. He finds a washcloth, wets it, and gently wipes my face. It feels cool and soothing after all my stress. I guess there were a few tears too. I hadn't realized it.

Next, he grabs my toothbrush and puts toothpaste on it. He wets it and hands it to me. "Brush."

I'm shaking as I take it from him. I brush my teeth while he fills the little cup next to the sink with water. He hands it to me when I'm finished and I rinse.

He points toward the toilet. "Use the bathroom. I'll tuck you in after that." He kisses my forehead before he leaves, shutting the door behind him.

For a moment, I stare at the closed door. *Holy shit. Holy... Shit...*

I do as he's instructed and wash my hands, staring at the woman in the mirror for a few moments, wondering who the hell she is. When I emerge, he's sitting on the edge of the bed. I go to him.

He removes my robe. Then he pats the mattress where he's pulled back the covers. "Get in."

I do as I'm told, only slightly self-conscious about my panties and tank top. "Are you going to bed too?" I ask, my voice small.

"I need to do some more work tonight, baby. I'll join you in a while."

I pout. I keep doing that with him. "Will you lie down with me until I fall asleep first?"

He holds my gaze for a moment, considering my request.

"Please?" I come so close to calling him Daddy. I know I did when I was half asleep last night, but it seems too bold to do so when I'm fully awake.

I'm nearly giddy when he nods and then rounds to the other side of the bed and climbs up on top of the blankets next to me. He lifts his arm out so that I can snuggle up next to him.

I shock him and myself when I kick the covers back and scamper over the top to flatten my body alongside his. I don't want to be under the covers. I want to be closer.

He chuckles as he wraps his arm around me and pulls me in tight. His large hand is on my hip, and he strokes the skin between my panties and my tank top absently with his thumb. "Imp."

I giggle.

"I realize I'm new to your world, Eve, but you're a manipulative little thing. I'm going to call Davis and get some tips from him before you steamroll me."

I giggle again. "At least I'm not as bratty with you. I'm usually bratty at the club."

"Surely you recognize that isn't going to work with me," he points out.

I shrug, not committed to that fact.

I want to be good. I want to go to sleep like he's asked me. But I can't do it. I want something else, something more. So, I slide my hand under his shirt and flatten my palm on his stomach before easing it up to his amazing chest. He's ripped. Like, hard-as-a-rock ripped.

He sets his hand over mine, his on top of the shirt, stilling me. "Eve..." he warns.

"What?" I ask all innocently as I slide my top leg up over

his thigh. I have no idea who I am or what I'm doing, but I need to be closer to him.

One second I'm half on top of him, touching him everywhere I can at once, and the next second, I'm flat on my back. My arms are pinned above my head, both wrists locked with one of his hands.

My eyes are wide and I gasp.

His other hand lands on my belly. My bare skin. My tank top is twisted and has risen up under my boobs. "You're playing with fire, Eve."

"I like fire." I'm panting now.

He searches my face.

"Please?" My voice isn't little or big. Somewhere in the middle. I squirm. I'm so fucking aroused. I need release. "Would you take off your shirt?" I ask, tentatively.

He shakes his head at the same time he rises over me. His hands come to the hem of my tank top, and two seconds later, he's shoving it over my head. "No, but I'll take off *your* shirt."

I gasp the moment my boobs are exposed. I want this. I've wanted him to fuck me for days. I want his mouth on me. I want my mouth on him. Why on earth am I suddenly bashful?

I whimper and squirm as his gaze lands on my small tits. He reclaims my wrists with one hand, tangling them in my tank top. Hovering over me, his other hand slides up my belly until he's cupping one globe.

"So pretty," he whispers. That doesn't help my adult at all. He's dragging out my little.

When he lowers his mouth to reverently kiss my hard nipple, I gasp. I was wrong earlier. I have a *new* level of arousal that is unsurpassed. I'm about to self-combust and he hasn't really touched me.

He flicks his tongue over the tip, and I cry out. "So you like that, baby? Do you like it when I lick your little nipple?"

"Yes, Sir." Nothing in my life has ever felt as good as this.

I'm conflicted. I don't have sex as my little. I've never been in this situation. I'm dominant in the bedroom. Or at least equal. Vanilla. My little never comes to the surface. What is it with this man? This *Daddy*.

He licks my nipple again before sucking it, letting his teeth nip gently.

I moan, my eyes rolling back. My panties are soaked, and my legs are pressed together as tightly as I can manage.

He shifts his weight slightly and cups the other breast. "Does this one feel neglected?"

"Yes, Sir." My voice is strained. I'm desperate.

Colt circles my nipples with his fingertip. Over and over. It's maddening. I want more. I've never been so wiggly in my life.

"If you stop squirming, I'll suckle it."

I whimper again. "Please..." my voice comes out as a whine and I arch my chest the scant amount of space possible before holding my breath and forcing myself to remain still.

He circles my eager nipple with his tongue before sucking it like he'd done to its twin.

"*Colt*," I scream.

He releases my swollen nipple and shakes his head. "Colton. If you're going to shout my name, I want you to call me Colton."

I swallow, blinking at him. "Okay."

He lifts that brow.

I flush. "Yes, Sir." Why does he still have his clothes on? Why wouldn't he take his shirt off?

"Good girl." He resumes tormenting my tits with licks and flicks and little bites.

"Colton..."

"Yeah, that's better."

"Please..."

After another love bite, he lifts his gaze. "If I release your hands, can you keep them above your head, baby?"

I nod fervently.

"If you move them, I'll find something to restrain you with. Understood?"

Jesus. Just restrain them now. I don't say this. "Yes, Sir."

He holds my gaze, a slow smirk lifting the corners of his mouth. "You're a naughty girl who's going to move both hands the moment I let go, aren't you?"

The flush climbing up my cheeks deepens. "Yes, Sir," I murmur.

"Do you want me to tie you down, baby?"

"Yes, please."

"Ask me, Eve. Ask me to tie your hands to the headboard. Ask me to do it because the idea is making you so damn horny you can't think."

I lick my dry lips and meet his gaze. "Please tie my wrists to the headboard, Sir."

"Why?" His smile is enough to get me to do anything in the world.

"Because I'm a naughty girl, and I won't be able to leave them above my head, Sir."

"Don't move." He climbs off me, grabs my robe from the floor, and tugs the tie out of the loopholes.

I watch in awed silence as he returns, wraps it around my wrists, and secures them to the headboard. My boobs are high and flat on my chest. I feel so exposed. I moan as he slides down my body. He pauses to tease my nipples again, then continues lower, kissing toward my belly button.

When he twirls his tongue in the little dip, I giggle.

"Are you ticklish, baby?"

I shake my head. Not usually. Not until just now.

He chuckles as he moves farther down. He lifts off of me

enough to reach for my knees, which he then presses toward my chest before opening them wide.

When he settles between my parted thighs, his hands gripping them, forcing them open, I start panting again. He licks along the edges of my panties, his tongue teasing me. "Your panties are soaked, baby."

I moan and buck upward. I'm going to come from his breath hitting my panties. How pathetic.

He drags a finger along the edges of my panties in the sensitive spot on my inner thighs, and then he glides it right down the center, flicking the tip over my clit.

I cry out unintelligibly.

"You like that? You like it when I touch you right…here." He strokes my clit again over my panties.

I buck. "Yes, Sir. Please…"

"You want me to take these panties off and kiss your pussy, baby?"

Jesus. Holy... God... "Please, Colton." Hottest damn experience of my life, hands down.

"Can you be a good girl and hold your legs open for me so I can kiss your greedy pussy, Eve?"

I nod. I'd climb a mountain without ropes if he asked me.

He releases my knees and rises above me to pull my panties down my legs. Before tossing them aside, he brings them to his nose and inhales my scent. "Mmmm."

I nearly die.

He's on his knees between mine, fully clothed. I'm naked and exposed. "Spread your knees apart, baby. As wide as you can."

He doesn't touch me while I do as I'm told. My pussy is throbbing. My heart is racing too. I whimper yet again as his gaze slides all over my body, landing on my pussy finally. "So pretty. Pink and swollen and wet for me. Do you like me looking at your naked body, Eve?"

"Yes, Sir," I murmur, unable to think of more words. Language has escaped me.

He touches me with his fingertip, circling my pussy far too wide to give me any relief. "You want me to kiss you, baby?"

"Yes, Sir."

"Where? Here?" He taps my thigh.

I shake my head. "Please kiss my pussy, Sir."

"I love that it's shaved bare. It makes you feel exposed and naughty doesn't it?"

"Yes, Sir." I can't think. I have no idea how I'm managing to answer his questions.

He parts my lower lips, and heaven only knows what kind of sound I make.

"I love the little noises you make, baby." He finally lowers between my legs and drags his tongue through my folds until he finds my clit. He flicks it over and over.

I'm writhing. It's too hard to remain still.

He takes pity on me and grips my inner thighs, holding me down while he sucks my clit into his mouth. Good thing he restrained me so thoroughly first or I would have shot off the bed. I know I screamed.

"Such a noisy little girl," he murmurs before sucking again.

I'm so close, but he doesn't let me come. He keeps stopping to lick somewhere else. It's so maddening.

"I'm going to push one of my fingers into your tight little pussy, baby, okay?"

Like he needs permission… "Please, Sir. Please put your finger in my pussy."

As he slides one finger slowly into me, his thumb rubs my clit, and there is no way to stop the orgasm that consumes me. "*Colton.*" I scream his name as my body pulses against him, as he gently torments my G-spot, his thumb driving me mad with pressure, his forearms holding me down.

It's heaven, and I'm panting and shaking when it subsides. "You're still wearing your shirt," I murmur.

He chuckles. "Yeah." His lips land on my pussy and he reverently kisses me there. "And you're so very gorgeous when you're naked."

When I can focus on him, I fake pout. "But I wanted you to take your shirt off."

He smiles. "Make you a deal."

"Okaaaay..."

"I'll take it off if you put it on." His brows lift. "I'd like it if you slept in my shirt. Just that. Nothing else. Can you do that for me, baby?"

I nod. "Yes."

He rises onto his knees and pulls it over his head with one hand in that way men in movies remove their shirts by reaching over their back to slide it off. The move is sexy, and so is his chest.

He leans over me with those amazing pecs and unties my wrists before pulling me to sitting and tugging the shirt over my body. "There," he declares like we just solved world peace.

"But..."

He chuckles again as he climbs off the bed. He hauls my body to my side of the bed, pulls the covers over me, and kisses me gently on the lips. "Go to sleep, Eve."

"But..."

He taps my nose. "No buts. Just sleep."

I grab his hand before he can walk away. "But you were going to hold me while I fell asleep, and I wanted you to get naked, and—"

"Your falling asleep time got used up with my mouth all over your delectable body. Not a chance in hell was I going to get naked with you yet. And, I still need to get some work done. So... You need to sleep. I'll slide in next to you when I'm done working."

I humph. "Okay, but will you wake me when you come to bed?"

"No, but I'll pull you into my arms. How's that?"

"Okay," I groan.

He stands and looks down at me for several seconds before kissing me. He again slips from the room. He even leaves the door ajar.

I stare at it for a while as I snuggle under the covers with Jessie, wearing Colt's shirt, which smells like him.

I'm only marginally aware when he comes in some time later and does exactly as he promised—pulls me into his arms.

CHAPTER 15

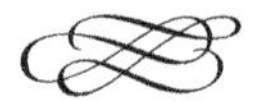

Colton

Even though I've only slept about six hours, I awake before Eve for the first time since I started sleeping in her bed. I'm staring down at her gorgeous features at rest when she blinks awake.

She slowly smiles. "You finally beat me."

"Yeah." I brush a lock of hair from her face. "You're so peaceful when you sleep. It's a huge change from how you are when you're awake." The truth is I've been awake watching her for a while. We crossed into new territory last night, and I'm concerned.

She glances down. "You didn't have sex with me."

"I didn't think you were in the right state of mind to make a decision like that. My instincts told me we needed to have a serious discussion about sex before jumping into it."

"What's to discuss?" she asks casually. "We like each other. We're attracted to each other. We're grown adults. Why can't we just have sex?"

I sit and scoot to the headboard, pulling her up alongside me. "First of all, we're never going to 'just have sex' so wipe that out of your mind. When and if we have sex, it won't be 'just' anything. Second of all, you're confused. It's written all over your face. I knew you weren't fully in your adult body."

She winces. "Did I make you feel like you were with a child?"

I shake my head. "Not at all. I'm clear you're an adult. I don't mind if you submit to me while we're in bed. I don't even mind if you're in your little space. But we need to discuss it first because you were more shocked than me. I know whatever is between us isn't the norm for you. You've made it clear you don't sleep with any of the Daddies you play with. And yet..."

She sighs and rubs her fingers along the edge of the sheet absently. "It's different with you."

"I get that. And that's okay, but we need to take our pulse on it first. I'm new to this lifestyle. I need some advice. I suspect you do too, based on your reactions to me."

"Yeah," she admits. "You're probably right."

I kiss her and then pat her butt. "You need to get in the shower, or you're going to be late for work."

She groans. It's adorable. It's the sound of her defiant little. "Will you come with me?"

I lift a brow. "Into the bathroom? Yes. Into the shower? No." I don't hesitate. I'm going to have to learn to be decisive and quick if I'm going to dominate her. I slide off the bed, lift her into the air, and toss her over my shoulder.

She squeals. "*Colt*."

I carry her into the bathroom and set her on her feet. Before she can protest, I remove my shirt from her and drop it in her hamper. I kind of like the idea of my clothes mixed with hers. Maybe I'll put the rest in there instead of back in my bag.

I turn on the shower and wait for it to warm up while she crosses her arms, pretending to be all modest on me again.

My smile is filled with mirth. “I’ve seen every inch of your body, you know. Tasted it too.”

She bites her bottom lip, her arms still crossed.

I decide to push her. “Hands at your sides, Eve,” I warn.

She sucks in a breath and slowly lowers them, a shudder wracking her body.

“That’s better.” I grab her hips and tug her closer, leaning down to kiss the tips of her amazing nipples.

She shivers in my grasp, her hands fisted at her sides. “When you dominate me, my little comes out. She pushes my adult self out of the way and fully emerges. She’s shy and nervous about being naked.”

“I gathered that, and it’s okay. I don’t mind her being shy.” I give her a little shake. “I don’t mind *you* being shy. It’s cute. And I feel like I’m getting to see a side of you no one has ever seen.”

She nods quickly. “You are.”

“That’s precious to me. The flush on your cheeks from embarrassment makes my cock hard.”

She gasps and glances down at my crotch. “I can fix that.”

I chuckle. “Stop trying to get in my pants, baby. If I have to warn you again, I’ll be increasing the number of swats you take the first time I spank you.”

She winces. “How many are you up to now?”

“A lot.” I turn her around and open the shower door, shoving her into the enclosure. “Take your shower.” For some reason, I can’t bring myself to leave the bathroom. I want to be in her space while she bathes. What I really want is to wash her myself. I won’t though. Not today. That would be dangerous.

I’m going to have blue balls by the time I drop her off at work this morning, but I’ll live. Tonight, I’ll consult with

Davis again about this dynamic between us. I need some advice before I have sex with Eve. Being a Daddy to her is one thing, but I'm uncertain about this new dimension. I hadn't expected to sleep with her when she's in her little space.

I know Davis does it with Britney. It's not that it feels wrong. It doesn't at all. It feels more right than it probably should considering how long I've known Eve and how fast I've fallen under her spell.

Her little is endearing to me and the joy it gives her is attractive. Is that strange? I don't know. I'm concerned though. Even though I get that other littles do have sex in that headspace, it's not something Eve expected to do, so I'm worried about her. I don't want her to have regrets or end up more confused than she already is.

I lean against the counter and watch her shower. I know it's unnerving to her. That's half the reason I do it. Her body is amazing. She's petite, but proportionate. When she lifts her arms to wash her hair, I can't keep my eyes off her tits and the sharp points of her nipples. Her bare pussy is calling out to me, but I'm not going there again this morning. She's shaking, clearly affected by me watching, but I like the effect I have on her.

When she's done, I grab a towel and dry her myself, ending by squeezing out her hair. I don't give her the towel. I love seeing her naked. She's so fucking sexy. I could stare at her all day. I already knew she would be this sexy from the glimpses I've gotten over the last several days, but naked... Shit. She's divine. And the addition of her misplaced embarrassment is even hotter. I like that I can get her all flustered so easily.

I have to leave the room and let her get ready for work, so I force myself to tip her chin back, kiss her briefly, then pat her naked bottom. "I'll leave you alone to get ready while I shower in the other bathroom this morning. We'll leave at the usual time."

She sighs. "I thought I'd drive myself."

I lift a brow, loving how she reacts every time I do so. "Why would you think that?"

She looks down. "Because I need the time to transition. Otherwise, I'll end up walking into my office straddling both worlds like yesterday. You'll dominate me in the car, and I'll end up hot and bothered and little when I get there."

"Then I guess we better leave a few minutes earlier than usual so you'll have a chance to regroup before you start working."

"Colt..."

I lift her chin again. "Not debatable, Eve. Don't mention it again. It's not safe. You're not leaving my side until I'm certain you're no longer in danger. That means, wherever you go, I take you. No exceptions."

"But, you could follow me like you did the first day," she hedges.

I grip her chin harder, not letting her look away. "Things changed. Did you forget a man was stalking you at lunch the other day? He's not just hanging around your apartment, Eve. He's watching your office."

She swallows.

"He's more than twice your size. You think you could take him on in the parking lot and get away?"

"No." Her voice is soft.

"Then don't challenge me on this issue again, understood?"

"Yeah."

I dip lower, meet her gaze, and lift that brow that makes her shudder.

"Yes, Sir." She gives me that gorgeous tremble as she submits to me, and her nipples are hard little points.

"Surely you understand the concept of human trafficking. I don't need to spell it out for you. If someone succeeds in kidnapping you and selling you as a commodity, your life is over. They aren't planning to sell you to someone local, Eve. The plan is to sell you to the Middle East. Do you get that? You won't even understand a word anyone is speaking." I'm scaring the hell out of her, and that's my intention. She's not taking this situation seriously enough.

She's shaking as she looks down, chagrined.

"So, no. You may not drive yourself anywhere. We'll leave ten minutes earlier so you have extra time. Are we done with this argument?"

"Yes, Sir."

"Good girl." I release her and point toward her closet. "Get ready."

An hour later when I pull up outside her building, I grab her hand before she can open the door and climb down. "Do you have any plans to leave the office today?"

"No. I'll order lunch in."

I nod. "Good. Text me if you change your mind so I can escort you."

She sighs. "Okay." Her voice comes out a bit whiny.

"Are you sassing me again today?"

She fidgets. That's her little taking over her adult. I know the signs. I shouldn't have pushed her like this again today. I know she's going to struggle to shake her little off when she gets out of the car. But I have two reasons for being so demanding. One, her life is truly at stake, so I need her to do as I tell her. And two, God forgive me, but I love a flustered submissive Eve.

She shakes her head. "No, Sir. I won't leave the building. I promise."

"Good girl. Have a great day. I'll see you at six unless you need to change anything." I slide my hand up to cup her face and lean close, kissing her lips before sitting back. I probably shouldn't have. It was too risky. Someone might have seen us.

But—and I might go to hell for this too—I don't care. I'd

kind of like someone to see us. I'd kind of like for her to claim me as her man in front of her coworkers. Damn the consequences.

She's beyond flustered as she exits the SUV, and I kick myself as I watch her walk away. I do not own her. Telling her coworkers she has a boyfriend is a horrible idea. How is she going to undo that when my job is done? In theory, that could be any day. People would have whiplash if they thought she was dating someone and then I disappeared.

I really need a head exam.

As I watch the confident, professional woman I just kissed walk toward the building, I can't help but compare her to the little I dominated last night. The woman disappearing in front of me is wearing a thong under the pencil skirt. My gaze travels down her legs to the heels that take my breath away. So different from the barefoot little she'd been last night wearing cute lavender cotton panties with hearts on them and a twirl dress. I smile at the memory of her spinning around in the kitchen so fast I thought she would fall on her butt. The smile on her face. The innocence. So carefree. Both of those personas appeal to me. Equally. It's a lot to process.

CHAPTER 16

Evelyn

"You're holding out on me." The teasing voice belongs to Lacy, and I spin around from the coffee pot to meet her gaze.

I'm not completely level-headed yet this morning. I was hoping not to run into anyone until I at least had my first cup of coffee. Arriving early hasn't done me a bit of good because apparently, Lacy is early today too.

Her eyes are dancing.

I frown. "What am I holding out on you about?" I force myself to stand taller and shake off my little.

She rolls her eyes. "Oh, come on. I saw that sexy hunk of man who dropped you off out front. And he kissed you. How long have you been seeing him? Long enough that he dropped you off at work." She wiggles her brows. "Details, girlfriend."

I chuckle as I spin back around to grab my cup from under the spout. Why the hell didn't I plan for this and come up with something to say?

When I turn back around, she's leaning casually in the doorway, smirking.

I shrug. I'm going to have to wing it. "It hasn't been long, and I'm not sure if it's going anywhere, so I don't want to jinx it." I sip my coffee, finding my adult. Thank God. My mind wanders to the man who kissed me fifteen minutes ago as I got out of his SUV. Damn, that was hot.

She lifts both brows. "You're not sure if it's going anywhere, but you obviously slept over at his place or he slept at yours if he's driving you to work. Interesting. I think I'm jealous. I want a man to fuck me all night, drive me to work, look at me like he did you, and kiss me as I start my day. Even better if it never goes anywhere." She sighs dramatically. "Where do I get one? Does he have a brother?"

Finally, Lacy comes all the way into the room and heads for the coffee pot. "Okay. Okay. I won't bug you for more details yet, but if you're still climbing out of that man's car in a week, I'm going to demand a night of drinks and information."

"You've got it." I'm relieved, but also uncertain. Will I still have him in my life this time next week? The idea of him not being with me every waking moment I'm not at work already stings. I'm getting too attached to him. He's not mine to keep.

When I get to my desk, my phone pings, and I smile as I reach for it, assuming it will be a text from Colt. If anything, I should be nervous. Yesterday when he texted me, he caused me to slide under his thumb for nearly half an hour. I can't have him doing that every day or I'll get nothing done.

It's not from Colt. It's from Owen. Jesus. I haven't spoken to Owen all week. Neither of us has contacted the other since we left the club last Saturday. Though we have a standing appointment for tonight, I cringe as I realize we don't usually go all week without chatting at some point or meeting for coffee or a drink. We're friends.

I open the text.

Hey. Sorry I've been so busy at work this week I haven't had a chance to talk. Are we still on for tonight?

I release a breath. He's been busy too. Good.

Hey, yourself. It's been crazy here too. And yes, I'll see you tonight.

He knows where to find me. We have an arrangement. I arrive at the club, change into my little in the locker room, and check myself into the daycare. Most of my club hours are spent in the daycare where I interact with other littles, playing and coloring. Owen will find me there and steal me away for an hour to do a scene. After I recover, he'll take me back and I'll continue to unwind by lounging on a beanbag chair and mindlessly watching cartoons in the corner, or reading.

Perfect. See you soon.

I close my eyes and inhale. Tonight isn't going to be like other nights. Colt will be there. He'll be with Davis, who has agreed to show him around as if he's a prospective member. His presence will always be on my mind, distracting me. What is he going to think when he sees Owen dominating me?

I need to do this for multiple reasons. One of them is that I'm aware Colt thinks someone at the club might be watching me. If that's the case, I need to stick to my routine and not cause anyone to become suspicious. I'll try hard to pretend he's overreacting out of an abundance of caution. The thought of someone at Surrender plotting my sale makes me want to vomit.

I'm struggling with the idea of submitting to Owen too. I've never once paused to worry about a scene like this. I'm not interested in Owen sexually, even though Leah doesn't understand my dynamic.

I rub my temples. Leah. Dammit. I haven't spoken to her all week either. Should I call her before I see her tonight? Tell her what's going on? Probably not. There are already several people involved. The fewer people who know about my situation the better. Leah's not going to be pleased when she finds out I kept this from her though.

When I think about her mistrust of Owen, I cringe. Does she have a sixth sense I should have listened to? Speaking of which, Colt mentioned some distrust for Owen also. I somehow managed to ignore this fact all week. Now, I'm feeling a little freaked out.

Granted, even if Owen is a serious suspect, that doesn't explain the large man who's been stalking me. That man is definitely not Owen. Owen is too slender to be the man in the ball cap. But maybe Colt has more than one suspect. Or maybe the stalker and Owen are working together.

I need more information.

I yank up my phone and send a text to Colt.

Do you still think Owen is a suspect?

I stare at the phone for several moments, fidgeting nervously while I wait for him to return my text. Finally, I get a response.

What makes you ask that suddenly?

I'm furious and texting back and forth with Colt is not going to suffice. I close my office door and dial his number.

He picks up on the first ring. "Eve?"

My voice wobbles as I speak. "Tell me the truth. Do you think Owen might be involved in trafficking?" I accuse.

He sighs heavily. "It's possible. Still not ruling it out. I have no evidence though."

"And you don't think this might affect my ability to submit to him tonight?" I'm angry, trying to keep my voice low, but probably failing.

"Eve... I don't have anything on Owen. Everyone is a suspect right now."

"But you want me to go on with my plans with him as if nothing is out of the ordinary while you watch to make sure he doesn't intend to kidnap me?"

"Eve, baby, calm down. It's not like that. I'm suspicious, yes, but I'm suspicious of every damn person who glances at you."

"I don't want to talk about this anymore. I'm hanging up." My hands are shaking and I'm close to screaming.

His voice firms. "Eve, don't hang up. Please. You either talk to me or I'm coming to your office to meet you face-to-face. Your choice."

I lean back in my chair and rub my temples. "You're not playing fair."

"And I'll *never* play fair when it comes to you. You're not like any other woman I've been tasked with protecting before, Eve. Not even close. I'm out of my mind worrying about you. I should have removed myself from this case the moment I met you and had the captain put someone else on it. I'm not impartial. I'm a fool for not calling my boss right now and telling him to assign someone else."

I gasp. "Don't you dare."

He sighs. "I won't, but for all the wrong reasons. I can't stand the idea of another man protecting you, so it's not going to happen, but you need to listen to me, baby. This is *not* a game. It's fucking serious shit. Yes, Owen is on my radar because you've known him only a few weeks and you've been seeing him both in and out of the club. That's all. I have nothing else on Owen. He's obviously not the man stalking you out front. But I am concerned about the possibility that someone inside the club might have their eye on you. So I'd like to be able to set my sights on every damn person who belongs to Surrender, and the best way to do that is to go tonight and keep a close eye on who pays attention to you."

I'm deflating. "Okay."

"Do I need to come over there and convince you face-to-face?"

"No."

"Pardon?"

My heart is racing and I'm trembling all over as I glance at my closed office door. "No, Sir," I murmur.

"Good girl. Now get back to work. Stop panicking about something that may or may not be true. I'll see you at six."

"Yes, Sir," I whisper. How does he do this to me? How does he manage to turn my anger and frustration into total submission?

I squirm in my seat as we end the call. My thong is soaked and I'm so aroused I can't possibly concentrate for a while. Thank God nothing urgent needs my attention today and I don't have any client meetings.

CHAPTER 17

Colton

I'm marginally concerned about arriving at Surrender with Eve. I don't want anyone at the club to suspect we know each other or have ever met, but I'm also not willing for her to arrive on her own.

To help dispel this idea, I've arranged to arrive at the same time as Davis and Britney. That way we can all walk in together. It will appear that I have come as Davis's guest and Eve has coincidentally arrived at the same time.

I park in the shadows. We've beaten Davis and Britney. After I turn off the SUV, I unfasten my seatbelt and turn to face Eve. I'm damn nervous, but I don't want her to know it.

I reach for her hand. She's been incredibly quiet since I picked her up from work. She's also remained in her adult persona all evening. When she changed, she put on jeans and a sweater, telling me she would take a bag to the club. She doesn't come and go from the club in little attire. Makes sense.

We ordered Chinese takeout and ate in near silence. I know she has a lot on her mind, but I'm worried about her and I don't want to go inside with tension between the two of us. It's going to be stressful enough without adding to it.

I stroke her knuckles. "Talk to me."

She shrugs. "Nothing to say."

"I beg to differ. Are you mad about our conversation earlier?"

She shakes her head. "No. You're right. I'm nervous and a little scared." She meets my gaze. "You really think a member of the club might be planning to sell me?"

"I have no idea, Eve. I just don't want to rule anything out. I'm going to watch every damn person in there to see if they're paying too close attention to you."

She offers me a strange coy smile, tipping her head to one side. "You know, it's possible someone might pay attention to me because they think I'm cute and they want to do a scene with me."

I chuckle, glad the mood has lightened. "In which case, I'll knock them out with my fist and drag their limp body out back."

She giggles. "How chivalrous."

"That's me."

"Or possessive."

"That's probably me too." I'm grinning at her.

"You do realize you can't interrupt my scenes here, right? It's against the rules. So, suck in your misplaced jealousy and hold your tongue and your fists."

I sigh. "I've read the rules. I know. I won't interfere. Promise. But, it's going to be very strange watching another man dominate you."

"Think of it as a learning experience. In the fetish community, it's not uncommon for even married couples to go different ways inside the club and scene with other people.

It's not even odd for their partner to watch. He or she might want to learn or maybe even gets off on watching. Anything is possible in the club scene."

"Really?" I'm kind of surprised. I have a long way to go before I'm going to grasp the dynamic. "A lot of swingers then?"

She shakes her head. "Not necessarily. That's something else entirely. It's just that often people like to get a rush from a scene their partner isn't proficient at. Like I've told you before, it's not always sexual. Often it's not."

I nod slowly. I'm not even close to understanding, probably because all of my experience in the fetish community has been with Eve, and there is no doubt everything between us is steaming hot sexual. Even for her, and she's the one who told me she doesn't mix sex with her kink.

I squeeze her hand. I don't relish the idea of letting go of her and pretending for the next several hours that we don't know each other. And as much as she's explained her relationship with Owen, I loathe the idea of watching the man dominate her.

I'm beyond glad that she's mostly been in her adult mindset since I picked her up, but I'm also aware that I'm largely responsible for her frame of mind. If I dominate her, she'll drop into a submissive mode, automatically aiming for her little because that's the type of submissive she is. If I speak to her as my equal, she can maintain control of her adult. I've put this to the test for the last few hours and proven it.

Granted, we also didn't talk much, and I'm itching to dominate her because I love how she responds to me. It's been challenging keeping my thoughts to myself. And my resolve is slipping.

What I *should* do is let her go so she can transition into her little space on her own in the changing room inside. But I can't quite bring myself to do it. I want her to go into this club knowing that I'm her Dom, not some other man. That she will leave here under my control. Macho much? Yes. Apparently.

"Eve, look at me, baby." I slide that word in to set the tone.

She lifts her gaze, her grip on her adult self already wavering behind her eyes.

"Don't worry about me. I've got this. I'm going to hang with Davis and learn the ropes. It's going to be fine. I promise I will not interrupt your scene in any way. You won't even know I'm here. But…" I release her hand to cup her face. I'm so going to step over a line I should not have drawn. "You're *my* submissive. For as long as we're together, you're mine. When we leave here, you'll be over my knee with my palm on your bottom. And even though you've never mixed sex with your little side, you will with me. When I spank you, you'll squirm with the need to come so badly that you'll be begging me to give you the release you crave."

She trembles so hard that my cock can't stand it. She's panting. Her eyes are wide. And she starts to fidget.

"Are we on the same page?" I love to make her say it out loud. I love it because it makes her squirm and I know it increases her arousal when I do it. It's a look I want to see as often as possible.

She licks her lips. "Yes, Sir."

"Good girl." I stroke her cheek and consider leaning in to kiss her but decide against it.

I'm staring at her lips when she speaks softly. "One of my coworkers saw us this morning."

I jerk my attention up to her eyes. "Oh shit. Sorry. What did they say?"

"Luckily, it was a friend of mine. Lacy. We hang out together outside of work sometimes. She was just teasing me. Said I was holding out on her. Wanted more details about the mystery man who dropped me off and kissed me out front. She was jealous."

I hold her face and lean closer. "I'm sorry. I shouldn't have kissed you. You bring out a possessive side in me I didn't know existed."

"It's okay. I told her I wasn't ready to talk and that I didn't want to jinx anything because I don't know you that well yet and it might not work out." She shudders as she finishes.

My chest tightens. I hate that she had to tell her friend she had no faith in our relationship. It shouldn't bother me. She's right. It's not going to work out. I'm going to solve this crime and then the captain will put me on a new assignment, and I won't see Eve again. I can't. It's not possible. But it hurts. Eve is the first woman I've ever considered having more with, but I would never drag another human being into the shitty world I live in. It wouldn't be fair.

I want to kiss her even more now, but suddenly a car pulls up next to us and I glance over to see Davis and Britney. It's time for this charade to begin.

I turn back toward Eve. "You okay, Eve?"

She nods.

I grip her face and hold her gaze. "Words, baby."

"I'm okay, Sir."

"Good girl." I open my door and search our surroundings. I see no signs of anyone lurking around the area. Not on foot or in a car. The only other people in the parking lot right now are Davis and Britney.

Eve exits the car, grabs her bag from the back seat, and lifts it onto her shoulder. I have no idea what she's brought to change into, but I'm looking forward to finding out.

She gives Britney a hug before the two of them link arms and head for the entrance. I hang back with Davis and enter behind them. My heart is racing. This is going to be a long night.

When we step inside, I'm shocked to find Eve's friend Leah working at the front desk. She greets us and checks her notes in front of her before waving us through. I know Julius left her my name and told her I was an invited guest.

While the women head off to the changing room, Davis and I wander around the club. It's kind of early so not many people are playing yet, but we pause to watch a couple doing a spanking scene.

Davis stands very close to me so he can talk without disrupting the scene. "So this particular woman is more like Eve than Britney. She really likes to get spanked, but it's not sexual for her. It's cathartic. Like a massage."

I watch closely as the Dom peppers the sub's butt with a steady stream of swats. He covers every inch of her skin so that a pink glow rises on her upper thighs and all over her cheeks, much like Davis did to Britney after dinner Tuesday night.

The woman is secured to the spanking bench, her wrists and ankles cuffed so that she can't escape. Her only movement is a slight wiggle back and forth. Her lips are parted and her face is relaxed.

I turn to Davis as he motions for us to step away from the scene.

He leads me to the break room where we sit on one of the sofas and turn to face each other. "Questions?" he asks.

I glance around, but no one else is in the room, so I feel confident I can speak candidly. "Turns out it's not going to be that way between Eve and me. When she submits to me, it's sexual. I get that it's not like that with other Doms for her, but it is when she's with me."

Davis smiles. "Have you spanked her yet?"

"No. I wanted to wait until after tonight. I feel like I need to watch several more times and get a better education first."

"Good plan. How about if we secure a private room for later and then I can go with you and help you the first time."

"That would be great. If Eve doesn't mind."

Davis chuckles. "I can tell you a few things about Eve. One, she doesn't mind who watches her. She has been spanked in front of the entire club many times. Two, she would want you to have every possible tool at your disposal, including solid instruction. And three…" He wiggles his brows.

I widen my eyes. "What?"

"Based on what you've told me, she's already under your control. Do you really think she would turn down the opportunity?"

I smile, then chuckle. "Good point."

Roman steps into the room. "Ah, there you are. I saw Eve and Britney in the daycare when I dropped off Lucy, so I figured you two were around here somewhere."

"Thank you again for allowing me access to the club."

"No problem. This is important." He sobers. "By the way, Julius and I looked over the picture Davis sent us. Neither of us recognizes the man."

Davis nodded. "I showed it to Blade too. He's never seen the guy either."

I sigh. "One step forward. Two steps back."

Davis glances past me as someone else enters the room. He smiles. "Speak of the devil."

I turn to see Blade coming toward us. The man is tall. Six-three. Dark hair, cut short. Dark eyes. I figure he's at least partly Hispanic. He holds out a hand. "Good to see you again. Though I hate the circumstances."

I shake his hand. "Yes. You too. Do you go by Blade in the club?"

His eyes dance. "Nope. Around here, I'm Master Andres."

I nod. "Good to know."

"Not a big deal. Most people in all walks of life call me Blade."

Davis chuckles. "It's impossible for me to think of him as anything other than Blade. I tend to not notice when I hear Andres."

I smile. "Trust me, I've had so many pseudonyms over the years that I barely know who I am anymore."

Blade claps a hand on my shoulder. "I'll be low-key around here tonight, but rest assured I will keep my eyes peeled on everyone who comes through the door. If they even so much as glance wrong at Eve, I'll let you know."

"Appreciate it."

"On that note, just ignore me. I'll catch up later." He turns and leaves the room.

I'm glad to have Davis's boss on my team. Another set of eyes is always welcome. And I know how the man feels about human trafficking. Of all possible crimes he finds himself investigating, that one really gets under his skin. It does all of us.

Roman motions over his shoulder. "You want to see the daycare?"

"Yes. Thank you." I wipe my hands on my thighs. I hope I don't appear half as nervous as I feel.

Davis follows us as we head down a hallway toward the elusive daycare all of them have mentioned. I'm stunned and amazed. It's exactly like a daycare would be anywhere except that everyone in the room is an adult in a role.

The room is large and divided into many sections with a variety of activities. There are three walls. Where we're standing is more like a fence. It makes up the entire fourth wall and allows people on this side to watch while pretending to keep the occupants safe from escaping.

I spot Eve quickly, and my breath catches in my throat. She's wearing a lavender dress. It's very youthful, barely reaches below her bottom, and will flare out like she enjoys if she spins. I smile as I remember her designating such dresses as twirl dresses and wonder what she's wearing underneath tonight.

She's sitting at a small table with two other littles. The dress is not tucked under her. It's hanging off the back and sides of the chair. She has on white knee socks and white patent leather shoes too. Her hair is in the usual pigtails she has worn at home a few times.

The woman across from her is Britney who looks equally young. I'm not sure who the other woman is, but I don't have to wait long. Roman points toward her and says, "That's Lucy. My little."

"Ah." Lucy is even shorter than Eve and very petite. She's also dressed similarly. "How long have you two been together?" I ask him.

"It will be seven years in May," he responds.

"Wow. That's amazing."

Roman chuckles. "It wasn't easy at first. We've had our rocky patches. I wasn't very diplomatic when I decided I wanted her to be mine."

I smile. "Looks like it worked out."

The girls spot us and wave.

We wave back.

Eve looks very sweet. She even shrugs her shoulders up and giggles when she sees me.

I stare at her, wondering how the hell I'm going to watch her get spanked by another man.

CHAPTER 18

Colton

When we turn around, Leah is heading toward us. "You wanted to see me, Sir?" she asks Roman.

"Ah, yes. I was wondering if you wouldn't mind doing a spanking scene for our guest to watch." Roman nods toward me. "You probably met at the entrance, but Leah, this is Colt. Colt, Leah."

I extend a hand because it seems polite.

She smiles. "Nice to meet you, Sir. I'd be happy to help out."

It feels strange for random people to call me Sir. It's also weird that I spied on this woman with Eve last week at lunch. She doesn't know it. I doubt Eve has told her.

She turns toward Roman. "Who's going to dominate me, Sir?"

"I was going to ask Stephan, if that's okay with you. You two have chemistry that draws a crowd."

"Sounds good, Sir."

"Perfect." Roman leads us back into the main room and Davis and I hang back while Roman speaks to Stephan and Leah. Finally, he nods toward the far corner of the room, and we head that direction.

"What's special about Leah getting spanked as opposed to anyone else?" I ask Davis.

Davis smiles at me. "You'll see. She's the polar opposite of the woman we saw earlier. She finds spanking extremely sexual and will orgasm for a crowd."

I nod. Interesting. "Is she little?"

Davis laughs. "Not even close. Though I'm pretty sure Eve has tried to get her to turn to the dark side on more than one occasion."

Even more interesting.

Roman joins us to one side and we talk while Leah and Stephan discuss their plans. The entire process is fascinating. These people negotiate every detail in full before they do a scene. I never realized how incredibly diligent the fetish community is about safety.

More people are starting to arrive, and I glance around, carefully noting everyone I see.

Roman is frowning when I look back in his direction. "It unnerves me that someone among us might be considering such a heinous crime," he murmurs.

"I know. Let's hope I'm wrong," I respond. "But in the meantime, I'm going to watch closely."

"You don't think any one person is working alone to snatch women though, do you?" Roman asks.

"Not a chance," Davis responds. He knows as well as I do. The man who attempted to sell Britney eight months ago was not working alone. I'm certain we're dealing with the same outfit this time. It was only a matter of time before they attempted to grab another woman.

No chance it's a one-man operation. Since no one at the

club recognizes the stalker from the photo, my inclination is that someone inside the club is still in on this crime. They are thorough. Their MO is to scope out a woman and then track her until they're ready to move. Just like was the case with Britney, I wish I knew the actual date the exchange is planned. But once again, I do not.

Roman steps closer and glances around. Luckily no one is near us. "So, all you know still is that someone is stalking her and you have a tip that came in warning you she was a target. And you're thinking there's an incredibly good chance that an accomplice to the kidnapping is a member of the club. Nothing new?"

I sigh. "That's correct." I'm not one bit closer to solving this crime than I was a week ago—or three weeks ago, to be honest.

Roman winces. "Hate it." He glances around. "Just fucking hate it. There are a lot of vulnerable women here, my own wife included."

"I noticed a man standing outside the daycare," Davis points out. "Not a coincidence, is it?"

Roman shakes his head. "No. I wanted extra security. He's a friend. Craig Darwin. We go way back. He's retired Army. He was gracious enough to do this for me. I don't like the littles unprotected in that daycare. Not Lucy or any of them. They are more vulnerable than anyone in the place because they get left alone."

Davis nods. "I did pin him as military. How much does he know about the BDSM community?"

I noticed him myself, but I had no way of realizing he was out of place. I'm glad to know he's here.

Roman chuckles. "More than the rest of us combined."

Davis smirks. "Okay then."

"Trust me. He's solid. I've been trying to get him to visit the club ever since his divorce five years ago, but he wouldn't do it. If I'm lucky, he'll get lured back into the scene while standing guard."

Movement to my right causes me to shift my attention toward Leah and Stephan. He's guiding her toward what I know to be a St. Andrew's cross. Leah is dressed nothing like Eve or Britney or Lucy. She's not a little. She's wearing a tight black skirt, platform heels, and a red corset that pushes her breasts up and gives her amazing cleavage.

Stephan lifts her chin with one finger.

When she looks at him, I see a very submissive woman, nothing like the woman I saw at lunch Sunday or at the front desk when we arrived. She has transformed, much like Eve does when she switches to her little.

Stephan is speaking to her in a soft voice I can't hear, and she's nodding. When he's done, he angles her toward the cross face first and lifts her arms one at a time, securing them spread high and wide.

I watch with curiosity as he trails a finger down her cheek and then between her breasts. He teases the edge of her corset before dipping his finger into one of the cups and flicking her nipple. Leah arches her neck and whimpers.

"She's amazing to watch," Roman whispers. "I'm going to go swap places with Craig for a bit so he can watch."

Davis chuckles. "Playing matchmaker today?"

Roman shrugs. "Leah is not his type. Craig is a Daddy through and through. Doesn't change the fact that the show you're about to see is going to be erotic and sexy as fuck."

I return my attention to Stephan as Roman leaves us. I'm marginally aware of Craig taking his spot a few minutes later. When I glance at him, he nods toward me and Davis. I'm betting Roman told him who we were. He's intense. Arms folded. Looks like a bouncer. Big guy. Serious.

Once again, I focus on Leah and Stephan. He's slowly strolling around her from one side to the other and back again. He touches her randomly. Her shoulders. Her neck. Her back. Her butt. Eventually, he plants himself right behind her, so close she can feel his heat, and he unfastens the back of her corset.

I'm surprised as it falls away, leaving her naked from the waist up. She's a gorgeous woman with breasts about the same size as Eve—more than enough to get a palm around, but pert and high at the same time.

When Stephan strokes the undersides with one finger, she moans.

He plants his hands on her hips next and leans in to whisper in her ear.

She nods. "Yes, Sir." I can read her lips even though nothing she says is audible from my distance.

He slides his hand to the small of her back and eases the zipper down on her skirt. He lowers it down her legs next and taps her feet to encourage her to step out of it.

I don't move a muscle. Intellectually, I knew I would see naked women here tonight. But knowing and seeing are two different things. Leah is now wearing nothing more than a black thong. She's stunning. This is a form of art.

Watching Stephan flow around her, stroking her skin, teasing her into submission is just gorgeous. Every time he speaks to her, she nods. I imagine he's checking in with her. Making sure she's still on the same page. Consenting.

Finally, he steps back and to the side and cups the globes of her ass, molding them, warming them up. The first swat takes her by surprise, and she whimpers as she sways forward.

He plants one foot between hers and nudges both her ankles until she spreads them apart several inches. She's panting. This is incredibly sensual to her. I'm oddly fascinated, but not aroused. Not as aroused as I would expect anyway. Not as aroused as Eve made me in the car with one simple whispered, *yes, Sir.*

Stephan begins to spank her in earnest now, swatting back and forth, high and lower. I'm understanding about the sweet spot more and more because every time he hits that exact place where her butt cheeks meet her thighs, she moans.

After a bit, her butt is delightfully pink and obviously hot. Stephan pauses every now and then to check in with her. They whisper quietly to each other. It's very sweet and special.

Leah is obviously aroused, and she can't keep her legs parted to his satisfaction. He eventually says something in her ear that makes her nod and whimper. A moment later, I watch him attach a bar to her ankles and spread it wider so she can't close them.

While Stephan speaks to her the next time, he slides his hand down over her heated cheeks and reaches between them. The moment he touches her pussy, she tips her head back and moans. Her body stiffens. She's desperate for release.

Stephan spanks her several more times, but he begins to stroke her pussy in between swats. Not enough. Just the slightest touch. He's edging her. It's a beautiful sight. She's sliding deeper and deeper into subspace. I've read about subspace. Now I'm witnessing it firsthand.

Finally, Stephan stops spanking her, steps much closer so that his body is lined up at her side, his foot between hers. He wraps one arm around her waist, holds her steady, and reaches between her legs with his other hand to rub her pussy.

She arches into him and comes moments later. I'm pretty sure he ordered her to. It's the most amazing thing I've ever witnessed. Hands down. "Jesus," I murmur, unable to stop myself.

The man next to me, Craig, responds to me in a whisper,

"You're not kidding. She's the most gorgeous creature I've seen in a long time. I'm humbled."

"Yeah. She is a sight to behold. That's for sure." Davis has witnessed her many times. For Craig and me, this is a first.

Craig swipes a hand down his face and turns toward us. He smiles and extends a hand toward Davis. "Roman told me to join you two. Craig Darwin." He keeps his voice low.

Davis shakes his hand. "Davis Marcum." He nods toward me. "This is Colt."

Craig grins as he shakes my hand. "That's all I get? Just Colt? How mysterious."

I chuckle.

Davis does too. "Hey, I've known him eight months, and that's all I get too."

Craig nods as he glances around, apparently making sure we're alone. "I'm just needling you. Roman told me to find you immediately if I notice anything remotely suspicious."

"I'd appreciate it. I'll be wandering around trying to stay under the radar. I might even begin to fit in after a few days with Davis's instruction."

"You must be a natural. I don't think you look out of place at all." He nods behind him. "Gotta get back to my post. I'll see you two later."

"Thank you for doing this," I tell him as he walks away.

"Shall we wander?" Davis asks.

I glance at Leah. She's no longer attached to the cross. In fact, she's now wrapped in a blanket and Stephan is carrying her out of the room. Her eyes are closed and her face is blissful. "Aftercare?" I ask Davis.

"Yep. He'll take her to a quiet room and give her water until she pulls herself out of subspace."

"How long does that take?" I wonder how this works for Eve.

"It's different for everyone. Leah can rebound fast. She'll be dressed and back at the front desk in no time."

"What about Eve?"

"Well, it's different for her. She doesn't go to the exact same place as Leah because she doesn't get sexual gratification from a spanking. But it's similar. She still slides into subspace and needs snuggling and fluid replacement. I'd say it takes her about fifteen minutes or so to feel oriented."

I nod. Everything about this experience is eye-opening. "Like I mentioned at lunch, I don't think her normal dynamic exists with me."

Davis grins. "I can't wait to witness this."

"You're not helping," I point out.

He chuckles softly. "Sorry. Tell me more."

"We haven't had sex yet, but we came close last night. She wants to, but I'm worried because she doesn't step out of her little space."

"That's okay. Not everyone does. As long as it doesn't bother you."

"It doesn't bother me. I'm concerned that she's out of her element and might make choices she wouldn't normally make. I don't want her to have regrets."

"You've been in her home five days, Colt. Surely she knows her mind."

I run a hand over my head and sigh. "Maybe. I just feel like I'm a catalyst in her life, inadvertently causing her to step out of her comfort zone."

"And you're worried about her recovering after you're gone."

"Yes."

He lifts a brow. "Maybe don't go?"

I groan. "You know that's not an option. Can we not go there now? I need to deal with the present right now. A present that includes a woman who wants to have sex with me."

Another chuckle from Davis. "What a horrible problem to have."

I can't help but smile. He's right. I'm overreacting. If Eve's life has been shaken up in any way, it was meant to be. Surely she wasn't living authentically in the first place. After all, her complicated world leaves no room for a permanent relationship. She deserves to have someone in her life who knows all her sides. Someone who loves all of her.

That someone can't be me, but opening the door to the possibility hopefully won't hurt her. Right?

We wander from one scene to another for a while. The club is filling up now. Out of the corner of my eye, I see Owen arrive. I've been watching for him. Though I've seen him several times outside of the club, coming and going from both Surrender and his bar, this is the first time I've been able to study him closer.

He looks like an ordinary enough guy. Nothing about him screams criminal. Not that there's a particular look per se, but it takes a very disturbed human being to sell another into sex slavery. I do not get that vibe from Owen. I'm also not going to rule him out. I hate that he recently started spending time with Eve. It feels like too much of a coincidence that someone called in a tip about her in the same time frame. It worries me that Owen might be involved.

I know from Roman, Julius, and Davis that Owen is a newer member. He greets several people as he works his way through the growing crowd of patrons. Every step brings him closer to the hallway that will lead him to Eve.

It doesn't matter that I really don't think Owen is a deranged madman, I still hate that he's going to dominate her tonight while I watch. I need to watch someone else with her for personal and professional reasons, but I don't have to like it.

Davis and I pass by him and head for the daycare so that we are casually milling around near the fenced area when he arrives.

Eve glances at me so briefly no one else would have noticed. She goes back to coloring.

I watch her closely, my chest tightening. If someone would have told me a week ago that I would enter into a relationship as a Daddy to someone who enjoys pretending they're little, I would have laughed them out the door. But that was before I met Eve. She's such a delight to be around. So genuine. I think that's what tugs at my heartstrings. She's authentic. Precious.

I set a hand on the fence and grip it as Owen arrives and enters the daycare area. I hope the level of my stress is not apparent to anyone else around.

Britney skips over to the fence and leans up on tiptoes to hug Davis over the side. He smooths her hair back and cups her face, speaking to her in a low tone that makes her smile and nod. Finally, she leaves him to hurry back to her coloring. Lucy is still with her, but Eve is standing now. She takes Owen's hand and lets him lead her out of the daycare.

I don't look at her directly, nor she at me. I can't. Nor should I. Damn, this is harder than I expected. I shouldn't feel this possessive of her. It's irrational and dangerous. How many days will I get to spend with her? Single digits? Maybe two weeks tops?

Besides the fact that my heart is going to be ripped out when I get reassigned, I'm going to hurt her too. I feel guilty, but I can't stop myself.

Davis steps in front of me as Eve and Owen disappear out of sight. "You okay?"

"Nope."

He grins. "I didn't think so. Gonna be able to fake it?"

"Yep." I have to.

"Let's go then."

He turns around, and I follow him. For the next few minutes, we pretend to wander and observe while Owen and Eve talk in the far corner of the room. I'm not quite sure what to expect. "Any last-minute words of wisdom?" I ask Davis.

He shakes his head. "Not really. I've watched Eve many times. She's going to have a mock tantrum of sorts, and Owen is going to spank her. Afterward, he will hold her for a while, then she'll go back to the daycare."

I nod. It sounds so simple when he lays it out. How the hell do other men do this? Besides the fact that Eve has told me couples do scenes with other people at the club, I can't see it myself. I've watched several couples come in and go their separate ways. I've seen them touch base with each other and wander off again. It's intriguing. It doesn't feel like something I could do. Share? Share Eve? Fuck no.

If she were mine, which she is not. But if she were, and even if she needed to be dominated as a little with no aspect of sex involved, I still wouldn't be able to share her. I'd move mountains to make sure I could give her what she craved without her needing something from other people.

Several people gather around Eve and Owen before he nods that direction.

"Why are so many people watching? They haven't done anything yet," I whisper.

"They know what's going to happen. They want to watch. It's like a performance."

I draw in a deep breath and release it slowly as we merge with the crowd. My gaze takes in everything. There's a spanking bench in the center of a matted area. It's simple. Nothing more than a padded place for the recipient to put their knees with a second padded platform for them to lean their upper body over.

Owen and Eve are done talking. He's standing near her, his brows furrowed, rubbing his chin.

"They're starting," Davis murmurs.

I'm not sure how he knows this but I take his word for it.

"What did you say, little girl?" Owen asks.

Eve sticks her tongue out at him, crosses her arms, and stomps her foot. "I said no. I don't want to go to school today. You can't make me."

Even though at least a dozen people have gathered to watch, it's very quiet around me. A palpable hush.

Owen narrows his gaze further. "Evelyn, that's enough. I *can* make you, and I will. The question is, do you want to get in the car now, or would you rather I spank your bottom until you're convinced?"

I gasp when he calls her Evelyn instead of Eve. I hate it. I should have been prepared for that. Davis told me she lets Daddies call her by her full name, but hearing it coming from Owen makes me cringe.

She humphs dramatically. "I'm not going."

He steps closer. "I guess that answers my question. You're going to have a long day explaining to your friends and your teacher about why it hurts every time you sit." He takes her by the arm and leads her over to the bench.

I can't breathe. This is nothing like how I play with Eve. It's completely fabricated. It's exactly what she told me to expect, but somehow it was hard to imagine since she doesn't fake her little when she's with me.

"On your knees, little girl."

Eve struggles a bit but it's all for show. Owen eventually lifts her off her feet and sets her on her knees on the padded section. "Lean over."

She grumbles but obeys him. "Fine."

Owen presses between her shoulder blades until she

relaxes fully against her chest over the bench. It's angled so that her head is lower than her butt.

My gaze shifts that direction, and I take in the fact that her dress is no longer covering her panties. It can't. It's too short. And it doesn't matter because Owen lifts the hem and pulls it high up her back.

Now I know what's under that dress. This pair of panties is not like any of the others I've seen her wear. They're plain white cotton. Something about that makes them even sexier.

Eve squirms, but to me, it's still fake. I'm not sure if her actions seem more authentic to other people, but I've been living with this woman for almost a week. Sleeping in her bed. Cooking for her. Holding her on my lap.

I shake the possessive thoughts away. They have no place here. I'm intellectually aware that she's performing with Owen, nothing more. She's not attracted to him sexually, and she's not going to get off from this spanking. At least I sure as fuck hope not.

A slight panic emerges from my depths as I suddenly worry if I've inadvertently unleashed something new inside her. Maybe she *will* get off on Owen's touch this time. Maybe now that she's had a taste of submitting sexually she'll feel those same responses to Owen.

"Down, boy," Davis whispers. "Seriously."

I draw in a breath and rein in my impulse to stop this nonsense. It's not my place. This is what Eve wants, I remind myself. I can't deny her this. I would never deny her anything. Never mind the possessive instinct I'm feeling. I must shake it off. I have no right to feel the angst I feel right now.

Is she going to enjoy this the same way she did last weekend? Has our time together influenced her in any way? Enough that maybe she won't be able to get into the scene like she normally would?

I feel like an ass, hoping my latest idea is correct and she hates submitting to Owen tonight. I pray that something has shifted in her over the past week and she doesn't crave this kind of thing anymore. Or at least that she won't after tonight.

I'm going to spank her sweet bottom myself later tonight. It's going to be sexual. She's going to come hard. Then I'm going to fuck her until neither of us can see straight. I'm so confident that I'm cocky.

Owen smooths a hand over her butt and pulls her panties down to expose the globes. My globes. *Jesus.* I knew this would be hard, but I'm in over my head.

"You want to walk away?" Davis asks quietly.

I shake my head. I'm going to watch. I'm not a jealous boyfriend. Good God.

I flinch when Owen lands the first swat. He hasn't even struck her very hard yet. He's warming up.

She has her legs squeezed together, so no one can see her sweet pussy. I've seen it. I've tasted it. I intend to again. Tonight even. But first I need to endure watching her scene with Owen.

The man is following all the usual protocol. He has checked in with her several times, whispering in her ear. He is fulfilling the fantasy she has requested of him.

It's hard to grasp that she also meets him for coffee or drinks as a friend. How bizarre. She hasn't met up with him since I moved in with her on Monday. I'm not sure how I would react if she wanted to see him outside of the club now that I'm in the picture. On the flip side, how the hell am I supposed to observe him and ensure he's not a suspect if she doesn't spend time with him?

I really need to get a better bead on the large man who stalks her and follow his ass. ASAP. It would help if I at least knew who the asshole was.

As Owen lands a firm spank, I flinch and force myself to

pay closer attention. It's hard to see Eve's face from where I'm standing. I should have thought of that and chosen a better spot, but it would draw too much attention to me to do so now.

She flinches every time he swats her, but I don't see evidence she's aroused. Granted, how the hell could I know from here? And her thighs are pressed so tightly together that she might be doing so because she's aroused. She's not squirming though.

After a few more spanks, Davis winces.

I jerk my gaze to him. "What?" I whisper when I see his face.

"She's off tonight. Not into it," he murmurs.

I look back at her. I have no idea how he can tell. But I'm glad. Pleased as punch.

Owen pauses and squats down near her face, his hand on her back as he speaks to her. She shakes her head a few times. He rubs her back. Finally, he scoots closer and lowers his face farther. Inches separate them.

I stiffen.

Davis touches my arm. "It's fine," he whispers. "Trust me."

I do trust Davis. I also trust Eve. Hell, most of me even trusts Owen. But what the fuck?

Finally, Owen stands and rounds behind her as she lifts her upper body so she's kneeling but no longer leaning over. She reaches down and pulls up her panties. Owen helps her to her feet and wraps her in a hug. He smooths his hand over her pigtails.

I grit my teeth.

When Owen leads her away from the bench, I watch them go, but don't move.

"Stay put," Davis insists.

I nod, but it's hard to do as he suggests.

In a moment they're out of sight and the crowd disperses.

Davis is grinning at me. "You broke her. You stud."

I don't think this is funny. I scowl at him. "I didn't do shit. What the hell are you talking about?"

He shakes his head. "Don't get all defensive. I meant that in the nicest possible way. She couldn't get into it. I'm sure it's because you're all up in her head. That's not a bad thing."

"I need to see her."

Davis sighs and follows me as I head toward the same room where Leah had gone for aftercare. Sure enough, Eve is in there. She's sitting in the corner of a loveseat, her knees drawn up to her chin. A blanket is draped around her, and she's rocking forward and backward slightly.

Owen is squatting in front of her, his hand on the armrest. He's speaking in a soft tone. I can't hear him.

I shouldn't be here, and I know it, but I can't help myself. At least I have the good grace to stop in the doorway. I just want to be sure she's okay. I need to know. Even if I can't be the one to comfort her, I need to see her.

She spots me and smiles. When she reaches out a hand toward me, my heart stops. Thank fuck.

Owen turns to glance at me and smiles also. Weird. He stands as I approach apprehensively. Davis has remained in the doorway.

In the oddest twist of events, Owen reaches out to shake my hand. "You must be Colt."

"I am." Call me confused, I want to add.

Owen sighs. "Eve told me a little about you."

"She did?" I glance at her. She's smiling sheepishly.

"Not much. Enough though. I could tell she wasn't into our scene. She was apologizing to me, though it wasn't necessary. Said she's actually met someone and he was watching and she couldn't get out of her head to enjoy having me spank her." Owen shrugs. "It happens. I'm happy for you."

I glance at Eve again.

She lowers her face and starts rocking again. She's stressed. It's palpable. Does she think I'll be mad?

Owen turns back to her. He squats down again to meet her gaze. "Eve? Will you be okay if I leave you with Colt?"

She nods.

"You sure?"

She nods again. I've only been dominating her for a few days, and I would never let her get away with a non-verbal. I have no idea why. It's instinctive. Or maybe I just like to hear her voice. I love the tremble in her tone when she submits to me verbally.

Owen pats her shoulder and stands. "Come find me if you need me."

She nods again. "Thank you," she murmurs. No *Sir*. Just thank you.

I'm dumbfounded as Owen leaves after patting me firmly on the back.

I ease around next to her and sit at her side, putting my arm around her shoulders.

She leans into me, burrowing her face in my chest. "I couldn't do it," she murmurs.

I hold her close, kissing the top of her head. "It's okay, baby. Why are you so upset?"

She shrugs. Nonverbal.

I let her get away with that for a few minutes, holding her close as she pulls herself together. Finally, I lean back and tip her head so I can see her eyes. "Talk to me. Use your words, baby."

"Are you mad?"

I frown. "Why on earth would I be mad?" I'm elated. I'm seconds from thrusting my chest out and going all Tarzan on her.

She swallows. "Because the plan was for me to go about my usual routine so you could observe. I'm ruining it."

I slowly smile. I lean down to kiss her gently on the lips before responding. "The only thing you're ruining is the likelihood that I might have eventually lost my mind and punched a hole in the nearest wall from watching you perform with another man. If anyone should apologize, it should be me."

She giggles. "You wanted to punch a wall?"

"At least one." I smirk. "Don't let my possessive jealousy go to your head. It's not very responsible of me. I should have been able to observe without putting off vibes so strong that Davis had to call me off like a pack of rabid dogs a few times."

Her face is lit up and she reaches her arms toward me.

I pull her into my lap and hug her closely, nuzzling her neck. "I'm sorry, baby."

"Me too."

I lean back a few inches so I can see her face. "So, we need a new battle plan. And this is totally unfair and irresponsible of me too, but can you live with people at the club believing you met me recently and we've entered into a D/s relationship?"

Her smile melts me. "Yes, Sir." She flushes. "I mean you can't stop that train now. It left the station. People saw what happened with Owen and people are aware you and I are sitting here together right now."

I take a quick glance around to make sure we are still alone, stroke her cheek, and search her gaze. "I'm no less concerned that someone here might be watching you."

"Surely you don't still suspect Owen?"

"Not really, but if people are watching you, there's a good chance one of them is inside this club either planted recently or even an older member. I'll feel much better if I always have my eye on you."

"Okay." She sounds very little when she says that one word.

"I have a question." I hold her gaze, hoping she won't be offended by my inquiry.

She widens her eyes. "What?"

"How come Owen was allowed to call you Evelyn?" I need to hear her tell me.

A slow smile spreads across her face. "Because, silly. I was in trouble. Didn't your mama call you by your full name when you were in trouble?"

I chuckle. "Yes."

She shrugs. "If you ever call me Evelyn, I will know I've been very naughty."

I stare at her in awe before giving her pigtail a tug. "I'll keep that in mind. Also, I took the liberty of letting Davis book us a private room. He's going to monitor me so I can spank your bottom until it's a delicious shade of pink and you're squirming off the bench." I grin.

Her eyes light up. "Tonight?"

"Yes."

She claps her hands together.

"And you don't even have to pretend to misbehave. The list of reasons why you deserve a spanking from me is long from the last few days."

She giggles. "Okay." That one word is a whine.

I lift my usual brow.

She corrects herself. "Okay, Sir."

I pat her bottom. "Good girl. Now, I have another question." I set her on her feet as I speak.

"What?" Her brows furrow with curiosity.

I pinch the edge of her dress. "Is this a twirl dress?"

She smiles broadly. "Yes. Want me to show you?"

"I do."

She takes a step back and then excitedly spins around and around. The hem of the dress flares out so wide that I can see her panties and even her belly.

When she's about to topple, I reach out and grab her around the waist, pull her against my chest. Since the hem of her skirt gets caught up high on her waist, I take the opportunity to tickle her tummy, making her squirm and giggle.

She is truly delightful.

CHAPTER 19

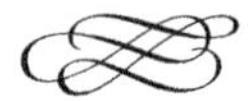

Evelyn

Colt escorts me back to the daycare even though I'd rather stay with him. He says he needs to do his job, which means he needs to wander around paying close attention to everyone in the club. He can easily do so under the not-fake guise of learning the ropes of the community since he's a guest of the club and a potential new member as well as being a newer Dom. My Dom.

I pout anyway when he returns me to the daycare. He sits me down at the same table where I was coloring earlier, sets his hands on the surface, and leans in close. "Pull that lip back in, baby. I can't focus on my job if you're tagging along with me."

"Yes, Sir."

He nods toward the entrance to the daycare. "Don't look, but did you notice the large man at the entrance?"

"Yes. I don't know him."

"Roman hired him to keep you safe. You can trust him."

My eyes go wide. "Seriously?"

He nods. "Yep. Not just you, baby. He needs to know that everyone in this club is safe. It's in his best interest."

"Okay."

"As long as you can see Craig, you'll know nothing is going to happen to you."

"Yes, Sir."

He taps the coloring book in front of him. "Color me a picture. When it's our turn in a private room, I'll come get you."

I smile. I'm beyond excited about this plan. So excited that I bounce in my seat.

He kisses the top of my head and leaves me in the daycare.

Lucy is still nearby and she joins me at the table. "How did your scene go?"

I wince. "It didn't."

"Why not?"

I sigh. "I couldn't get into it. My headspace is filled with Colt." I'd told Lucy about my weird relationship with Colt earlier.

Lucy beams. "That's so fun. I'm excited for you."

I lower my face. "It's also scary and I'm sad because it's temporary. As soon as he finds the man trying to sell me, he will be gone."

Lucy cringes. "Why? Why does he have to leave just because he solves the case?"

I shrug. "It's his job. He works mostly undercover. He says he would never string someone along in his life because it wouldn't be fair to them. He's sometimes gone for months. I wouldn't even be able to reach him."

"Oh. That's awful."

"Yeah." I absently color my picture, but my heart isn't in it. I'm sad now.

"I'm sorry."

"It's probably for the best. I'm not myself when I'm with him anyway. He's shaking up my well-organized life." I grin at her, though I know it doesn't reach my eyes.

Lucy frowns. "Maybe your life needed a bit of shaking?"

I shrug. "Probably, but it was working."

"How was it working? I mean you deserve to have a Daddy more than two hours a week. You've kept everyone at arm's length for years, not letting anyone get close to you. I don't think it was really working," she says gently.

I know she means it in the nicest possible way. I stare at my picture, absentmindedly coloring. Maybe she's right, but what I've been doing was safe. I've kept my personas separate for years. No one in my vanilla world is aware of my fetish life and, to a certain extent, vice versa. I haven't let the two collide. As an adult, I've dated—albeit intermittently—but I've also given my little what she needed.

I've never considered the possibility that the two could collide in a functional way. I'm not even sure I like the idea. It seems complicated. How on earth would I keep everything straight if I was always submitting to a Daddy even while I was at work?

And none of that even matters because it's not an option that's on the table. It's not like the perfect Daddy is someone I'll encounter on every street corner. This is a fluke. And Colt is not my Daddy. He's a newish Dom who happens to click with me and isn't staying in my life.

I need someone's advice though so I look at her and set my crayon down. "Something is different with Colt. It's like I can be myself with him. Both sides of me. And the lines are blurring and that makes me nervous."

Lucy grips my hand. "That's okay. You're evolving."

I lick my lips. "I've never felt sexual with other Daddies. With Colt… I mean… I get mixed up. My little gets aroused with him. I want to have sex with him and not worry about which side of me is present. Does that make sense?"

Lucy smiles. "Of course. My little has sex. I'm almost never an adult when I'm with Master Roman. Maybe I'm not as babyish when we get naked, but I still have a piece of me that's submissive and little at all times. There are no rules. Just do what feels right. Does Colt mind if your little comes to bed?"

I shake my head. "He doesn't seem to. I think he enjoys both sides of me."

"Then there's your answer. Maybe he's just the first Daddy to come along with whom you felt that kind of attraction. Maybe it's a gift." She smiles warmly.

"Maybe." I try to shake off the maudlin. I also try not to think about how long I might get to have him in my life.

Lucy gives my hand a squeeze. "Don't give up. Maybe there's a way to make things work out. You never know."

I don't respond. I can't. If I try to say anything else on this subject, I will start crying. I don't want to cry right now. I'm going to do a scene with Colt, and that's exciting.

Lucy colors silently next to me for a while before she nudges me. "Colt is waving at you."

I turn my head and light up when I see him. I pick up my picture and skip across the room toward him, holding it out.

He smiles as he takes it from me. "Love it, baby." He lifts me over the fence without opening the gate, hugging me tightly. He kisses my forehead. "Ready to do a scene with me?"

"Yep."

He takes my hand and leads me down the hallway toward the private rooms. After glancing through the window, he turns to me. "Davis and Britney are already inside. They said we can watch them and then they will watch us. Is that okay?"

I nod. "Yes. Sir."

He squeezes my shoulder before he opens the door and we step inside.

"Hey," Davis says as he lifts his gaze. "Hope you don't mind, but we're going to try something new tonight." He lifts up a paddle.

Britney is standing near him, her hands clasped behind her back, swaying slightly from side to side. She looks uncertain. I don't blame her. I've never had a Daddy spank me with anything other than his hand. Maybe I would like it. I don't know.

Colt leads me to the loveseat that's along one wall. He sits, but instead of settling me next to him, he spreads his legs and positions me between them, facing out. He wraps an arm around my middle, holding me close against his chest. I'm short enough that his cheek can rest near my shoulder against my biceps.

Davis tips Britney's chin back and meets her gaze. "Ready?"

"Yes, Sir." Her voice is not strong.

He chuckles. "You sure?"

"Yes, Sir."

He leads her toward the bench in the middle of the room. It's the kind that's like a pommel horse with four padded sections for elbows and knees.

Davis grabs the hem of Britney's dress and pulls it over her head.

She shivers and pulls her biceps in close to her boobs. I know that look. It's the same thing I've done on occasion if I was artificially embarrassed by people staring at my tits but knew I would get reprimanded for blatantly covering them.

Davis squats in front of her and tugs her arms away from her sides. He cups her breasts next and thumbs her nipples, making her rise onto her toes.

My nipples stiffen at the same time as hers, and Colt flattens his palm on my belly, letting his thumb absentmindedly stroke the underside of my breast. My boobs are covered with smocking. I never wear a bra when I'm in my little space, so the only thing between me and Colt's fingers is the thin material.

Britney is wearing yellow panties with little ducks on them. That's all that's left, and only for another few seconds because Davis finally pulls them down her legs and sets them on top of her dress.

When he stands, he lifts her by the waist and settles her on her belly on the spanking bench. As he moves around her, attaching her wrists and ankles to cuffs, he glances at us. "Like I said the other night, I don't usually spank Britney for no reason. It's not part of our dynamic. What I have been known to do, however, is keep a tally when she's disobedient and cash them all in whenever I choose."

Colt chuckles. "I wondered what that chart was on your refrigerator the other night."

"Yep. She has a chore chart and a naughty tally. I enjoy making her stew for a few days, wondering when and how I might discipline her. Sometimes I let them accumulate. I don't spank her every time she doesn't make her bed or put her dishes in the sink, but they add up. Tonight, she's going to experience something new."

He finishes attaching her ankles and pulls a strap over her lower back too, cinching it tight.

Britney whimpers as she tries to wiggle. Her breasts jiggle along the sides of the bench.

Davis checks the strap to make sure it's tight. "I don't want her to have any movement for the first time I paddle her. Wouldn't want to risk her hands getting in the way or me striking her in an unintended spot because she jerked to one side."

Colt is holding me so close and so tight that I feel like I'm just as restrained as Britney. His left arm is around my body, his left hand teasing my right boob. He slides his right arm around my upper legs and smooths his palm up my opposite thigh until that thumb is teasing the sensitive skin of my inner thigh an inch below my pussy.

I'm panting already and we haven't watched or participated yet.

Davis kisses Britney on the lips and cups her face. "Ready?"

"Yes, Daddy."

He rounds behind her until he's standing between her thighs, sliding his hands up and down her skin until he cups her butt cheeks. He even parts them several times, exposing her tight hole.

She squirms the slightest amount possible.

"Your bottom is going to be so pretty after I paddle it, sweetie."

It's impossible not to watch intently as he continues to stroke her skin, his fingers coming very close to her pussy over and over but never touching her directly. I'm sure she's dying of lust. Hell, I am from watching. And judging from Colt's grip, he is too.

Finally, Davis picks up the paddle and stands to one side of her. He pats her bottom gently in several places before giving a firmer tap that makes her flinch.

He sets one hand on her lower back and taps her again several times, warming her up. I know it doesn't hurt at all. He's just getting started.

Sure enough, he gradually increases the pressure, keeping a close eye on her face after every few strikes. Pink lines rise across her skin, the width of the paddle. Eventually, her entire bottom is dark pink and each strike no longer leaves definitive lines.

It's mesmerizing.

Colt whispers in my ear. "You're aroused."

I nod and bite into my bottom lip.

"What if you were the one strapped down and I was spanking you like that?"

I would probably come without him touching my pussy. I don't respond.

"Are your panties wet?" he whispers softly so that we aren't disrupting their scene.

I squirm.

"Shh. Not a sound." He surprises me when he slides his hand from my thigh to my pussy. He cups me there, finding out that I'm soaked. He strokes a finger over my panties, grazing my labia and my clit.

It's hard for me to remain standing, but he's got me.

My vision clouds for a moment but I jerk back to attention when Britney cries out, just in time to see Davis has dropped the paddle and his hand is between her legs. Judging by the movement, I assume he's thrusting his fingers in and out of her.

Her head is lifted off the table and she's moaning. "Daddy..."

He keeps fondling her. "Tell me what you need, sweetie."

"I need to come, Daddy. Please."

"Good girl. Go ahead. Come around my fingers."

Her orgasm is immediate and palpable in the room.

Colt stops stroking my pussy as she orgasms.

I whimper.

"Shh. Not your turn, baby."

Not my turn to come? I'm so horny. I'll never survive my own spanking, and I know that's what's coming next.

I shudder as I remember that I've never been aroused with a Daddy. I've never had an orgasm from a spanking. That is about to change right now. At least I certainly hope so. The very thought of Colt spanking me makes my nipples hard. I know I'm going to get even more aroused the moment his hand makes contact with my bottom. If he doesn't permit me the release...

I can't imagine that scenario.

CHAPTER 20

Evelyn

I'm entering new territory here for the millionth time this week as Davis and Britney trade places with me and Colt. I'm nervous, not because I have any hesitation about this or any concern about my reactions to Colt. I'm nervous about Colt's reaction and whether or not this is something he wants or if he's doing it for me.

He leads me to the bench and then circles me, keeping a hand on my shoulders. Finally, he stops in front of me and lifts my chin. "I'm not always going to pause and double-check your consent when I spank you, Eve, because I don't think it's part of our dynamic. You aren't the sort of little who steps out of the role in the middle of the evening for a pulse check."

I nod. He's right.

"But tonight I want to check in with you often and make sure it's working for you. Tonight we're doing a scene inside the club. This isn't real life. This is a small performance."

"Yes, Sir." He's done his research. He's also watched a lot this evening.

"Do you have a safeword you like to use?"

"Broccoli," I tell him, shuddering.

He chuckles. "Your little doesn't like broccoli."

"Bleh." I make a face. I'm totally aware that this is a strange detail about me. My adult is perfectly fine with broccoli, but years ago I decided little Eve wouldn't like it, so she doesn't.

"Broccoli it is then. Use it if you need me to stop at any time."

"Yes, Sir."

"Since I'm the newbie in this room, there are a few things I'm not sure of. I assume Davis and Britney have seen you naked more than I have."

I flush. It's a strange fact. "Yes, Sir."

"So, you're okay with me taking off your clothes?"

"Yes, Sir." *Looking forward to it.*

"How do you feel about restraints?"

"Either way." I bite my lip and add, "Usually I behave enough to do as I'm told when I'm being spanked, but there is nothing usual about our dynamic, so I can't promise how I'm going to react. You'll have to wing it."

He smiles. "Noted. On a scale of one to ten, what's your pain tolerance? How hard do you like to be spanked?"

I meet his gaze. "Seven?"

"Are you asking me?" he teases.

I shake my head. "No. I'm just not sure. This is…different."

"Okay, winging that one too then. Ready?"

I nod.

He lifts a brow.

"Yes, Sir."

"I think I want more, Eve."

"Please spank me, Sir."

"Good girl." He lifts my dress over my head, leaving me in

my panties, knee socks, and shoes. I shiver. My nipples harden immediately. Already, this is different. I'm so aroused by Colt. I've never been down this path. It's going to be interesting.

He cups my boobs and flicks his thumbs over my nipples, making me whimper. It's hard to keep my hands at my sides. "Even though Davis and Britney have seen you naked, they aren't used to seeing you aroused, are they?"

I swallow and shake my head.

"They don't see you moan and whimper, do they, baby?"

"No, Sir," I murmur. He's making me feel like this is the first time I've been naked. He's doing it on purpose. It's hot.

He circles me and angles me so that I'm facing my friends where they're sitting while Britney recovers. From behind, he cups my tits before pinching both nipples and twisting them slightly. His lips come to my ear as I lift onto my toes, writhing under his touch. "They've never seen your pretty little nipples hard and needy, have they?"

"No, Sir," I whisper.

He strokes them several more times before rounding back to stand in front of me. He squats down so that we're eye level, his hands on my hips. "Are your panties wet with anticipation?"

"Yes, Sir."

He slides his hands around to my bottom and grips it, the cotton of my panties the only barrier between us. When he kisses my belly button, I shiver. When he lowers his mouth to kiss my mound, I grab his shoulders.

"Do you like knowing your friends are going to watch me spank you, baby?"

"Yes, Sir." My voice is wobbly. I can hardly form words.

"They're going to watch you come so hard that you scream. Does that excite you?"

I nod this time.

He trails his fingers between my legs at the elastic along

the sides of my pussy. When he pulls it away and releases it with a snap, I gasp. "Shall I take these off now?"

"Yes, Sir."

He slides them down my legs and I step out of them, leaving me still in my socks and shoes. It would seem he wants to keep those on me. After stuffing my panties in his front jeans pocket, he grabs my hips and leans forward to kiss my pussy again, his tongue reaching out to flick over my clit.

I hold his shoulders to keep from falling. My legs will give out if he keeps this up.

"Do you remember how wet Britney was while Davis spanked her the other night and again tonight?"

"Yes, Sir," I whisper.

"I bet you're that wet now, aren't you?"

I nod, biting my lip. How does he do it? How is he so dominant after less than a week of education? It's natural to him.

He finally stands and takes my hand, leading me to the bench. When we arrive, he lifts me onto it, and I settle my knees and forearms on the padded platforms. He circles around me, slowly adjusting the four padded sections so that I can comfortably reach each of them. He notably spreads my knees wider than necessary.

My butt is facing Davis and Britney. I know they can see my glistening arousal. It's weird for me because they've never seen me so raw and sexual. Just little. But I'm not embarrassed. In fact, I'm kind of excited for someone to witness my strange unveiling. A new side of me. I might not understand it, but at least someone will know it happened. When I doubt this experience ever occurred months from now, I can always double-check with Britney.

Colt strokes my butt cheeks with his palms for a long time, helping me settle down and relax. I wonder if he knows this. He's preparing me mentally. Finally, he steps to one side and sets his hand on the center of my bottom. The first swat makes me flinch, but it doesn't hurt. It was very gentle. He peppers me with several more like it, warming me up.

After a few minutes, he increases the pressure, spanking me all over. I can feel the heat and the sting, but it's more soothing than painful so far. He stops, rubs the skin, and leans toward my face. "How are you doing, baby?"

"Good, Sir."

"Can I strike harder?"

"Yes, please."

"Good girl." He resumes, his swats coming less frequently but with more intensity. It feels so good. There's nothing like this feeling in the world. As I slide deeper into the experience, I think—not for the first time—about how vanilla people are really missing out.

He spanks me all over but stays high on my butt for a long time. When he pauses to check in with me the next time, I'm far more subdued. "Okay?"

"Yes, Sir," I murmur.

"More?"

"Yes, please."

The next spank lands closer to my thighs, and I moan, the sensation rushing to my pussy. After two more like that, I'm panting. My clit is vibrating. *Holy shit.* This. This is what people speak of.

Three more swats to that juncture between my cheeks and my thighs send me close to the edge. Just like that.

But then he shifts his attention lower, spanking my thighs now. Back and forth. I'm vibrating with need. In fact, I'm pretty sure I'm moaning constantly and it's reverberating in my head.

I need to come. I want Colt to make me come. I don't care who's watching or that I've never done this before and I'm shocking them. I'm going to shatter, and Colt knows it. He's stroking the small of my back with his free hand. I think he's murmuring words of encouragement, but I can't hear them.

The final two strikes land right where I need them, on that sweet spot, one on one side, one on the other. He slides his hands between my thighs, thrusts two fingers into me, and thumbs my clit.

"*Colton,*" I scream, my head lifting off the padding.

He keeps pumping his fingers as I ride the waves of my release, easing the pressure right before I would have winced.

I can't breathe. My fingers are wrapped so tightly around the padding that they ache. My legs are stiff. My toes are curled in my shoes.

Colt lifts me off the bench seconds later, and I'm aware that Davis is there too. Davis wraps a blanket around my shivering frame as Colt carries me to the loveseat and cradles me in his arms.

I bury my face in his chest and curl up, unable to stop shaking. I hear the door to the room open and close, assuming Davis and Britney have left.

Colt tries to lean me back, but I'm gripping his shirt tightly.

"Baby, you need to drink some water." He holds a water bottle low enough for me to see it, perhaps hoping it will jog my memory about what water is. In any case, it works. I finally tip my head back and let him angle the top of the bottle to my mouth. "That's it. More, baby... Good girl."

I drink as much as I can before turning my head away and burrowing against him again. I just want to snuggle, and luckily Colt gets that. He rocks me back and forth, stroking my hair. "I've got you, Eve. Just relax."

CHAPTER 21

Colton

It's late when we get back to Eve's apartment, and I'm grateful that no one seems to be lurking outside. I'm exhausted, and I know Eve is too. She rode home with her knees pulled up and her eyes closed. Hell, Britney had to help her change back into her street clothes in the locker room. She was still dazed.

Somehow she manages to walk to her apartment on her own. I thought I might have to carry her, which would have been difficult to explain to anyone we passed. As soon as I lock the door, I lift her into my arms and cradle her, making my way to her bedroom.

In the bathroom, I set her on her feet, remove her clothes, and fix her toothbrush. She takes it from me and goes through the motions of brushing, at least marginally.

After she rinses, I point to the toilet and leave her in the bathroom while I change into sleep pants.

She looks very shy and embarrassed when she emerges. It's oddly endearing.

"Come here, baby."

She shuffles toward me, and I pull one of my T-shirts over her head before swinging her up onto the bed and pulling the covers around her. She's still halfway in subspace. I understand it much better after talking to Davis while the women changed clothes.

I quickly use the bathroom myself, pull the door to the bathroom almost shut with the light on, and turn off the bedroom light before climbing into bed with Eve. For the first time, I don't remain on top. I slide under the covers and pull her intentionally against me.

She wraps her arm over my chest and snuggles closer.

I've never been so happy nor so scared in my entire life.

Eve is the best thing that's ever happened to me, and I'm going to hurt both of us when I leave.

The room is still dark when I suddenly jerk my eyes open. It's not because there's a threat. No sudden noises or braking glass or even a ringing phone. It's that Eve is between my legs under the covers, and my cock is in her mouth.

I thread my fingers in her hair as I moan. "Eve..."

"Mmm," she manages around my erection, the vibrations making me even harder.

How the hell did I sleep through her tugging my flannel pants over my cock? She has one hand wrapped around the base, moving it up and down in sync with her lips. I'm so damn hard, I'm already about to come. Granted, I spent half the evening with a hard-on, so it wouldn't take long to bring me right back to the plateau.

When she increases the suction, I arch my body and stiffen. I don't want to come in her mouth. I want to be inside her tight pussy. "Eve…" I try to dislodge her, but she swats at my hands and continues.

I'm shocked by her brazenness. She is not little right now. This woman is in total control. Determined. And I'm not going to stop her. I'm not sure I could if I wanted to. I'm too close to the edge to convince my hands to pull her off.

She grips the base of my cock tighter with her small fingers and hollows out her cheeks. That's when the world stops spinning. I come so hard and so fast that I can't even warn her. But she doesn't seem to care. This was her intention. She's still sucking and now swallowing at the same time. It's fucking hot, and I pulse into her throat until I'm completely spent.

Eve eases off my dick and lifts her head. The covers have slid down our bodies. I'm breathing hard. She's grinning at me.

"Come here, baby." I reach for her with arms that are still not ready to take orders from my brain.

She climbs up my body and lays on top of me, planting her elbows on my chest and setting her chin in her palms. She's grinning like a Cheshire cat.

"Imp," I tell her.

"Mmm."

"Welcome back to earth." I stroke her back through my shirt.

"I hardly remember getting home or climbing into bed."

"I did most of the work," I tease her.

"I bet I shocked the shit out of Davis and Britney."

"Probably, but I didn't pay close enough attention to them to tell you." I mentally acknowledge she has cussed. If she were in her little space, I would reprimand her. But this woman on top of me is definitely Eve the adult.

"You made me come from a spanking," she states as if this is already featured on billboards all over town.

I chuckle. "I was there."

She smiles, her cheeks flushed. "You're an amazing spanker for someone who's so new to the lifestyle."

"Thank you." I give her a squeeze.

She sighs and slides her arms up around my neck and rests her cheek on my chest. "You're ruining me for other men."

I purse my lips and thread my fingers in her hair. Inside, I'm fist-pumping. Outside, I think I'm a heel. It would be absurd to respond. What would I say? I'm sorry? Good? That's a shame? Give me ten minutes and I'll show you how much more I can ruin you?

I swallow, hating this situation. How on earth have I allowed myself to fall for the woman I'm meant to be protecting?

Then again, how could I not have? She's amazing and multi-faceted and gorgeous and precious and sexy and smart and powerful and greedy and delicious and confident and timid. She's so many things.

She's not mine.

The next time I wake up, the sun is streaking across the room. I panic for two seconds before remembering it's Saturday. I'm always working, but Eve doesn't have to go into the office today. I get to lounge in bed with her as long as I want, and I intend to start our day by making her scream.

We've accumulated a list of sexual activities, but I have yet to be inside her, and that's about to change right now.

I stare down at her peaceful body. She has rolled onto her belly, facing away from me at some point. I carefully ease my sleep pants down my body so as not to disturb her. She woke me with her mouth around me in the night. Time to return the favor.

I lean over the edge of the bed and snag a condom from my discarded jeans. Moments later, I'm rolling it on. Once I get started, I don't want to have to stop touching her to find a condom.

I ease the covers down her body until her bottom is revealed. My shirt has risen up over the globes in her sleep. Her skin is still pink from my spanking. It's sexy as hell.

I ease up closer to her side and palm her bottom, letting my hand slide between her parted thighs until I'm stroking her slit.

She gasps as she comes awake, lifting her head and twisting it toward me. Her eyes are wide, but as soon as she sees me, she smiles and relaxes, dropping her cheek back to the pillow, but facing me this time.

I ease a finger into her, and her lips part.

As her eyes slide closed, I nudge my knee between hers, parting her legs.

She lifts her butt into the air when I add a second finger and whimpers when I remove both of them to focus on her clit instead. She's already wet, but the arousal I've gathered from inside her makes it easy for my fingers to glide around her swollen nub.

She gasps as I pick up the pace, her hands fisting the pillow on both sides. When she tries to lift her bottom again, I hold her down. The moan that escapes her lips is musical, so I keep focusing on her clit until she's writhing. "Please..."

"Please what, baby?"

"Please fuck me."

"What a potty mouth," I tease.

She groans and turns her face toward the pillow, pressing her forehead against the soft down.

I thrust two fingers into her again but pull them back out immediately.

The growl of frustration makes me smile.

"Colton, put your cock in me," she demands.

I chuckle. "Not yet."

Another grumble.

"Come for me first. I want to feel your orgasm on my hand then I'll join you."

Her body shudders as she grinds her pussy against my fingers.

I flick her clit rapidly until she's panting, and the moment she sucks in a sharp breath, I add two fingers to her pussy again.

"Colton…" God, I love that sound. My name vibrates in the air as she comes, her body trembling with every pulse.

I need to be inside her, and I want to catch her off guard, so I quickly climb between her legs and jerk her hips off the mattress, forcing her to her hands and knees.

"God, yes. Please," she begs.

I thrust into her without hesitation, and she cries out.

I hold her hips steady, keeping my cock buried deep inside her. It's been a damn long time since I've been inside a woman. I've overestimated my stamina. If I don't get a grip, I'm going to come too soon. I want her to reach another orgasm first.

When I finally ease almost out of her, it's my voice I hear echoing in the room. My moan. My pleasure.

I thrust in deep again, tipping my head back, knowing this is going to be quick. On my next thrust, I know I can't keep this up. Not in this position. It's too erotic. I pull out of her and shift back a few inches so I can flip her onto her back.

She whimpers as she lands, her eyes wide, lips parted.

I shove my shirt off her delectable body. I need to see all of her. I push her knees high and wide and press them into the mattress.

"Why did you stop?" Her voice is desperate, eager, shaking.

"Your pussy was strangling my cock. I need a moment," I

exaggerate as I lean down and kiss her sweetly. I thread my fingers with hers and plant our combined hands alongside her head. "You're fucking tight, baby."

She licks her lips. "It's been a while."

"I see that. For me too. I want this to last longer than three thrusts."

She arches her body. "Who cares if it doesn't? We can always do it again."

She's right, but damn. To distract myself, I dip my head and flick my tongue over her nipple. I love the sounds she makes when I play with her tits. The little bud hardens. I blow on it and then nip it with my teeth, making her squirm. I do the same to the other tit until she's writhing again.

I have no idea how I thought this would slow things down. If anything, her reactions are driving me just as close to orgasm as if I were inside her. By the time I give up and thrust in to the hilt again, I'm too close to the edge to stop. I pump hard and fast, groaning as I enjoy the grip of her pussy around me.

My one functioning brain cell reminds me that I want her to come first, so I release her hand and drag mine between our bodies, finding her clit and pinching it.

Her eyes roll back and she bucks her hips against mine.

"Come around my cock, baby. Milk me with that tight pussy."

It's fucking amazing how she's able to follow that demand, but I only get to enjoy the pulsing of her channel around me for about one second before I too reach my peak and hold myself deep as my orgasm shakes my foundation.

For a long time after my release, I hover over her, panting, watching her blissful expression. She's limp and sated beneath me, and I wish I could stay right here forever, but I'm about to collapse.

I finally ease out and drop down onto one hip alongside her, my lips coming to her shoulder.

She's still breathing heavily when she suddenly gasps and jerks her head up to glance down at my cock. A heavy sigh escapes her mouth as she once again lowers her head to the pillow. "Scared me for a moment. When did you put on the condom?"

"Before I woke you." I stroke her cheek. "Sorry. No need to panic."

She turns her head toward me and cups my face too. "I'm covered from pregnancy, but I've just never had sex without a condom."

I lay my hand over hers and slide it around so I can kiss her palm. "I haven't either, baby."

She nods. "Okay."

I finally release her to roll off the bed and go dispose of the condom. When I return a few minutes later, she's in the same position, on her back, staring at the ceiling, so open and sexy and warm.

I crawl back onto the bed, pull the covers over us, and haul her into my embrace so that she's draped over me. It's how she likes to fall asleep. My heart beats easier when her tits are pressed against me. It's even better naked.

I kiss her forehead. I've never felt this strongly about a woman. Sex certainly did nothing to change my opinion about that. It's worse now. I'm in deep trouble. I suspect she is too.

She's drawing circles on my chest, probably as deep in thought as I am. When she speaks, her voice is soft. "What do we do now?"

I hold her tight. "I don't know, baby." I'm being frank. I don't have answers. "Let's start with a lazy day together, okay?"

She tips her head back to meet my gaze. "I need to be little."

I nod. "I figured you would." I tuck a lock of hair behind her ear. "Will you let me take care of you?"

She nods. I can see her sliding into her little space already. It's fascinating. Her eyes take on a different glow. A youthfulness that wasn't present while my cock was inside her. I'm not sure I understand yet what triggers her to be in which headspace, but I don't think she knows the answers either. This is new territory for her just as it is for me.

She's been aroused and clearly sexual as her little. I've brought her to orgasm in that headspace. I wasn't sure where she might be during sex, but the blowjob she gave me in the night and the amazing sex we just had was in her adult space. I'll just have to pay attention and see what happens next.

After a few minutes more of lounging, her stomach growls.

I chuckle. "I need to feed you."

She snuggles against me. "Not yet. I'm cozy."

I lift a brow and tip her chin back. "Did you just tell me no?"

She licks her lips. "Maybe? Can we just stay here for a while longer? I'm warm."

"And you'll be warm in the bathtub too." I tap her nose. "I'm going to fill the tub now. You may stay here only as long as that takes. When it's ready, you'll come get in. Understood?"

"Yes, Sir," she murmurs.

I slide out of bed and tuck the covers around her as she curls into a ball. Half of me agrees with her. We could stay in bed for hours. But I know she needs to eat, and I'm starving too, so I take charge.

I pad to the bathroom, deciding to shower first. It will give her a few moments longer under the covers and give me time to plan our day. Or hell, at least our morning. It's hard to plan too far ahead since I'm only marginally grasping what her needs are yet. I've never spent as much time with her as I will this weekend.

I shower quickly before turning on the bath to let it start filling while I dry off. While it fills, I step into the bedroom and rummage through my bag to grab clean clothes. It's impossible not to chuckle at the lump under the covers. She's so buried that I can't even see her face.

When I return to the bathroom, I test the water. It's perfect and it's ready. I turn it off and call out. "Bath time."

I'm not remotely shocked that she doesn't come running. In fact, I suspected this would happen. I expect her to challenge me. It's who she is. It's part of her persona. She's going to test me every step of the way, and I'm equally clear that I cannot waver. I've done enough research and asked enough questions in the last few days to know that Eve's little likes boundaries and firm guidance. She's about to get that from me.

I step into the bedroom. "Evelyn." My voice is firm. "Now."

She flinches under the covers when I call her by her full name, but then she grumbles, "But I'm warm and cozy. Five more minutes."

"Nope. The water is hot now. I suspect your bottom is still feeling the sting from my palm last night too. I'm going to count to three. If you're not on your feet, I'm going to add to that burn."

She flips the covers back. Her eyes are wide as she meets my gaze.

I feel the challenge. "One..."

She jerks, but still stares at me.

"Two..."

Finally, she decides I'm serious and scrambles out from under the covers. She's on her feet in moments, and she stomps toward me, shoving past to enter the bathroom. "Fine."

Oh, this is going to be interesting. The defiant challenge in her is not unexpected but still just as interesting. I grab her arm as she tries to pass me, halting her progress to pull her back against me. "I'm glad you took me seriously and got out of bed, but your attitude has earned you a punishment anyway."

She huffs. "I'm up, aren't I?"

I spin her around and hold her shoulders. "What you are is sassy and disrespectful. Is that the way you spoke to any other Daddy you've been with?"

She crosses her arms under her tits in a defiant, exaggerated stance. "You're not my Daddy."

I flinch. I hadn't expected her to be quite *this* defiant. I falter for only a moment before recognizing this as the challenge it is. The ultimate challenge.

I direct her toward the toilet where I sit and pull her between my legs so our faces are level. I cup her face. "Look at me, Eve."

She meets my gaze, her lip trembling.

"I know we're wading into unknown territory together, and I can't promise you a damn thing past the here and now, but I do think you want me to be your Daddy for as long as we're together. Am I right?"

Tears form in her eyes and she swipes at them. "Yes, Sir," she murmurs.

"Then I expect you to behave like any Daddy would demand of you. I know you need boundaries, and I'm going to give them to you. I know you're going to challenge me today. I'm ready for it. But know this—I won't waver, not for an instant. I will be firm and demanding. You will be obedient or find yourself in a heap of trouble. Understood?"

She stares at me with wide eyes and slowly nods.

"Words, Eve."

"I'll be good."

I lift a brow.

"I'll be good, Daddy."

My chest tightens when she calls me that. The only other time she called me Daddy she was half-asleep. She's awake now. Coherent and choosing intentionally to address me as Daddy. I pull her closer and hug her sweet naked body against my fully clothed one. "That's my girl."

When I urge her to lean back, I meet her gaze again. "First, I'm going to give you a bath. We'll discuss your punishment after that."

Her eyes widen again. "I can bathe myself," she mumbles.

"I'm sure you can, but that's not what I said, is it?"

She shakes her head. "No, Sir."

I doubt anyone has ever bathed her since she only practices her kink inside the club. I doubt anyone has cooked for her either or any number of other things I'm going to insist upon today. If we're doing this, we might as well go all-in.

CHAPTER 22

Evelyn

My emotions are all over the place. I'm stunned speechless, excited, nervous, panicky, eager. My heart is racing as Daddy lifts me into the tub. I watch him in awe as he reaches for the bubbles and turns the water back on so he can add them to the flowing stream.

Moments later, I'm in a luxurious, warm heaven.

He leans me back to get my hair wet, then grabs the shampoo and massages my scalp.

I close my eyes and enjoy every moment. I know we've been dabbling in this world for several days, but it would seem he intends to dominate me completely today. As a Daddy. As *my* Daddy.

I grab the sides of the tub as he rinses my hair, and continue holding on as he rubs the conditioner in next. "Do you have any bath toys?" he asks.

I nod and point to the vanity. "They're under the sink," I tell him in my smallest voice.

He grins as he opens it and hands me several of my favorites, including a boat and the little people who go in it. I play while he washes my body, though I do hesitate when he runs the washcloth over my boobs. My nipples stiffen and I can't help but react.

He doesn't linger too long, but he does flick his thumbs over the tight tips before easing the washcloth down between my legs. With one hand on my shoulder, he rubs my pussy. "Spread your knees wider, baby."

I do as I'm told, instantly aroused.

"Good girl."

I'm sad when he stops touching me there, but I return my attention to my boat. "Do you want to stay and play for a few minutes?" he asks.

"Yes, Sir." I giggle as the passengers fall out of my boat. I reach under the bubbles to find them.

He tips my chin back, meeting my gaze. "Ten minutes. No arguments when I say it's time to get out."

"Yes, Daddy."

He stands and leaves the bathroom.

I stare at the door, wondering if I'm dreaming. Is this really happening? It's like my wildest dreams all in one. My adult had amazing sex less than an hour ago, and the same man has taken full control over my little. I'm already calling him Daddy.

I shiver at where this is heading, releasing the boat to grab the side of the tub with one hand while reaching for my pussy with the other. My clit is swollen and needy from the residual of having had sex as well as the most recent contact with the washcloth.

My eyes drift closed and my mouth falls open as I push a finger inside my channel. I'm slightly tender from Colt's cock. It really has been a while since I've had sex. The sensitive skin feels good though. Really good.

When I find my clit with my thumb, I let out a little gasp. So much sensation. I don't even need to visualize something imaginary to get off. I have so much material to work with from this morning alone, I could orgasm four times.

I picture Daddy washing my boobies, the way his thumb slid over the tips, making me gasp. The image urges me to release the side of the tub with my free hand and cup my little breast. I pinch my nipple, which causes me to cry out.

The noise startles me, and I jerk my eyes open, freezing when I see I'm not alone. I start panting, not moving an inch. My finger is still deep in my pussy, my thumb on my clit, my other hand cupping my boob.

Colt is leaning in the doorway, casually, arms crossed loosely under his pecs. He's got a slight smile, so I don't think I'm in trouble, but I'm completely embarrassed.

Finally, he speaks. "I was gone five minutes, and your naughty little fingers went to work."

I swallow as I remove my hands from their guilty locations and lower my gaze.

"Apparently two orgasms in the morning aren't enough for you, huh?"

I purse my lips.

He shoves off the doorframe and shuffles toward me. After grabbing a towel, he reaches into the tub and lets the water out. His hands come under my arms and he lifts me from the tub to set me on my feet on the bathmat.

Without a word, he sits on the toilet seat and dries me. I'm shivering from embarrassment and cold when he finally wrings out my hair and then turns me to face him. "What were you thinking about, baby?" His voice is soft, inquisitive.

I lick my lips. "You, Sir."

"More specifically?"

"I was thinking about when you were washing my boobies," I mumble.

"And that made you feel aroused?"

"Yes, Sir."

"I'm glad you enjoy my touch, baby, but I think we need a few rules."

I shudder. Yikes.

"From now on only Daddy gets to touch your pretty little boobies and your pussy, got it?"

Wetness leaks out of me at his demand. I'm trembling as I meet his gaze. He would really order me not to masturbate?

He lifts that brow.

I swallow hard. "Yes, Sir," I whisper.

"Your orgasms will be earned and I'll decide when you deserve them, understood?"

"Yes, Daddy."

"No matter how horny you get, whether we're at home, at the club, or you're at work, you'll keep your greedy little fingers away from your pussy and your tits," he reiterates, which adds to my arousal, and I'm certain he knows this.

"Yes, Sir."

"Good girl. Now, let's get these tangles combed out, find you something to wear, and get some breakfast in you." He stands and opens a drawer on my vanity, finding a brush.

I close my eyes as he works out the tangles, so carefully that it doesn't hurt. When he's done, he takes my hand and leads me to the bedroom.

I wait while he opens my closet and chooses a soft cotton dress. It's a simple one. Pale pink. Thin. Lightweight. The sleeves are three-quarter length.

"Arms up."

I lift my arms so he can slide the dress down my body. It reaches a few inches below my bottom.

"Perfect. Now, how about some breakfast?"

"I need panties, Daddy."

He taps my nose. "Not this morning. You've already

earned a firm spanking, and I suspect you intend to challenge me several times today. We'll leave your bottom exposed. It will make it easier for me to discipline you for the next few hours."

I'm so aroused as he takes my hand and leads me from the room that it's a wonder I don't moan. It's also out of character for me and therefore confusing and maddening. I can't wrap my head around my reactions to him. Not like any other Daddy I've ever been with. I don't just want him to spank me so I can get release, I want him to fuck me too.

When we reach the kitchen, he sits on a chair and guides me to his side. "I'm going to spank you first for your sassy attitude and defiance. It's going to hurt. Tomorrow you'll get out of bed when I tell you to."

"Yes, Sir." I have no doubt his spanking is going to hurt, nor do I doubt he realizes I'm going to need to come. Will he let me?

He takes me over his knees, pushes my dress up to my shoulder blades, and holds me down with a hand to the small of my back. "Knees wider, Evelyn."

I spread my thighs, unable to breathe when he calls me Evelyn. Every time he does that, I will slide into subspace. It's so arousing. My full name is filled with complete domination that makes me more submissive than ever.

Colt palms my bottom. It's still pink from last night, but that's only going to make this more arousing. He's more confident today. He starts out gentle, but doesn't waste time picking up the pace, peppering my bottom with his swats until I'm panting. The last few land at the junction of my bottom and my thighs, making me cry out.

He stops abruptly and stands me on my feet.

I'm swaying, unable to support myself, dizzy with need and so much more.

He steadies me with his hands on my biceps until I finally

stand still. His next act takes me by surprise. He stands and leads me to the corner of the kitchen, angling me toward the junction of the two walls. "You'll stand here in a timeout while I cook breakfast. Use the time to think about how often you want to be defiant today."

I'm shaking with arousal. So out of my element. He's caught me off-guard. I've never been put in timeout before.

"Pull your dress up to your chest, Eve. I want to see your pink bottom while I cook."

My fingers tremble as I gather the material and clasp it just under my boobs.

He shuffles away but returns a moment later, squatting down behind me. "Spread your feet, baby."

I step out.

"Farther."

Wetness is leaking out of me. It's going to run down my thighs.

When he's finally satisfied with the width of my feet, he sets a wooden spoon down between them, end to end. "Keep them this wide. Don't move." He rises and leaves me standing here. In the corner. Horny. Wet. My bottom is burning. Exposed. Tingling.

I'm whimpering because I can't help it, but he doesn't say anything. I stand as still as I can while I listen to the sounds of him making breakfast. The scent of bacon fills the air, making me realize I'm starving. I listen to the sizzle until it subsides and something else goes into the pan, reviving the frying sounds.

Finally, he speaks. "Breakfast is ready, baby. You can come to the table."

I release my dress and glance down at the spoon on the floor as I step back.

"Leave the spoon. I have a feeling we'll need it again today."

I hope not. Timeout wasn't my favorite pastime.

Daddy pulls out a chair and lifts me onto it, yanking my skirt out from under me before I'm fully seated. "Sit on your bare bottom, baby."

I wiggle. The cool chair feels good, but I'm going to get the seat wet.

"Stop squirming. Knees wider." He scoots me in as I comply. I'm so aroused that I could probably come if he ordered me to.

I grin as Daddy brings our plates to the table. Mine is a pink Mickey Mouse-shaped plate with two pancakes on it. Daddy cuts them up into bite-sized pieces and drizzles syrup over the top before sliding the plate toward me and handing me a chubby plastic fork.

"How do you know so much about what I like?" I whisper in awe as I pick up a piece of bacon.

He chuckles. "It's not rocket science, baby. You own two boxes of pancake mix, which tells me you like them well enough to have a backup box. I assume you don't own all those dishes if you don't normally use them. And..." He reaches over and tweaks my cheek. "Based on the dishes and clothes and toys you own, I'm guessing you're not old enough for knives, so there you have it."

I grin. He's amazing. "Thank you, Daddy."

"You're welcome, baby. Now eat before it gets cold."

I pick up my sippy cup and down half of my milk before continuing.

CHAPTER 23

Colton

My phone rings as I'm cleaning up the kitchen. I glance at Eve. She's busy coloring, which I've determined is her favorite pastime. I kiss her forehead and meet her gaze. "Daddy has to take a call in the other room. You stay here at the table, understood?"

"Yes, Sir."

I tap the screen as I walk toward the master bedroom, not wanting her to listen to my conversation with my boss. "Hey," I say by way of greeting. "Please tell me you've got something on that damn stalker."

He sighs. "No. Not yet, but I have something else you're not going to like."

I stiffen as I perch on the edge of the bed. "Give it to me."

"Got another tip."

"You're shitting me."

"I wish I was. Came from someone who saw you with her last night."

"Fuck." I fail to keep my voice down. I glance at the door and hope Eve chooses to obey me. I stand and start pacing, rubbing my forehead with two fingers. "What did they say?"

"Guy left a message with the non-emergency line. Jane just brought it to me a few minutes ago. I'll read it to you.

I know you've got a man guarding Eve. I saw him with her last night. Tell him not to let his guard down. These assholes still have her on their radar. First chance they get, I think they will still grab her.

"Fuck," I mutter again.

"You with her now?"

"Yes."

"Don't fucking leave her side."

"Wouldn't think of it." I'm seething though. This means someone at Surrender knows about this, they saw me, and they knew I was undercover. What the fuck?

"Wherever you went last night, don't go there again."

"Obviously." I scowl. "But we were at a club. The owner needs to know one of his members is involved." I pace some more. "Jesus. This is fucked-up." Why would someone who knows Eve is being stalked call in tips to the cops? Why not just fucking walk into the police station? Why the hell does this guy feel the need to stay out of it? I have more questions than answers. "We really need an ID on that stalker."

"Guy's not in the system. You know it takes time."

"What if Eve doesn't have time?"

My boss pulls in a breath. "You sound overly concerned, Marshall. Please tell me you aren't involved with this woman."

I have never lied to the captain. Nor have I ever gotten personally invested in anyone on the job.

"Shit," my boss murmurs when I don't respond. "Do I need to fucking pull you off this case, Marshall?" His voice rises.

"I'll yank you out of there in five minutes if you've gotten involved with this woman. You know better. Christ, Marshall, you can't keep her safe if you're fucking her."

I wince. "Don't talk about her like that, man." I don't like the tone of his voice or the implication.

Silence. Finally, he responds. "Shit."

"And don't even think about pulling me off. It's not an option. If you do, you'll find my resignation letter on your desk before the end of the day. She's my responsibility. I'm keeping her safe. No one else."

"I don't fucking believe it. Ten years you've been working for me. Never once have you made such a bad judgment call. This woman's life is at stake, Marshall. Do you get that?"

I stop pacing, facing out the window. I'm seething. I grit out my next words. "I understand that better than anyone alive, and I won't let anything happen to her if it's the last damn thing I do on this earth. You hear me?"

"Oh, I hear you. I just know you're wearing blinders now."

I close my eyes, my jaw so tight it's a wonder I don't break a tooth. "I've got this. Just fucking get me an ID on that guy."

"I'm doing my best. Please, for the love of God… Oh, Christ. You are not going to listen to me, are you?"

"No."

"Great," he drawls out sarcastically. "Be careful, Marshall. I mean it."

I end the call and drop my chin toward my chest.

"Daddy?" The timid voice behind me makes me spin around. Eve is standing in the doorway. She's shaking and looks like she might cry at any moment.

I rush over and sweep her off her feet to carry her in my arms back to the living room. I poke her belly as I sit in the armchair with her on my lap. "You weren't supposed to leave the table."

Her lip trembles. "I didn't mean to, but you were shouting

and cussing and… It was about me, wasn't it?"

I sigh. "Yes, but I don't want you to worry. I'm not going to let anything happen to you." Should I tell her everything that I know?

"Okay." Her eyes are wide, and I don't think she wants details right now. I don't think her little can handle them.

"Listen, Daddy needs to make a few more calls. Can you be a good girl and watch cartoons while I do that?"

She nods. "Yes, Daddy."

I lift her up and swing her around in a circle until she smiles. Finally, I settle her in the corner of the couch before grabbing the remote and flipping through the cartoon channels. "Which one do you like best?"

"That one," she announces when I pause at one with a pink pig.

I head back to the bedroom, find her stuffed unicorn, and return to snuggle it in her embrace. I lean over and kiss her forehead. "Stay right here. I mean it. Give me ten minutes."

"Okay, Daddy." She leans against the arm of the couch looking very small, her legs curled under her, her unicorn clutched tightly in her arms.

This time when I enter the bedroom, I close and lock the door before heading for the bathroom and lifting up my phone. I don't want her to hear me. I've done enough damage for one day.

The first call I place is to Roman who picks up immediately. "Colt. Everything okay?"

"No. Not even close. We need to talk. You have some free time today?"

"Absolutely. Can you come here to my home?"

"Yes. If you don't mind."

"Not at all. I assume Eve is with you?"

"Yes. She's…little."

"Good. Lucy is always little at home. They can play

together while we talk. Anyone else you think needs to hear this?"

"Yes. Julius, since he's your manager. Davis because he's been in the loop from the beginning."

"I'll call Julius. You call Davis. I'll text you my address. See you in an hour?"

"We'll be there. Thanks." I end that call and hit up Davis next.

Luckily, he too answers on the first ring. "Hey, Colt."

"You free this morning?"

"Of course. What can I do?"

"Meet me at Roman's. He's calling Julius too. I'll explain when we get there. The girls can play while we talk."

"Sounds good. See you soon."

I draw in a deep breath and head back to the living room. When I pick up the remote and turn off the television, Eve groans. "Hey, I was watching that."

I sit on the coffee table and level my gaze at her. "Television is a privilege, not a given, Evelyn. I turned it off because we need to go."

She humphs and crosses her arms. "Where are we going?"

"Master Roman's house."

She eyes me suspiciously. "Like a playdate?"

"Sort of. You can certainly play with Lucy. Britney will be there too."

"There's stuff you aren't telling me."

I take her hand and hold it lightly in mine. "Yes, there is, baby. I need you to trust me to tell you later, okay. You're not in the headspace for it now, and it's not urgent."

"Am I in danger?"

"No more than yesterday, and you have my word that I won't let anything happen to you."

"Okay, Daddy."

"Now, let's get some panties on you." I smile.

She glances down. "I'm going to wear this?"

"Yes. And a coat of course."

"I've never left the house little," she tells me, her eyes wide.

"Today, you're going to. Today, you're little all day. Besides, Lucy and Britney will be little also. You can play with them while the Daddies talk."

I sweep her off the sofa and carry her to the bedroom before depositing her on her feet. After grabbing a pair of panties from her drawer, I help her step into them before I find socks and tennis shoes. She seems okay with my selections. At least she doesn't say anything.

"Can I take Jessie?" She's still clutching the unicorn.

"Of course." I lead her to the living room and find her a full coat, helping her into it before I put on shoes and grab a thick sweater myself. "Ready?"

"Yes, Sir."

I hurry her down the hallway and into the garage, knowing she will be a bit unnerved until she's in the car, worrying about someone seeing her.

As I pull out of the parking garage, I scan the area, instantly spotting the same fucker. He's farther away, but I recognize his size and ball cap. "Fuck," I mutter. I take a right out of the garage, moving in the opposite direction. He clearly has me pegged by now though because I see him on the move out of my rearview mirror. He's jogging across the street toward his car.

"Daddy?" Eve glances over her shoulder.

"Face front, baby. It's safer in case Daddy has to hit the brakes." I take a left and then another right, hoping by the time he gets in his car, he can't find me.

Luckily, I never spot him again. I've lost him. Just to be safe, I drive around in circles for a while, taking strange turns several times before getting on the highway. He's not on my tail, and eventually, I sigh and reach for Eve's hand.

She's shaking.

I lift her fingers to my lips and kiss them. "It's okay, baby."

"It's not though, not really." Her tone tells me she's waffling out of her little space. And that's fine if it's what she needs or wants, of course, but it won't change anything.

When I get off the highway, I pull over into a parking lot and put the car in park, facing her. I cup her face. "You okay?"

She shakes her head. Her eyes are watery.

"Listen, baby, I won't make this decision for you. It's your choice. If you want me to tell you everything I've learned this morning, I will. Right now or when we get to Roman's or later today. But, here's the thing. Nothing has really changed. Not where you're concerned. I still don't know anything about who's after you or who the man is watching your apartment. I need you to know that nothing is ever going to happen to you because I won't let it. I know it's stressful, but I bet you'll handle it better if you stay in your little space and enjoy some time with your friends. I promise if anything ever happens that you need to know for your safety, I will tell you immediately. In this case, I think you should let Daddy talk to Roman, Julius, and Davis first. Can you do that, baby?"

She nods. "Yes, Daddy." Her voice is small.

"Good girl." I lean closer and kiss her forehead. "You good?"

She nods again.

I know she's only marginally good, but, even after spending only one week with her, I feel like I know her well enough to encourage her to stay in her little space, oblivious to the new facts that honestly don't concern her directly. Perhaps after speaking with the other men, I'll decide to bring her into the fold, but for now, I'd rather not worry her.

I pull back onto the road, look in every direction, and finish the drive to Roman's.

CHAPTER 24

Colton

We pull up to what would most aptly be described as a mansion. Wow. Not what I was expecting. After driving through a gated entrance, I park in front of the estate and stare at the older brick home for a few moments before removing my seatbelt. Eve does too.

I round to her side of the car and let her out.

She clutches her unicorn as we take the steps up to the front door. Before we reach for the knocker, the door opens. A man in his early seventies opens it. He's very formal and serious-looking, but he smiles wide as soon as he spots Eve. "Come on in. You must be Master Colton and Evelyn. My name is Weston."

Master Colton? I shake his hand and then help Eve out of her coat.

"My wife's name is also Evelyn. She's the cook here. She's in the kitchen. I'm sure she's going to love meeting someone with her namesake."

Eve grins. "I never meet anyone with my name," she tells him. "My mama said it was an old name." Eve flushes the moment those words come out of her mouth.

"Evelyn," I admonish her.

Weston chuckles. "Your mama is right. It is an old name. Much too old even for my Evelyn. She's only fifty-seven." He winks. "I married me a younger gal."

Eve giggles.

Weston hangs Eve's coat in the closet and nods over his shoulder. "Come on. We'll drop your Daddy off in Master Roman's office and go find the other girls in the kitchen. My Evelyn is so excited to have a houseful of little girls today. She's cooking up a storm, making you all kinds of treats for lunch."

We reach the office first, and I glance inside to find Julius and Davis have arrived before me. I reach for Eve's chin and tip her head back. It seems necessary to ensure she knows who's in charge here and assert my dominance firmly. "You'll be on your best behavior, right?"

"Yes, Daddy."

"Don't cause Evelyn any trouble. I know you don't want my palm on your already sore bottom again today."

She flushes and ducks her head, but I see the shudder at the same time. In addition, she squeezes her thighs together and her dress is thin enough for me to see her nipples have beaded. "I'll be good, Daddy."

I pat her bottom and turn to enter the office. When I make eye contact with the rest of the men in the room, I find them all smiling at me. "What?" I glance over my shoulder, but I know what they're thinking.

"Impressive," Davis states. "That's all."

I shrug. "Just giving her what she needs."

I shake hands with everyone, realizing I don't know much about Julius. "Do you have a little too? I didn't meet her yet."

Julius shakes his head and waves a hand through the air. "Nah. I'm not that kind of Dom. I do have a submissive though. Abby. And she might as well be little for as naughty as she is and as often as she gets into trouble."

"Did she come with you?" I definitely didn't meet her last night.

"Nope. I have a polyamorous relationship. I share Abby with two other men. We all live together. In fact, the three of us lived together before we found Abby. She is a breath of fresh air, but it takes three of us to corral her," he jokes. "She's with Levi and Beck this morning."

After everything I've learned in the past week, nothing shocks me. The man seems very happy, so lucky him.

I turn my gaze toward the doorway when Weston returns and clears his throat. "Your last guest has arrived, sir."

Craig Darwin steps inside. Good. I should have thought of inviting him. Luckily, Roman was on top of it.

We all shake hands with Craig before Roman points toward a seating area. "Talk to us," Roman says as we take our seats.

I run a hand over my hair. "My boss got another tip this morning about Eve."

Everyone's face scrunches up.

I glance at the door.

Roman stands immediately and strides over to close it. "Sorry about that. I guess you didn't share everything with Eve yet."

"No. I gave her the option, but advised she let me handle this for now. Nothing has changed really. She might as well play blissfully with the other girls."

Davis nods. "Agreed."

"What did the tipster say?" Julius asks.

"Basically that he saw her last night with me and knew I was a cop. He wanted the police to know that someone is still planning to grab her and to make sure I didn't slack off."

"Christ," Roman mutters.

Davis groans.

Craig frowns deeply.

Julius looks like he's going to punch something. Can't blame him.

"So, someone inside the club had to call in the tip," Julius points out.

I nod. "That's my assumption. That or he's following us. Also possible. But something leads me to believe he got closer than just stalking from across the street. Close enough to assess me and determine I'm a cop."

"Are you still keeping an eye on Owen as a possible suspect?" Davis asks.

I shrug. "He's unlikely. He doesn't fit the profile. In addition, if he's in the process of grooming her, he's doing a piss poor job of it. He wasn't in contact with her this past week."

Roman rubs his eyes. "So, chances are that Owen has nothing to do with anything. He just happened to join the club a few months ago and start playing with Eve."

"I agree," Davis says. "Plus, he's just so…"

"Nice?" Julius suggests with a chuckle. "He's a great Daddy —caring, kind, nurturing. The littles love doing scenes with him. Also, I vetted him. He's been in the fetish community for many years. No one at any of his previous clubs had a single complaint. It's super unlikely that he's selling women into human trafficking on the side."

I nod slowly. "I should probably get a list of his previous clubs and make sure no one has gone missing from any of them, just in case."

"Of course. I'll get you that." Julius pulls out his phone and taps the screen, probably making himself a note. "In fact. I'll check with all of them myself. The owners are more likely to respond to someone they know inside the community."

Roman turns toward Craig. "Did you see anything unusual last night?"

Craig shakes his head. "Nothing. Granted, I don't know the members like you do, but no one loitered around the daycare or seemed to pay extra attention to Eve. No one who watched her scene with Owen looked suspicious. And no one paid any attention to the fact that she went into a private room for a while with Colt, Davis, and Britney."

I tip my head back and stare at the ceiling. "It just doesn't make sense. I'm inclined to think Surrender has nothing to do with it at all. Why would a member call in a tip three weeks ago and again last night? And if it's a member who suspects Eve is in trouble, it would stand to reason that another member is the seller. That would mean two people at Surrender are involved, and no one has seen any evidence that even one person has her on their radar."

"If it's not someone at Surrender," Davis interjects, "who's calling in the tips?"

I shake my head slowly. "We know someone's following her. And none of you have ever seen him at Surrender. It makes no sense."

Davis nods. "Perhaps the stalker followed you to Surrender but never came inside."

"It's unlikely he followed me because I would have shaken him off, but it's quite possible he's been following Eve everywhere she goes for longer than I've been assigned to the case. He may easily know she's a member of Surrender." I flinch as an idea comes to me.

"What is it?" Davis asks.

"Perhaps the stalker is actually the one calling in the tips. What if he's the good guy instead?"

Everyone nods. "It's possible," Craig states. "Forward me a

picture of the stalker when you have a chance. I'll do some digging."

"Any chance he followed you here?" Roman asks, his brow furrowed.

"Not a chance in hell. He was on foot outside her apartment building when we left. I do know that he has realized I'm with her by now. He knows my SUV and takes action when he sees it. But he couldn't get to his car fast enough to follow me, and I drove all over the place just to be sure."

Davis rises from his seat at the same time as Craig. They look at each other and chuckle.

I groan. "You can sit back down. I've checked the SUV every day for tracking devices. It's clean."

They sit again, still smirking.

I roll my eyes. "I don't think the stalker much cares where I go or that Eve is with me. He's biding his time. I'm sure he's waiting to grab her as close to the day of the exchange as possible. That was the MO when Britney's boss was working his deal to sell her." I look at Davis. "You were there. You know the drill. That asshole kept close tabs on her, intending to wait until the date of the rendezvous so she would be easy to snag. These people aren't in the business of keeping a bunch of women hostage for days or weeks."

"Why not?" Roman asks.

Davis sighs. "Because they want the women to be in top physical condition at the exchange. If they take them too early, they run the risk of them not eating or drinking or having to struggle which leaves marks on them."

"Jesus," Julius mutters.

The thought of anyone snagging Eve and possibly torturing her brings bile to my stomach. "On that note, I'd like to set eyes on Eve now, if you all don't mind."

Everyone stands in agreement, and Roman leads us down

the hallway. We enter into a huge kitchen where Eve, Lucy, and Britney are sitting at a table. They all look up with bright eyes as we enter.

"Daddy!" Britney shouts. "Look what we're doing."

The woman I presume to be Evelyn is also in the kitchen. She comes over to the table from the island, a bowl of what looks like pink frosting in her hands. Judging by the sugar cookies I see scattered all over the table, I'd say my guess is accurate.

Craig sets a hand on my shoulder. "I'm going to run." He hands me a card. "Please call me if anything changes. I'll be at the club every night it's open until I'm certain it's safe for everyone."

"Thank you." I take his card and reach into my pocket to grab one of my own before handing it to him in exchange.

"I'm leaving too," Julius says as he turns from talking to Roman. "Judging from the incoming texts I've been getting, my submissive is currently restrained in an uncomfortable position awaiting punishment. Apparently, she wasn't pleased with me leaving this morning and let that be known to Levi and Beck."

I chuckle. "Good luck with that."

As both men leave, I follow Roman and Davis deeper into the kitchen to join the girls. I'm surprised to notice Eve is no longer wearing the dress she came in.

Evelyn obviously notices my glance at Eve's attire and explains. "I hope you don't mind I lent Evelyn one of Lucy's shirts. I didn't want her to get frosting on her white dress."

I smile and lean over the top of Eve to kiss her forehead as she tips her face back. She's wearing nothing but a tight yellow T-shirt and her panties. My cock is hard the moment I see how happy she is and how stiff her nipples are. I resist the urge to reach around and pinch one of them.

She's on her knees on the chair, a pillow under her so she

can reach the cookies easier. She has a plastic knife in one hand and a cookie in the other. Sprinkles and pink frosting are all over her fingers and forearms.

"Did you get any on the cookies, baby?" I tease.

She giggles. "Yes, Daddy. Don't be silly. See?" She holds one up. It is indeed frosted and has shiny silver sprinkles on it. "Evelyn says we can't eat them until after lunch, and only if we eat all of our lunch, and only if you say it's okay to eat them."

"I notice Evelyn also gets to call you by your given name, hmm?"

She grins as she shrugs. "We have the same name."

I can't stop smiling. What a delightful life Roman has here. He seems to have everything imaginable for a little in his home. In fact, the table where the girls are sitting is not a standard size. It's smaller. Just right for adult littles who are on the petite side.

Evelyn addresses Davis next. "You'll be delighted to know that your sweet girl let me know she isn't permitted to use knives. Not even plastic ones. I gave her a soft spatula."

Britney holds up the spatula to show Davis. She's beaming.

"Good girl, sweetie." Davis kisses the top of her head. "I can't wait to taste these cookies."

Lucy shifts her weight back and forth from one knee to the other. "Daddy, can we go in the hot tub after lunch? Please?"

He tugs one of her braids. "We'll see. I'm not sure how long everyone can stay, blossom. Plus, it's chilly outside. Davis and Colt might not want to stand out in the cold while you girls splash in the water."

Lucy pouts. "You could stay in here in the kitchen where it's warm, Daddy."

Roman's eyebrows reach clear to the ceiling. "How many years have you been my little girl, blossom?"

"A lot. Almost seven," she murmurs.

"And how many times have I permitted you to go outside unsupervised in that time?"

"None, Sir." Her voice is meek now.

"Why is that?"

She sighs, her shoulders slumping. "Because it's not safe for little girls to be near the hot tub without an adult present."

"Would you like me to spank you now in front of your friends or later after they leave?"

"Later, Sir."

"I thought so. Now, finish frosting your cookies and then you can have some lunch."

"Yes, Sir."

I watch this exchange in total awe, my gaze shifting from Lucy to Eve several times. Eve is flushed and biting her bottom lip. She's also shifting her weight back and forth like Lucy. Only in her case, it's because she's aroused. I can sense it. I can't speak for Lucy. She may be aroused too for all I know. Doesn't matter. Eve is the one who has my attention.

The girls finish frosting the cookies a few minutes later, and Evelyn hands each of us a warm washcloth to clean them up.

I wipe Eve's fingers and try to get most of the frosting off her forearms, but I'm going to need more than this cloth. "Can you direct us to the restroom, Roman? I think we're going to need some soap and water." I lift Eve to her feet.

She holds her arms out to keep from touching herself.

"I'll show them, Daddy," Lucy declares as she jumps down from her chair and skips toward the door.

Evelyn calls out to her. "Child, you are going to be the death of me. Stop running in the house." The older woman shakes her head, but she's smiling at the same time. I wonder how many times in the past seven years she's said that.

"Sorry, Ma'am." Lucy slows down.

I chuckle as Eve follows her with me bringing up the rear. We don't have to go far before Lucy points out a bathroom. She pushes the door open and skips back toward the kitchen, not one bit slower even though she just got admonished for running.

I usher Eve into the bathroom and shut the door behind us before turning her toward the sink and running the water. I get a squirt of soap and thoroughly wash her hands and forearms before rinsing. Her skin is still pink from the food coloring, but I can't fix that. After I dry her with a towel, I surprise her by lifting her onto the counter and setting her on her bottom.

She giggles and squirms as I push her legs wide, situate myself between them, and slide my hands up her waist. "Daddy..."

When I thumb her nipples, she shudders, her hands coming to my shoulders. Her expression changes instantly from mischievous to aroused. I pinch her hard little nubs next, making her arch and moan.

"I bet your panties are soaking wet, aren't they, baby?"

She purses her lips, not answering me.

I cup one breast and slip my other hand down to palm her pussy. Hot. Soaked. "Mmm. Tell me about this, baby. What made you horny?"

She lowers her face and plants her forehead against my chest. Embarrassed?

I stroke through her folds and flick her clit over the cotton barrier, making her moan again. "Tell me, Evelyn," I say sternly. "Tell Daddy why your panties are wet and your little nipples are so hard." I tease her again, knowing I'm making it difficult for her to talk.

When she still doesn't respond, I release her breast to slide my hand up under her shirt, pushing the material over her breasts before resuming my torment. The moment my fingers are directly on her nipple, she nearly shoots off the counter.

I have to hold her down with my elbow on her thigh. At the same time, I reach a finger under the edge of her wet panties and thrust it into her.

She cries out.

I stifle her noises by kissing her, swallowing her passionate sounds as I devour her mouth. I know she's bombarded with sensation because she's struggling to return my kiss. I'm not helping out. I'm still thumbing her nipple and thrusting a finger in and out of her. In addition, I've managed to flick her clit several times too.

It's not hard to sense when she gets close to the edge of orgasm. Her body stiffens and she sucks in a breath. I'm feeling ornery though, so I immediately remove my fingers from her panties and her nipple.

She whimpers. "Daddy…"

"Look at me, Eve."

She slowly lifts her gaze. Her face is flushed and she's trembling with need.

"Tell Daddy what made you horny in the kitchen and then I'll let you come." It's not like I don't know. It's that I want her to recognize and acknowledge what's happening here.

"It was everything," she whispers.

"Examples, please." I'm not going to back down. She wouldn't want me to anyway.

"It's just…different now. Now that you're here. I got aroused when Evelyn took my dress off and put Lucy's T-shirt on me."

"Why was that, baby?" I'm genuinely curious about this part. I hadn't expected her arousal to go back quite that far.

She glances down.

"Evelyn," I warn. I love the way she flinches when I call her by her full name. It makes my dick hard just to say it. "Eyes on mine."

She lifts her gaze slowly and licks her lips. "Because I knew you would eventually find me like that in the kitchen. Find me in my panties. I wanted you to see my bottom like that. It made me horny."

My heart is racing. *Fuck. Me.* I can't stop myself from closing the gap and kissing her gently. "That makes me horny too, baby." My voice is gravelly. "It's so sexy. You liked listening to Lucy get reprimanded too, didn't you?"

She nods. "It's different. She's not acting exactly. It's a way of life. Not like when I submit to a Daddy at the club and pretend to be naughty. Lucy is genuine. It's just how their dynamic works."

"I can see that." I grip her waist again, teasing her nipples with my thumbs. "You want that don't you, baby?" An actual ache forms in my chest. She obviously wants that, and I can only give it to her until I solve this crime.

Part of me hopes she's learned some things about herself in the past week and can find a Daddy who can fulfill her new needs. Part of me imagines myself punching him in the face for daring to touch her or talk to her.

I'm fucked.

I shake the maudlin from my head and focus on giving my girl what she needs, which right now is an orgasm. With one hand cupping her breast, I once again slide the other down between her legs and ease my fingers under the edge of her panties. I reach in from the top this time, tapping her clit first and circling it until she whimpers.

"Can you stay really quiet for Daddy? We don't want everyone in the house to hear you come, do we?"

She shakes her head and purses her lips.

I doubt she can do this, but I don't care who hears her, so I thrust two fingers deep inside her without warning.

Eve arches off the counter, her legs coming around my waist. She's so fucking wet and hot that I know this won't take more than a minute. I thrust faster, grinding my palm into her clit while I pluck her nipple.

She gasps and holds her breath, her body shaking violently as her orgasm pulses against my hand.

There's nothing in the world sexier than this moment right here. My girl riding my fingers, her face pure bliss as she comes all over my hand.

How will I ever survive leaving her?

CHAPTER 25

Colton

Roman's cook clearly adores taking care of the littles. She bustles around the kitchen, making sure they have everything they need for lunch. Her husband, Weston, helps by doing whatever Evelyn delegates to him, mostly carrying things to and from the table.

When we returned from the bathroom, the cookie fiasco was completely cleaned up and lunch was about to start. Now, I'm seated at the regular table with Davis and Roman. We're helping ourselves to what can only be described as the most gourmet of sandwich fixings I've ever seen.

Roman only permitted his cook to fuss over us for a moment before waving her off and telling her we could manage. She has her hands full with the littles.

The girls are at the smaller table. They have a completely different spread of food. Evelyn has made them sandwiches on regular bread, even cutting off the crusts. She has given them sliced apples and carrots too. Each of them has a sippy cup of milk.

Roman isn't looking directly at the smaller table, but he clearly knows Lucy well enough to speak to her without a glance in a harsh voice. "Lucy, drink every drop of your milk before you touch that sandwich, understood?"

"Yes, Sir," she groans.

I look over to see her downing the milk. Afterward, she shudders while she makes a disgusted face.

"She hates milk," Roman tells us. "It's a daily battle."

Davis laughs.

I can't stop the stupid grin. Every moment of this day should be shocking to me. My jaw should be on the floor and my eyes wide, but I'm educated now. One week's crash course in age play and I'm sucked in deep. Too deep.

Roman swallows a bite and glances at us. "If you don't mind standing outside in the cold, we can let the girls play in the hot tub for a while. I don't like to make my staff stand out there. They have better things to do."

Davis and I both nod.

"It's not a problem. I'm impressed by how strict both of you are," I say.

Davis shrugs. "It's not the same for every little. They're all different. It just so happens that Lucy and Britney are happiest at a rather young age with extremely strict rules and boundaries."

Roman chuckles. "I couldn't have said for sure where Eve might fall in that spectrum since she's never been in a relationship outside of playing alone or doing a scene, but she seems to be thriving in the same environment as Lucy and Britney today."

I glance at her again. She's licking peanut butter off her thumb. The smile on her face lights up the room. I've only known her a week, and it's been a challenging one, but I've never seen her quite this pleased either. She's so happy here.

Once again, my chest tightens.

When I look back, Roman is watching me. His expression is serious. He doesn't say anything, but I know what he's thinking. He's worried. And he should be.

We're just finishing our food when the three girls rush toward us.

The cook is behind them with her hands on her hips. "Slow down, little ones."

Lucy ignores her and launches herself at Roman. "Did you ask them, Daddy? Did you ask if they can stay and we can go in the hot tub?"

He smooths his hand over the top of her head. "Yes, blossom. They can stay. I heated up the water. Take the girls up to your room and find them a swimsuit to borrow."

Lucy jumps up and down. "*Yay*," she shouts as she grabs both Eve's and Britney's hands. "Let's go."

Roman is shaking his head. "Sorry. She gets overly excited when people come over."

"No worries at all," Davis responds. "Britney is delighted."

"It's obvious Eve is too," I say.

Roman stands, grabbing his plate and utensils. "Don't worry about the water being too hot. I set it at about ninety for the girls. Hot enough that they won't shiver, but not too hot to harm them if they stay in a while."

He glances over his shoulder as we follow him with our plates toward the sink. "The three of us might freeze our balls off watching though."

Weston is at the counter, and he responds to Roman. "I set the space heater up on the patio for you. It's nice and warm out there by now. You won't even need coats."

Roman slaps the man on the shoulder. "Bless you."

The girls come rushing back into the kitchen moments later.

Weston sighs. "All this running is going to give my wife a heart attack."

I chuckle. Worrying about three grown women running in the house should be comical, but it's a lifestyle. It's fascinating on so many levels. And most interesting is that every single person living in this house is part of the age play.

Eve looks adorable in a pink one-piece swimsuit that has Strawberry Shortcake on the front and a frilly ruffle above her butt. I lift her into my arms and carry her out the door on my hip, not setting her down until we reach the hot tub so her feet don't get cold on the concrete.

She kisses my cheek. "Thank you, Daddy."

Once the girls are settled, I grab a seat around the heater with Davis and Roman. We're close enough to keep an eye on them and far enough to not be heard talking.

Roman glances every few moments. He's overprotective. As is his right. Hell, Davis isn't less attentive himself, and now I know he doesn't permit Britney to use knives. I decide to ask what that's all about out of curiosity. I face Davis. "I sense there's a story behind the no-knife rule in your house?"

Davis sobers. Shit. This is serious. Not random.

"You don't have to tell me."

He shakes his head. "No. It's okay. You met Britney in the same timeframe I did. You know a lot about her story. She wasn't little when I met her. Or she didn't know it yet. She had so many signs though, and she quickly let me become a Daddy to her."

He glances at her and back at me. "You've noticed her hair is very long. She had a traumatic experience as a young child with a foster mother who cut all her hair off when she got lice. She never cut it again and developed a phobia of scissors.

Once I learned that story, I forbade her from ever touching knives or scissors. It's calmer for her to know it's not permitted. She tends to panic when sharp objects are close to her. Even her adult side does."

I swallow. That's so sad and yet how fortunate for her that she's found someone who loves her and suits her so well. "You're a good man, Davis."

He smiles at me. "You are too, Colton. I hope you pull your head out of your ass and figure it out soon."

I stiffen and look down. "It's not simple."

"But it is."

I sigh. His insistence is warranted. He knows I'm going to hurt Eve and myself when this case is over. I'm not sure how he thinks it's easy though. My job is my life. I'm not trained to do something else. I'm good at undercover work. It's important to me. Sometimes things don't go my way, but more often than not, when I solve a crime, I sleep better knowing someone's life was saved or the course of their existence was improved.

It's in my blood to fix what's wrong. People count on me. People who don't know me yet or have never met me are counting on me. I could never be so selfish as to throw that away. The guilt would eat at me. Nor would I be so selfish as to drag Eve down into my gutter. She would never be happy, and neither would I. Plus I'd worry about her all the time. She needs a full-time Daddy, not a part-time undercover cop.

I turn my attention to Eve. She's giggling and splashing, so carefree and relaxed. A one-eighty from how she was earlier in the week before I encouraged her to be herself.

I suspect she's drastically different from before I came into the picture too. She'd been alone with no one guiding her at home. She craved this level of age play; she just didn't realize it. Or maybe she was kidding herself about keeping her life so compartmentalized because she hadn't met the right person who could give her what she wanted.

I inhale deeply at that last thought. My chest tightens. I'm going to hurt her.

I. Am. Going. To. Hurt. Her.

CHAPTER 26

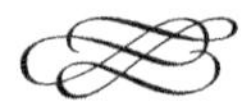

Evelyn

I'm having the best day ever. Hands down. If I totally ignore the reason why we're here and pretend my life isn't in danger, that is.

I've never been in my little headspace for this long at a time. Evenings are the longest I've ever gone, and even then, I've never had an actual Daddy around to take care of me like this.

Colton is a natural, and I know from the way he looks at me that he's enjoying our dynamic as much as I am. When he doesn't know it, I've caught him staring at me in awe. As if I'm the special one when really it's him. He's so dominant and caring.

If I could have created a pretend day in my head that was perfect, I wouldn't have come up with anything as great as this one. Decorating cookies with two friends. Eating lunch with them. Giggling. Being doted on by Lucy's amazing cook. And now splashing in her hot tub.

I'm in awe and a bit jealous of Lucy's life. I've always known she lived as a full-time little at home. She works a regular job like me, but when she comes home, she transforms immediately and rarely steps out of her little space.

She's young. Four or five most of the time. I know her Daddy guides her to different ages to shake things up, but most often at the club, I see her in this age range. It suits her.

Britney is newer to age play, but it's been eight months. She's very deeply involved too, and also falls into the same age range. Her Daddy is super strict, same as Master Roman.

Maybe it's from being around the two of them for several hours in a relaxed environment, but I feel like they have exactly what I never realized I crave.

Granted, I knew they both found age play to be sexual and that thought never occurred to me. I've never mixed sex with my little space. Colt thinks it's because I never met the right Daddy. Maybe he's right. Or maybe he's cocky. That thought makes me giggle.

"You keep laughing," Lucy points out. She's bobbing up and down sitting on a noodle.

"I'm having fun," I tell her.

Britney is grinning. "You're happy. I've never seen you this happy."

"Me neither," Lucy agrees.

I shrug and glance at Daddy. His expression is very serious, which worries me. I know he's concerned about whatever happened this morning on the phone, but that's not the only thing.

"Eve? You okay?" Lucy asks. "I didn't mean to make you sad."

I jerk my gaze back to her. "It's okay. Just scared out of my mind is all."

Britney floats closer and pats my back. "That's

understandable. The unknown future sucks sometimes. Are you worried about the human traffickers?"

I shrug again. "Sometimes, but I try not to think about that. Did you worry all the time when they were after you?"

She nods. "I did, but I also knew Daddy would protect me."

I furrow my brow. "If the seller is still out there trying to sell me now, why did they give up on you?"

Britney licks her lips slowly before chewing on the bottom one.

"You don't have to tell me," I add quickly. "I don't mean to pry."

She shakes her head. "No. It's okay. It's just a little embarrassing." She glances down for a moment and then lifts her gaze again. "They sold my virginity."

I stare at her, trying to understand.

She clears her throat. "I was a virgin. And, now…I'm not."

"Oh." I get it. Now she's with Davis and they have sex.

Britney continues. "The man who was purchasing me wanted a virgin. He's dead, and so is the seller, so the police don't believe whoever was above my seller would continue pursuing me. I'm a liability now. Plus, Davis is incredibly careful all the time still."

"But… I'm not a virgin," I murmur.

She shrugs. "Not every buyer is looking for a virgin, but they do like women who look younger. Which you do."

I nod. After a moment I ask, "Why were you embarrassed to tell me you were a virgin?"

She shrugs, her face flushing. "I don't know. It's weird. No one my age is still a virgin."

"I was," Lucy says softly as she wraps an arm around Britney. "Master Roman is my only partner."

Britney slowly smiles. "Really?"

Lucy nods.

"So, I guess I'm the odd one out in this group," I offer.

"Well, you're thirty. I was twenty-two. I wouldn't have made it to thirty," Britney says.

"I was twenty-two also," Lucy states.

"True." I glance down and drag my hands through the water. "I wish I had a Daddy like you both have," I mumble. I envy them, and spending time with them like this reminds me that I'm playing house. Colt isn't really my Daddy. Not forever.

Emotions well up inside me, and I can feel tears forming. I spin around so that my back is to the men. I don't want Colt to see me upset. None of this is his fault. He was upfront with me from the beginning. He never offered me more than the few days or weeks it would take to catch the bad guys.

Nevertheless, it hurts when I think about it. The thought of him leaving and me never seeing him again makes my tummy upset.

"Do you really think he'll leave after he catches the bad men?" Britney asks in a soft voice.

I nod, sucking back my tears. "He has to. It's his job."

Lucy floats closer. "Why can't he do his job and stay with you?"

I swallow. "Because he works undercover a lot and doesn't come home and doesn't want to do that to someone."

"Oh. That does suck." She covers her mouth and glances at the men. "Oops. Don't tell Daddy I used a bad word."

"It does suck," Britney mimics. "And don't tell mine either."

They both smile, trying to cheer me up.

I force a smile back and shake off the sadness. "Tell me more about your life. It's fascinating. I love your bedroom." We went to her bedroom to borrow the swimsuits we're wearing. "Do you sleep in there alone at night?"

Lucy shakes her head. "Not anymore. I used to when I first moved in with Daddy, but I mostly sleep with him now unless

I've been particularly naughty or he thinks I need a night alone."

I turn toward Britney, curious to learn how full-time littles live. "Where do you sleep?"

"I sleep in both places. Whatever Daddy says. If he has to stay up late, he puts me in my own room. He also makes me take a nap when we're at home, and that's always in my own bed."

"I don't think I want a separate room," I muse. I've never considered having a little room like the two of them have. Mostly because I've never even considered having a Daddy in my home at all. My entire apartment can be a little space if I want. If Colt were my Daddy all the time, I'd want to sleep with him. I like snuggling up to him at night. It calms me.

Lucy shrugs. "Everyone is different. Every relationship is different. You just have to figure out what works for you and go with the flow."

We float in the water a bit longer until Master Roman comes to the edge. "Time to get out, girls. You're going to be prunes."

"Aw, Daddy, already?" Lucy groans.

"And you, my lovely little cherry blossom, have talked back to me a few too many times today. Unless you want to spend the entire evening standing in a corner after I spank you, I suggest you get out of the hot tub now. It's time to say goodbye to our guests. They have other things to do today."

Lucy climbs out first, but she does so pouting. Britney and I follow. I'm shivering as I walk toward Daddy.

Lucy's Daddy removes her swimsuit right away and wraps her in a towel. When I glance at Britney's Daddy, he's peeling her suit off too.

Colton pats me partially dry and seems to take his cue from the other men, pulling the straps down on my suit then bending down to pull it off my feet. I'm shivering when he wraps me up in the towel like a burrito and lifts me onto his knee to hold me close.

My teeth are chattering, but I warm up fast under the heater and in his arms.

He kisses my forehead. "Did you have fun in the hot tub, baby?"

"Yes, Sir. It was the perfect temperature. Not too hot. Not too cold."

He hugs me tighter. "Good. I'm glad you enjoyed yourself. You ready to go home?"

I nod, though I'm sad to end this fun day.

He sets me on my feet at the same time Master Roman and Master Davis set their littles down, and then he pats my bottom through the towel. "Go change. I think Miss Evelyn put your dress in Lucy's bathroom."

"Yes, Sir."

Davis calls out to us as we waddle toward the sliding glass door that leads into the kitchen. "Britney, use the potty before you come back down so you don't have to go on the way home."

"Yes, Sir."

My nipples stiffen at Davis's words. His commanding way is so sexy. Both he and Roman have a very dominant control over their littles that makes my pussy swell. Until this week, I never noticed anything like that or paid attention to anyone else's Daddy or his demands. But now…

Now that I'm experimenting in a more full-time little space, I find myself noticing these things. Simple things that remind me of my place. The accumulation of little commands like that makes me feel incredibly submissive in a shockingly sexual way.

I want what they have. I want the world. I don't want it to end.

I glance at Daddy. He's smiling at me. His smile lights up

my world. Taking his cue from Davis, he says exactly what I need him to say. "You too, baby. Use the potty so I don't have to watch you squirm in your seat."

"Yes, Sir." I shiver as a wave of arousal rushes through me. Luckily, I also turn around before a different wave of emotion hits me. Sadness. It seeps back in on the heels of my arousal.

I shake off the emotions that suffocate me as I follow Lucy and Britney up the back staircase that comes out next to Lucy's little girl room on the second floor.

The three of us change back into our dresses and panties, each of us using the toilet as we've been told. Evelyn has set our shoes and socks in the bathroom too, and I sit on the floor to put them on.

"Today was so much fun. I wish you could stay longer," Lucy says, her voice sorrowful.

Britney giggles. "That's because your Daddy is going to spank you good as soon as we leave."

Lucy sighs. "Yeah. That too." She leads us back downstairs, and we find the men near the front door.

"What do you say to your friends, Lucy?" Master Roman says.

"Thank you both for coming. I had a great time." Lucy beams.

"Thank you for having us," I return.

"Yes. Thank you, Lucy. It was most fun," Britney adds.

Evelyn comes rushing from the kitchen holding something in her hands. She also has Jessie tucked under her arm. I almost forgot my unicorn.

I take her from Evelyn and hug her tightly while Evelyn holds up baggies of the cookies. "Don't forget to take some cookies home with you." She hands a baggie of cookies to each Daddy before turning toward me and Britney. "You girls make sure you have permission before you eat those. You'll end up with a tummy ache if you eat too many."

"Yes, Ma'am," we both state at once.

"And please come again. You were a delightful group." Evelyn smiles broadly. I know she really did enjoy having us.

Daddy helps me into my coat and holds my hand as we head to the car. He even lifts me into the seat and buckles me before rounding the car.

My heart is full as I watch him. I think I'm in love with him, and I'll never even have the chance to tell him.

CHAPTER 27

Evelyn

I'm nervous when we get back to my apartment. I'm not even sure why. It's been an amazing day so far, but I feel like something is about to change. Colt is quiet on the drive home. He holds my hand and strokes it often, but he's tense. I don't like the vibe.

The moment we're inside, I decide to tackle whatever is on his mind. "Is something wrong?"

He turns toward me, combing a hand through his hair. When he's done, he reaches for me, grabs my hand, and tugs me closer. As he removes my coat, he smiles, but it doesn't reach his eyes. "No, baby. Nothing new." He tugs me against him with his hands on my hips. "I need you to do something for me."

"Okay." I'm worried. Scared.

He slides his hands up my arms and cups my face, meeting my gaze. "I need to talk to Evelyn the adult. Can you do that for me?" His brow is furrowed.

I nod. "Yes. Of course."

He blows out a breath as if he's been incredibly worried to ask this of me.

I frown. "I can do it anytime you want, Colton." I wrap my arms around him, calling him by his full name like he's done to me. "I cherish every second of our time together, and I can't ever thank you enough for letting me be authentic with you. It's been amazing. The best week of my life. I'll never regret it. But I have two sides. I can flip into my other self. I did it every day before I met you. I can do it with you too. Give me ten minutes to change and shift my headspace okay?"

He stares at me in awe as if I've stunned him with this information. Finally, he kisses me on the lips and then nods. "Thank you."

I slip from the room when he releases me, calmer than I was five minutes ago. This isn't too much to ask. I should be worried, of course, but the truth is that he hasn't told me yet what happened this morning, so I should be expecting him to explain that, and it's logical he would want to talk to my adult self.

When I reach the bedroom, I close the door and remove my clothes. I drop everything in the hamper and head for my closet. Granted, my casual wardrobe doesn't consist of many things that are adult, but I've managed with Colt before, and I can do it now.

I grab a thong and matching bra from my dresser drawers and a pair of jeggings and a black sweater from my closet. I head to the bathroom next to comb out my still-damp hair and add a touch of lip gloss. I don't think Colt needs more than this.

I'm barefoot when I head back to the living room, but my head is in the right space.

Colt is sitting on the couch and he stands when I enter.

His gaze roams up and down my frame, stopping at my feet before he grins.

"Do I need shoes for this?"

He chuckles. "No, and you have sexy feet. You never need shoes." He reaches for me.

I come to him and let him tug me onto the couch next to him.

"I just want to bring you up to speed so you're not in the dark."

"Okay."

"That was my boss who called this morning. They got another tip this morning. Someone called in on the non-emergency line."

I swallow. "What did they say?"

"That they saw me with you last night and knew I was a cop and that someone should warn me that you're not safe and I should remain diligent."

I gasp. "Shit."

"Yeah." He grabs my hand. "I'm not going to let anyone near you, Eve."

I nod slowly. "Okay." I glance at the window. "You think that man who's following me has anything to do with this?"

He sighs. "He definitely has something to do with it. The question is which side is he on? Is he working for the seller or is he keeping an eye on you and calling in the tips?"

"Right. I hadn't thought of that. But you're worried someone from the club called in the tip, aren't you? That's why you met with Roman, Julius, and Davis."

"Yes. Or at least I want them to be aware of the possibility. Part of me thinks it's not related to the club at all. But someone is watching us. On the other hand, if that's the case, how has anyone gotten close enough to peg me as a cop?"

I bite my lip and release it. "Maybe since that same person

called in the first tip, they're just assuming I have a cop with me?"

He shrugs. "Perhaps. Something doesn't add up though. I don't like it."

"I don't either." That's an understatement. "What do we do now?"

He meets my gaze. "You're not going to like my idea."

I cringe. "Tell me."

"I don't want to leave you unprotected during the day anymore."

I stare at him. "You want to go to work with me?"

He nods. "Yes."

I groan as I tip my head back and stare at the ceiling.

"I know you hate that plan, and it's horribly inconvenient for you, but I can't in good conscience leave you alone. I can't be sure someone in your office isn't the seller at this point, Eve."

I jerk my head up. "You think one of my coworkers is going to sell me to human traffickers?"

"I don't know. I've never met any of them. I've only seen them once, at lunch the other day. I can't begin to know that. I just don't want to take a chance." He watches me closely before continuing. "Look, I know this will be hard on you. I know that you have trouble staying in your adult persona when I'm around. I get that. I'll do my best to stay out of your way so you can work, but please let me protect you."

I jerk my hand out of his grasp and jump to my feet.

"Eve?"

I take several steps backward, putting some space between us. "Colt, my hesitation has nothing to do with your dominance. All you have to do is turn that shit off and I'll be fine. It's when you fucking go all Dom on me that I struggle to hold my adult space. You're not doing it now, and see? I'm fine. As long as you're my equal, or—God forbid—below equal to me, I can be an adult just fine."

He flinches. "Why are you so upset then?"

I throw my hands in the air. "Colt. You're not the invisible man. What the hell am I supposed to tell my coworkers? Huh? That some asshole is trying to sell me and you're my bodyguard? Or, wait, let's not forget that at least one of my coworkers saw us kissing the other day. What will she think? That I'm fucking my bodyguard? And even if everyone did know all that, then what? In a few days or a week, you end this and disappear. Then what do I tell them? That I was fucking my bodyguard and I fell for him and now he's moved on?" I shake my head. "Because no fucking way, Colton. Not a chance in hell. I'm a respected member of the team. They see me as strong and independent with my head fully screwed onto my shoulders. I'm not the sort of person who needs protection from anything, especially not at work. Already, I have no way of knowing who saw us kissing that morning. If Lacy saw us, who's to say ten other people didn't and they just haven't said anything?"

Colt stands slowly, seeming to be unwilling to make any quick movements, and that's a good thing. "Eve, you're human. Surely no one thinks you don't have a life outside of the office. Why do you care if they find out you have a boyfriend? Everyone has a life."

I shake my head. "No. Not really. I'm in the middle of climbing the ladder in an industry that doesn't recognize women as equals." I roll my eyes. "Like all industries. I have to work longer and harder than anyone else to get the same promotion. So, no. I'm not really permitted to have a life. I can have pretty things I keep on a shelf but not anything that might affect my job."

He jerks, hurt by my words. Good.

I stand firm, my hands on my hips, wishing now I'd put on a pair of heels. I'm fierce in heels. "It's not the end of the world that Lacy saw me with you. She's a woman. She's my friend. She won't mention it to anyone. But men… Colt, men don't see things the same way. If they got wind that I wasn't pleasantly single, all they would see when it came time for promotions is someone who could potentially show up pregnant and put a wrench in all their plans."

"Jesus, Eve." He's staring at me like I have two heads. And so what if I do?

I'm shaking now. And I sound like a lunatic. A crazed lunatic. It all sounds so ridiculous out loud. It's not like I ever really considered all of this. I never planned to fall for a man in the first place. Who the fuck would be able to manage me and my duplicity? No one.

Except Colt.

Dammit.

I draw in a slow breath, trying to rein in my crazy side and soften my voice before I speak again. "It's not going to happen, Colt. No matter how you slice it, it will hurt my career. Even if not one person suspected we were sleeping together, I'd still look weak for needing fucking protection. No one will care what the reason is. All they will see is a damn bodyguard outside my door like I'm a prima donna."

Colt's head drops toward the floor. I'm exasperating him. Too bad.

"I'm already in way over my head here. I'm already trying to figure out how I'm going to pick up the pieces—both professional and personal—after you disappear. I simply can't add anything else to my plate, Colt. I can't do it." I turn around and stomp from the room. I'm not even close to being little right now. I'm a full-grown adult having a meltdown.

I head for my bedroom, slam the door like a goddamn

toddler and pace the floor, trying to think and calm the fuck down. There are a dozen reasons why I just shouted all that nonsense, and none of them have a thing to do with Colt trying to protect me.

I'm furious with myself and the situation and the world.

When I'm worn out, I climb up onto the bed, prop myself against the headboard, and draw my knees up to set my chin on them.

Eventually, Colt knocks on the door. "Eve? Can I come in please?"

"Yes." What the hell other options do I have? Plus, I need to apologize to him. I'm being a brat and I'm not even little.

He enters cautiously and shuffles over to the bed, taking a seat as far away from me as possible. He hangs his head, then lifts it. "I'm sorry."

"I know. It's not your fault."

"I'm not a woman, so forgive my naivete, but do you really think your job opportunities are going to be thwarted because some asshole would like to kidnap you?"

"No."

He jerks back, his eyes wide.

I sigh. "I exaggerated. My office is a wonderful place to work. Everyone is treated fairly, male or female. I do worry frequently about how much harder I have to work to climb the corporate ladder, but I've never seen or heard of any direct evidence that would insinuate that I would lose opportunities with this particular team simply because I got married or had a baby."

He's staring at me. Can't blame him. I just spent fifteen minutes telling him a giant pile of shit and tore it all down in two minutes.

"Then..." His brows are raised in confusion.

"I'm a hot mess because I'm in love with you, and you're going to destroy me."

There. I said it. It wasn't like I could keep that a secret forever.

He gasps and doesn't move a single muscle for several seconds. Finally, he jumps into action, climbs onto the bed, and crawls toward me. He doesn't say a word as he yanks me into his arms and gathers me against him.

I'm stunned by his reaction.

His lips find mine and he kisses me senseless, with a desperation only seen from two lovers who've been separated for a year and just got reunited. He cups my face and angles his head to one side, kissing me fiercely.

When he finally releases my lips, we're both panting. He looks deep into my eyes, holding my head. "I love you too, baby."

Tears form in my eyes and fall down my cheeks. It's like a ten-ton brick has been lifted off my shoulders. We don't have a single answer that would even begin to solve our problems going forward, but at least we're on the same page on that one issue.

Colt swipes at my tears. "Don't cry. I'm so sorry. I didn't mean to make you cry."

I chuckle as I reach around him to grab a tissue off the bedside table. I blow my nose, not even remotely delicately, and wipe my tears away.

Colt eases me down onto my side and lines himself up next to me so we're facing each other. He strokes my hair from my cheek and forehead. "I don't have more than that right now, Eve. Not a single answer. Just that I love you."

I nod. "Okay." I get it. He can't possibly have thought this through.

"I'm not saying it changes anything, but no matter what, I can't walk away without you knowing how I feel. The truth. It would be a lie to tell you otherwise. I've fallen so hard for you, *both* of you." He grins. "I love them both. I love the woman who reigns like a lion in the office and the little girl who curls up in my lap and needs to cuddle."

I smile. My heart is racing because this changes nothing, but it's also everything.

"Now, my immediate concern is keeping you safe. That's all that matters. I've learned over the past week exactly what I do to make you tick. I get it. As long as I don't dominate you, you can hold on to your adult persona just fine. I promise I can be the demure boyfriend slash bodyguard who stands outside your door as if I work for you and not the other way around. But you have to let me do that, Eve. Please."

I sigh heavily. "Okay."

He lifts a brow. It's different somehow. When I'm little it puts me in my place. When I'm an adult, it signals his confusion. It's subtle and would be comical to someone else.

"So, I'm a horrible liar. I'll have to tell my coworkers the truth. That you came into my life to protect me and I fell for you and now we're dating. I'm sure half the office will get a kick out of it. Half of them will think I've lost my mind. Half of them will talk about me behind my back. And half of them will think it's romantic and be jealous."

He chuckles. "For a woman who spends her days working with numbers, your math sucks."

I laugh.

He draws me closer and kisses me sweetly. His hand runs up and down my back. He searches my face.

I lick my lips. "If you're wondering how often I have an irrational meltdown like that, probably once a year. You won't have to worry. You'll be long gone." I look away, wishing I hadn't said that. It was snarky and unnecessary.

"Let's worry about today and tomorrow for now. We'll see what we can do about the future after I extract you from this mess, okay?"

I nod against him and relax into his embrace, my heart

rate settling into a more reasonable pace as the minutes tick by.

Colt kisses the top of my head. "Now, my extensive research and education tell me that I cannot punish you for infractions that occur when you're in your adult persona, so…"

I jerk my face up to look at him. "No, you may not."

He grins evilly. "I can't discipline you for cussing or having a tantrum, but I do think you would relax and feel better if you shifted back into your little space and let me spank you."

I swallow. God, he's so right. So very right. It's scary how well he knows me and how quickly he has understood not just how to manage a little but how to manage this particular little. I nod.

"Good. I want you to take these clothes off. I'm going to find something else for you to wear, and then you're going to stand in the corner in the kitchen for a while to get your headspace straightened out. When I decide you're ready, I'm going to spank you hard enough to chase out all the bad things. Then you'll be able to calm down."

"Yes, Sir." This is exactly what I want.

He pats my bottom. "Clothes off."

I shove off the side of the bed and strip while he pads across my room and opens a few drawers. He returns to me holding up a pair of panties—pink ones covered with tiny white clouds. He squats down in front of me, and I hold his shoulders as I step into them. He pulls a white tank top over my head next. It's tight and makes my already hard nipples beyond obvious.

Colt takes my hand and leads me into the kitchen. He points toward the corner. "Stand there until I tell you to move."

I shuffle to my spot and lean my forehead against the corner where the two walls meet.

"Do you think I left that spoon on the floor for my health, baby? Spread your legs."

I tremble as I do as I'm told, already sliding deep into my little space. It's amazing how he manages me. Amazing and wonderful. I'm scared out of my mind.

CHAPTER 28

Colton

I need this timeout almost as much as Eve. I need the time to get my head on straight. Or at least as straight as possible under the circumstances.

She loves me.

I can't stop grinning when I remind myself of that fact.

I love her too.

And I can't stop panicking when I remind myself of *that* fact.

I don't know what we do now. Where we go from here. I can't see a path for us. But I wasn't kidding. For now, we have to worry about only one thing, making sure Eve has a future. Nothing else matters if I can't protect her.

I pace slowly while she stands very still, exactly as I've instructed her. She's one of the sexiest women I've ever seen when she is in heels, a pencil skirt, and a professional blouse. But damn, she's just as sexy when she's in panties and a tank top. Her most comfortable little attire.

And I'm the lucky bastard who gets to love both sides of her.

She has her arms tucked up against her chest right now, but I don't care. She needs the comfort of being able to hug herself. It would have been cruel to insist she clasp her hands behind her back. It's enough that her feet are wide.

I know she'll be very young and vulnerable after I spank her. She'll need a long session of cuddling and aftercare. I'm up for it. I can't wait to hold her in my lap and rock her while she recovers.

But first, she needs to be spanked harder and longer than I've done so far. It's cleansing to her. I get it now. It's cathartic.

I'm ready.

"Eve, baby. You can come out of the corner now."

She turns away slowly and takes her time coming to me.

I take her hand and lead her into the living room where I sit in the middle of the couch and pull her between my legs. She meets my gaze. "You feel better after having some time alone, baby?"

She nods. "Yes, Sir."

"But you'll feel even better after you get your bottom spanked, won't you?"

"Yes, Sir." She flushes.

I love that it embarrasses her to voice her needs. It's part of the process. "Tell Daddy what you need, baby."

"I need you to spank me, Daddy, so that I'll feel better. Make all the icky bad feelings go away."

I cup her face. "Okay, baby." I lean down and pull her panties off. I don't want them around her knees. I want her to be able to spread her legs wide. When I guide her to one side of me, she whimpers. It's expected. She's also shaking a bit as I lower her over my lap.

I consider removing her shirt but decide against it. She's going to be aroused enough without the extra exposure, plus I can still toy with her nipples through the thin cotton if I want.

I palm her naked bottom. It's so pretty. So perfect. Smooth. Flawless. It will look even more delectable after I pepper it until it's hot and pink. "Give me your hands, baby."

She reaches behind her back and I clasp her wrists in one hand at the small of her back.

As I palm her bottom, I continue instructing her. "I want your knees parted, Eve. Wide enough that I'm certain you aren't able to get yourself off from rubbing your clit on your own. If you disobey me and pull your thighs together, I will flip you over, part your knees, and swat your clit, understood?"

She gasps. "Yes, Sir."

"What are you going to do then?"

"Keep my legs parted, Sir."

"Good girl."

"Are you wet, Eve?"

She nods against me.

"Words, baby." I want her deep in her space.

"I'm so wet, Daddy. My pussy aches."

I know my cock does. Glad I'm not alone. "Good. You don't have permission to come while I'm spanking you. I decide when and if you get to come, understood?"

"Yes, Sir."

"Good girl." It's time. I lift my hand and give her the first round of swats, peppering her all over without enough pressure to do more than warm her up.

She moans and squirms a bit on my lap, trying to get comfortable. That's okay.

"May I continue?" I ask.

"Yes, Sir."

Damn, her bottom is pretty as it turns a darker pink. I love the feel of her skin warming under my palm as I spank her, hitting the sweet spot at the juncture of her thighs intermittently.

She's panting and wiggling when I pause to rub her bottom again. "Feel better, baby?"

"Yes, Sir." Her voice is soft. She's sliding into subspace.

"One more round? A little harder?"

"Yes, Sir."

I hold her tighter and nudge her knees farther apart before I resume spanking her bottom and her upper thighs. I keep it up until she starts whimpering and squirming more consistently.

The moment I stop spanking her, I reach between her legs and find her soaked pussy. When I thrust a finger into her, she cries out. She's so close to coming. I love that I did this to her.

I continue to hold her down across my lap while I finger her, thrusting in and out of her soaked channel while teasing her clit with every pass.

Her legs start shaking, and she arches her chest upward on a low moan. "Colton..."

"That's it, baby. Let it feel good. Come on Daddy's fingers."

She goes completely rigid at that command, her orgasm consuming her a moment later. The pulses of her release make my cock harder than it's been all day. I need to be inside her, but I need to make sure she's okay first.

As her orgasm subsides, I release her wrists and carefully turn her around so that I'm cradling her in my lap.

She grabs onto my shirt with her fist and holds on tight as her labored breathing slowly ebbs. When she eventually tips her head back to look at me, her eyes are clear, and I know she's no longer in a deep subspace. "Thank you, Daddy."

"You're welcome, baby." It warms my heart to see her sated and relaxed.

She bites her bottom lip. "Would you mind if I..."

I cock my head to one side. I have no idea what she's about to say. "If you what, baby?"

"Could I suck your cock, Sir?"

A slow smile spreads across my face. "Is that what you want, baby?" How often has a woman asked me if she could suck me? I'm going with never. My dick is suddenly ten times harder.

She nods. "I really really want to taste you."

"Then by all means." I release her and hold out both arms as if to indicate there is no way I would interfere with such a suggestion.

She slides down between my legs and goes to work unfastening my jeans.

While she does so, I lean over and pull her shirt off. If she's going to give me a blow job, I want to see her naked tits bouncing with the effort.

Eve is very cautious as she releases my cock. When I lift my hips and tug my jeans down to my thighs, she touches me very tentatively and then blinks up at me and gives me an embarrassed grin.

I start to speak, but then realize she's little. She's in a role. She's in a headspace of innocence and awe. I won't interrupt her, but I find it fascinating how she can have sex with me in either persona.

When she flicks out her tongue to taste the precome on the head of my dick, I lose a piece of myself to her. This woman fucking owns me. It may be the other way around in her mind, but the truth is that she owns me. Hands down.

Every move she makes heightens my arousal. I can't take my eyes off this precious woman who is licking my dick and palming it like she's never seen one before. Like she hasn't seen *mine* before either. It's fucking hot.

I groan the first time she covers the tip with her lips and sucks me into her warmth. I've never been this close to orgasm with so little stimulation. Her every movement is tentative and naïve. Gentle.

She glances up at me every few moments as if asking me if she's "doing it right." I stroke her hair gently and convey just how precisely right she's "doing it" with my eyes and my ragged breaths.

She resumes, increasing her efforts until I can't hold back another minute. I cup her face. "I'm going to come, baby. If you keep that up, you'll be swallowing."

She hums around my cock and draws it in deeper, so deep that my eyes roll back and I lose the battle. My orgasm slams into me, and my God does it feel good when Eve swallows over and over, stimulating my cock even more as she does so.

I'm gasping for air when she finally pulls back. She licks her lips and kisses my dick before climbing up onto my lap and straddling me. Her hands come to my shoulders.

I'm still hard, and her rubbing her pussy over my cock doesn't help.

"Ride me, baby," I tell her. I reach between us and line my erection up with her pussy.

She lowers over me slowly, her head tipping back and her mouth dropping open as she does so.

I grip her hips, mesmerized by her every movement. She's so fucking sexy bobbing on and off me. Her tits jiggling. Her back arched. Her pink lips wet from licking them.

She's so gorgeous. Every inch of her. Both sides of her. Emotions well up inside me as I stare at her. There's no way I can come again so soon, but I can stay hard while she rides me. And it feels amazing. I might decide I enjoy fucking her after I've come even more than before. I get to enjoy the show because I'm not up inside my head.

I slide my hands up and cup her breasts, thumbing her nipples, then pinching them as she moans. The tight pink tips are enticing, and I slide one hand to her back and steady her for a moment so I can suckle her.

She squirms against me. "Colton..."

I know she wants me to let her come, and I will, but I can't resist tasting her sweet tits first. I know she's enjoying it too. After a minute I switch to her other nipple, treating it to the same seduction.

Eve grips my shoulders and whimpers. "Please, Sir..."

I finally release her breast. "Go ahead, baby. Make yourself come on my cock."

She resumes lifting and lowering over me, her thighs tight from the exertion.

When I see her breaths coming more infrequently and her face softening, I know she's close. That's when I slip a hand between us and find her clit. "Come for me, Eve."

She's such a good obedient sub. Her pussy grips my cock as her release takes over, and I watch every single second.

CHAPTER 29

Evelyn

The rest of the weekend can only be described as amazing and relaxing. I spend most of my time little because, in my little space, I worry less. Daddy spends most of his time on the phone and looking out the windows. He doesn't say a word to me about the imminent threat to my life because there's no need. He's handling it, and he worries enough for the both of us.

On Monday morning, I have to go back to work, and I'm not enthusiastic, to say the least. I shower and dress in the skirt and blouse that make me feel the most powerful and in control.

Colt jumps in the shower after me.

I'm in the kitchen making a cup of coffee for Colt when he emerges from the hallway, and I nearly drop the mug. My eyes bug out and I'm at a loss for words. The only reason I know my mouth is hanging open is because Colt smirks when he reaches me and subtly lifts my bottom jaw. "You're drooling." He takes the coffee from my hand, sips it, and sets it on the counter.

"You're wearing a suit."

He shrugs as if this is no big deal. I was aware that Davis went to his apartment and dropped off more clothes here yesterday, but I hadn't thought much about what clothes those would be.

My man—at least for the time being—is wearing black dress pants, black dress shoes, a lavender shirt, and a black tie. So, yeah, I'm drooling. He's clean-shaven too.

He glances down and smooths his hand over his tie. "This okay? I thought maybe the purple was a bit much."

I stare at him before shaking myself out of whatever place I've gone to. "It's..." I grab him by the tie and drag his face down to mine. I don't give a fuck that I'm going to have to redo my lipstick, nor that I'm getting it all over him. I need to kiss him like I need my next breath.

He's smirking again when I release my death grip on his tie. "If I'd known how you'd react to a tie, I'd have worn it all last week too."

My gaze goes down his body and back up again. "Damn."

His hand slides behind my back to rest just above my ass. "You're going to have to come up with more vocabulary before we get to your office or people will think you've had a small stroke."

"How am I going to get any work done with you hanging around looking good enough to eat?"

He lifts a brow. "You could eat me now before we leave and get it out of your system." He's joking, but I consider the offer anyway. He laughs as he sets me back a few inches and reaches for the coffee again. "I promise to stand outside your office out of your line of sight if it will help."

I shake my head. "Not a chance. There are several single

women working in my office. They'd spend the entire day hitting on you, and I'd have to kill them."

He shrugs. "I'll stand wherever you want, baby."

I shiver. "Could you do me a favor and not call me *baby* when I'm in full-on adult mode? It's jarring for some reason."

"Okay. Done. Anything else?"

"Not that I can think of. Just don't...dominate me."

"I'll do my best." He cups my face. "If I say or do anything that doesn't work for you, just let me know, okay?"

"Yes."

He kisses me again and then turns me around and aims me toward the hallway. "Go fix your lipstick."

I groan as I do as instructed.

An hour later, we walk into my office building and take the elevator to my floor. We've gone over what we're going to say several times. In addition, I called my boss at home yesterday to give him a heads up. He was extremely sympathetic and concerned. I know from our conversation that he sent out an inner-office email to the top partners, alerting them to the situation.

When we step out of the elevator, no one is around yet. I've intentionally arrived early to avoid answering twenty questions before my first cup of coffee, and thank God I manage to snag a cup and make it back to my office before the first person stops by.

Luckily, it's Lacy. She's already talking as she enters. "You're bright and early this morning. How was your—" She stops talking mid-sentence when she sees Colt standing in my office. He's leaning casually against the wall near the window, one ankle crossed over the other.

He gives her a winning smile and shoves off the wall. "You must be Lacy." He extends a hand.

Lacy's mouth is hanging open and her eyes are as wide as I imagine mine were earlier this morning. It takes her a moment to clear her throat and find her voice. "Are you the guy I saw kissing Eve the other morning?"

He chuckles. "Lucky for Eve, yes. What if I wasn't?" He glances at me. "Imagine explaining that."

Lacy's face flushes. It's so unlike her. Then she laughs, nervously. "Yeah, Eve doesn't date even one guy, let alone two, so..." She clamps her mouth closed and palms her forehead. "I'll shut up now." She turns to me. "Is it bring-a-hot-hunk-to-work day? I missed the memo."

I glance at Colt, but he gestures for me to explain myself however I choose. I look back at Lacy. "Actually, here's the thing..." I rub my temples. What I'm about to say sounds absurd. "So, it turns out someone has been calling into the police tip line with an anonymous threat against me. Colt was assigned to keep me safe. And then, well, you can guess the rest."

Her face is priceless. "You— I mean— Oh, my God. You—"

Colt chuckles. I can't blame him.

I shrug. "Hot guy shows up to protect you. Whatcha gonna do?"

Lacy glances back and forth before sighing dramatically. "I'm calling the cops right now and telling them there is a threat to my life." She spins around and leaves the room, still chuckling.

One down.

The rest of the morning isn't quite as dramatic. I do have to explain myself to a dozen people, but none of them are as close to me as Lacy, so I don't elaborate and insinuate I'm sleeping with my bodyguard.

Most people just assume I hit the undercover cop jackpot and move on. They don't say this. It's in their expressions. Especially the women. No one besides Lacy insinuates they saw Colt kissing me the other morning.

By ten o'clock, my world is almost normal. I'm at my desk. Computer open. Files in front of me. Deep breaths.

But, Colt is also in the room. He's sitting at my small conference table, focused on his laptop, staying as quiet as he promised, but he's still there. I can't avoid seeing him. And he doesn't get any less sexy as the minutes tick by.

If anything, he gets more attractive.

I love how he is with my coworkers. He lets me tell them our weird story, never interfering. He's overly polite with each person, endearing the entire office to him. My boss and both of his partners stop by to meet him even.

Overall, I'd say it's going better than I could have dreamed. I'm certain several people are suspicious, but they're not wrong, so how can I blame them?

The start of my week is far less painful than I expected, and when we get back to my apartment that night, I jump Colt's bones while he's still locking the door.

Fifteen minutes later, we're still against the door, Colt is breathing heavily, and he grabs my face, meets my gaze, and says, "I'm going to buy some more suits."

This is how our week goes. Colt and I settle into a comfortable routine. Shower, dress, work. Undress, fuck against the door, shift gears.

In the evenings, after I'm beyond satisfied by our antics in the foyer, I change clothes and spend a few hours in my little space. Colt—the champion—takes care of my every need. He's a God. And it scares me more every day.

Several times a day and in the evenings, I stop what I'm doing and stare at him when he doesn't know I'm looking. He's too good to be true. I have to pinch myself, then I remind myself that I'm right. He *is* too good to be true. He's not mine.

On Thursday, my boss pops into my office and asks me if I'll be able to attend a seminar about the latest tax laws on

Saturday. It's six hours long and includes lunch. It's being held in the conference room of a nearby hotel.

I glance at Colt. He's frowning, and I know he hates when we deviate from our routine. We haven't gone anywhere for any reason other than work and home since Saturday. He stares at me for a moment before glancing at my boss and nodding.

My boss steps all the way into my office and shuts the door. He looks concerned. "If you think it's too dangerous..." He glances from me to Colt.

I interject. "No. It's fine."

"I'll get another guy or two to watch the exits," Colt says. "No one will know we're there, so it won't upset the other attendees. Not a problem."

I know he's lying to my boss, and I know he's doing it for me. He doesn't want to do anything to upset my career, but he's going to worry the entire day too.

After my boss leaves, I turn to Colt. "You hate it."

"It's fine."

I come around my desk, shut my door once more, and flatten my palms on his perfectly starched white dress shirt. I try not to touch him while I'm at work, but he's stressed right now, and I'm hoping my touch will bring him down a notch. "Who's going to abduct me from a crowded accounting seminar?"

He stares down at me. "No one. I won't let them."

I sigh. He's rigid, not touching me even though I'm smoothing my hands up and down his pecs now.

His brow is furrowed, and I nearly laugh at his dead-serious expression. Even though he's not reacting outwardly to my flirting, he's breathing heavier, and his fists are clenched.

I finally stop tormenting him and back up. "Sorry. That wasn't fair." I head for the door, but before I reach it, he grabs my hand and yanks me back so that I slam into his chest. His hands cup my face and his lips are on mine before I have time to react.

He kisses the daylight out of me before releasing me, smirking. "There. Now we're even."

I lick my lips and turn toward the door once more, shaking as I open it. I wish I could say that he doesn't play fair, but I did this to myself, and besides, I'm not sorry.

CHAPTER 30

Colton

I've made arrangements with the captain to have a second cop stationed at the seminar tomorrow. I've also spoken to Davis, and Blade is sending a guy too.

This doesn't keep me from pacing Eve's office most of the morning on Friday. The hair on the back of my neck is on end. I'm not even sure why. Nothing out of the ordinary has happened.

It's after lunch, after Eve and I have finished eating takeout at the table in her office, after Lacy and a few other of her coworkers have stopped by to flirt with me, after Eve has once again shut the door and kissed me just to "remind you who belongs to you," after she safely returns from the ladies' room.

That's when I get the call. From my boss. I yank my phone up and connect to him as I step out into the hall. I tell myself it's so that I don't disturb Eve while she works, but that's not entirely true. The way my hackles have been up all day, I answer the call with a high level of anticipation.

"What's up?" I say all casually.

"Swat moved in on the seller an hour ago."

I stop pacing and freeze in my tracks. "Pardon?"

"Yep. Got another tip. This time it was for the seller. Not a middle man. The whole tamale. Name's Antonio Russo. Goes by Tony. We raided his estate and found three women in his custody. In cages in the basement. We took his computers of course, but there was a printout of the women he was selling in two days. Evelyn Dean's name was on the list."

I can't breathe, but I somehow manage to step back into Eve's office and continue toward her. She lifts her gaze and freezes at the expression on my face. "You're sure?" I ask my boss.

"Positive. It's over. If you want to swing by here, I'll show you everything."

I slowly lower onto the chair across from Eve's desk. "Why didn't someone call me before the raid?"

"Ten reasons, Marshall, and you know it. Starting with the fact that we couldn't possibly know the tip was good. Then let's move to the fact that there was no way I would have trusted it enough to pull you from Evelyn to chase squirrels. What if it had been a decoy to lure you from your post?"

I sigh. He's right. Of course.

"Now, it's over. Come in this afternoon if you want visual proof, or take the fucking weekend off and I'll see you Monday morning."

"Got it. Thanks." I end the call and meet Eve's gaze. She has rounded the desk and is leaning against it, close enough for me to grab her and pull her closer. I'm sitting, but I hold her hips and tip my head back to look at her. "It's over. They got the seller."

She gasps. "Seriously?"

I nod. There is a lump in my throat. It's insane. Of course,

I'm beyond relieved that they caught the guy, but this means my time with Eve is over. I can stay with her for the next two nights, but then I have to return to my real life on Monday morning.

"How did they get him?"

"Someone called in a tip. Probably the same guy."

"Was it the man who's been following me?"

I realize I don't know the answer to her question. "Not sure." Why the fuck didn't I ask that? It's possible the guy following her either works for the seller and will now disappear because his source of income just dried up, or he might have also been the tipster. No idea. I still want to hunt him down though, so I'll make sure the captain or Davis's boss eventually makes an ID.

She feels unsteady, so I pull her onto my lap, hug her tight, and stroke her back. "It's over," I repeat as much for myself as for her.

"What happens now?"

"You get your life back and don't have to spend every second of your day with an undercover cop breathing down your neck." I'm trying to sound light and comical.

Eve doesn't laugh. In fact, her eyes are watery. Her voice trembles. "Do you think that's funny?"

I shake my head. "No, baby. I'm sorry." I said I wouldn't call her that at work, but I can't help it. She looks like she's about to fall apart, which is so backward since we should both be relieved. A man who intended to sell her into human trafficking has been caught.

Neither of us feels elation.

"Is there anything you need to finish this afternoon? Or could you take the rest of the day off?"

She sniffles. "I don't even know. I can't think."

I stand, helping her to her feet. "Get your stuff together and turn off your computer. I'll go tell your boss what happened and that we're leaving and you'll be at the seminar in the morning."

She nods. "Okay."

I tip her head back. "You'll be all right for a few minutes?"

"Yes. Of course." She dabs at the corners of her eye, sucking back emotion.

"I'll be right back."

I make my way toward her boss's office, glad to find the door open and that he's not on the phone or with a client. "Do you have a moment?" I ask him, leaning in the doorway.

"Yes, of course. Everything okay?"

"Yes. I just got word they caught the guy. Eve is shaken up. I'm going to take her home. She'll be at the seminar in the morning."

Her boss stands. "Of course. Yes. Take her home. I'm sure that's a relief and stressful at the same time. Tell her we'll see her tomorrow."

"Thank you." I hurry back to Eve, finding her organizing her desk. She grabs her purse. "Ready?" I ask her.

"Yes. I think so."

I set a hand on the small of her back when she joins me and we leave without saying anything to anyone else. A few people look up, but they seem to wisely know now isn't a great time to chat.

It's not until we're in the SUV and pulling away from the parking lot that Eve loses it. She tugs a pile of tissues from her purse, but they won't be enough judging by how hard she's crying.

I'm helpless. All I can do until we get to her apartment is grip her thigh. She's using both hands to wipe her cheeks and dab at her eyes.

It seems like it takes ten years to get to her place and another decade to get inside from the car. I note that her stalker is not around, but then again he wouldn't expect her to be returning from work at this hour of the day.

I also know he didn't follow us from her office. He wasn't lurking around the office building. And no one is capable of tailing me. I've got a sixth sense when it comes to being tailed.

As soon as we're inside, I take her purse and toss it and her keys on the end table before lifting her off the floor and carrying her to her room. I head straight for her master bathroom where I carefully strip her work clothes off. Everything. It always has to be everything because she owns the sexiest bra and thong sets I've ever seen, and neither suits her little.

I know she needs to be in her little space right now.

"Don't move," I tell her and leave her there shivering while I rush back into her room and grab white panties and a pale blue T-shirt that says Spoiled Rotten on it in white letters.

She doesn't protest or fight me as I pull the shirt over her head and help her step into the panties. When I'm done, I lead her closer to the vanity and help her remove her makeup. Mascara is running down her face. I've watched her remove it enough times to know which bottle to grab and where she keeps the little flat cotton circles. I douse the cotton with the remover and gently wipe the rest of the makeup off her face.

When I'm done, I take her bun down and brush out her hair. I don't feel like taking the time to braid it or put it in pigtails right now, so I leave it long and wavy as I sweep her off her feet and cradle her.

I consider putting her to bed so she can sleep off the hysteria, but I don't want to release her, so I carry her to the armchair we often sit in in the living room, drop down with her on my lap, and tug the throw blanket from behind me around to my front.

I tuck it all around her trembling body and hold her close, kissing the top of her head every once in a while. She cries for a long time while I say nothing. She's been through a lot. I can't imagine how stressful it's been for her to keep up with her job, maintain her little, and start a new relationship with a man who knew nothing about her lifestyle two weeks ago.

When she finally wears herself out, she burrows deeper against me and falls asleep.

I feel beyond privileged to be the man she trusts enough to let me take the reins and hold her through this. The Dom. The Daddy. Whatever she needs, it's hers. I'm helpless. All I can do is stroke her hair while she relaxes. I have nothing else to offer her. Literally.

The sun is dipping in the sky when she rouses. She startles and lifts her face, rubbing her eyes. "I fell asleep," she murmurs.

I smile. "Yes, you did. You were exhausted. You needed it."

"I don't know why I got so emotional. I mean you told me the best news in the world and I cried like a baby."

I kiss her forehead. "It's not unusual, baby. You've been worried for two weeks. The relief when trauma is finally over has a letdown involved that's not much different from the subspace you go to after a spanking."

She nods. "That kind of makes sense."

"Are you hungry?"

She shrugs and leans her head on my shoulder again, her arms tight around me. "You're going to leave," she whispers so softly I can hardly hear her.

I rub her back, my chest tightening. "Well, not today. Unless you want me to." I stiffen, not moving.

She shakes her head. "No. Please, Daddy."

I lick my lips. "I'm all yours for the weekend."

"I have that seminar."

"That's okay. It's only for six hours. I'll drive you and pick you up. The rest of the weekend, you're mine." I don't know what else to say. I'm as lost as she is. I can't imagine leaving her. I've been here two weeks, and already her place feels more like a home to me than my own dreary apartment with very little furniture and nothing personal. All I needed when I got it was a place to sleep in between cases. I'm not home enough days a month to warrant anything fancier.

"How about we order pizza and watch a movie?"

She nods against me. "Can I pick the movie?"

"As long as it's PG," I remind her.

She pouts adorably. Her eyes are red and puffy, but she's shoving our elephant to the side for now, and I'm glad. I don't want her to spend the rest of our time together sad.

"Will you spank me later?"

"Of course. If that's what you want."

"I do. It will make all the bad feelings go away for a while."

"Okay, baby. I can do that."

CHAPTER 31

Colton

I'm uneasy once again as I drop Eve off at the hotel where her seminar is being held. It's not rational. I'm just used to worrying about her. As soon as she's safely inside the building, I head for the crime scene. Ever since my boss called to tell me about the arrest and subsequent raid on Antonio Russo's home, I've been uneasy. I know the captain still has several people at Russo's house this morning, so I head that way. Maybe if I see some of the evidence myself, I'll feel like it's real.

When I pull up, several investigators are on the scene. Yellow tape surrounds the house. I park and duck under it, shaking hands with a few of the guys as I put gloves on and cover my shoes.

A detective I've worked with on several cases, Roger Durban, greets me as I enter the house.

"Captain send you over?" Durban asks.

"Nah. I'm just curious." I rub the back of my neck.

He chuckles. "You gotta see for yourself, don't you?"

I nod, my brow furrowed as I wander in deeper, following him. He leads me downstairs, and I'm shocked by what I find. Fucking place is definitely ground zero for a human trafficking sting. "Jesus," I mutter to myself as I slowly wander around.

The main room has all kinds of information tacked to the walls. In fact, the walls are made of corkboard. Whoever this asshole is, he's meticulous. Each victim has a square on the wall. There are dozens, which leads me to believe he was either planning on picking up several women in the near future, he plans way in advance, or some of them have already been sold.

I turn toward Durban. "Have all these women been located?"

He shakes his head. "Not yet."

"Anyone know if any of the cases are older?"

"Could be. But most of the information on the walls is current. Judging by the filing cabinets in that office over there," he pauses to point in the direction of the indicated room, "I'd say he's been in this business a long time. There are dozens of closed files."

"Fuck." Tightness forms in my chest as I realize one of those files is undoubtedly for Davis's woman. "Can you see if there's a file for Britney Heath?"

"Will do. Be right back."

I keep wandering, my heart stopping when I come to a square dedicated to Evelyn. Pictures of her coming and going from work and her apartment. Recent ones if I'm not mistaken, undoubtedly taken by the guy who's been stalking her. Makes my skin crawl. I look closer, reading the details. This guy was thorough. He knew every damn thing about Eve. Including the fact that she belongs to Surrender.

When I can't stand to look any longer, I turn away and

head for the office. This room is immaculate. Unlike the larger space outside of the office, there is not a paper in sight. Everything is in its spot. Pens lined up on the desk. Files all put away. "Guy has OCD," I comment.

Durban lifts his gaze from a filing cabinet as he pulls out a file and holds it up. "Found it. Britney Heath. That's the woman you rescued eight months ago, right?"

"Yes." I tentatively take the file from him, forcing myself to open it and absorb the details. I know it will give Davis closure in a way. He can decide if he thinks Britney needs to know, but the important thing is finding out the seller has been arrested. No matter what, I'm sure this has been hanging over Davis's head. It would mine.

I hand the file back to Durban and aim for the bookshelves. Even these are dust-free and organized in alphabetical order. Every other shelf has pictures or trinkets on it.

I pick up a group shot of a bunch of guys all smiling drunkenly at the camera. It looks like a fraternity picture. It's hard to imagine a man so vile that he sells women on the side but he used to be a regular guy in college with his friends. Or maybe he never was a regular guy.

I glance at Durban. "Which one is he?"

"Oh. There's a better picture over here. Close up." Durban snags it from another shelf and holds it out, his finger pointing to the guy on the left.

My blood runs cold as I yank the picture out of his hand. "*Fuck*," I shout.

"What?"

I jerk my gaze toward him as I pull my phone from my pocket. I can no longer see Durban though. I drop the picture and take off running as fast as I can back through the larger room and up the stairs.

As I run, I call Eve, but it goes straight to voicemail. I'm sure her phone is off. I call my boss next.

He's already speaking when he answers. "Heard you couldn't resist and headed to the crime scene," he jokes. "Oh hey, we got an ID on your stalker too. Bates Roberts. Heard of him?" All this rushes out of my captain before I have a chance to interrupt.

I'm at my car now, hands shaking as I enter. I put the phone on speaker and slide it into the holder as I start the engine and peel away from the curb.

"Marshall?"

"Those fuckers are in cahoots."

"Who?"

"Russo. Bates. And the fucking guy I've been keeping an eye on all this time. Owen Karplus."

"How do you know?"

"Frat brothers. Saw a picture of them in Russo's office."

"Fuck. I just sent a team to pick up Bates at his home, but I didn't make the connection to Karplus. Sending someone now."

I hear muffled voices while he shouts out orders to several people. When he comes back, he asks, "Where's Evelyn?"

I'm on the highway now. "Fucking seminar I told you about."

"Shit. That's right. I pulled my guy from that."

"I'm on my way there now." Though I can't seem to get there fast enough. The car in front of me is going too slow. I speed around it.

"Son of a bitch," my boss mutters. He shouts more instructions at whoever's nearby, then he's back again. "Got two guys on their way to the hotel now."

I tap the damn steering wheel nervously as I exit the highway and come to a stoplight. *Fuck. Fuck fuck fuck. If anything happens to her...*

"Marshall, you still there?"

"I'm pulling up to the hotel now. I'll get back to you." I end the call as I squeal into a parking spot and barely take the time to turn off the engine before running full speed toward the hotel. I don't give a single fuck that I look ridiculous. I keep jogging until I reach the entrance to the large conference room where Eve should be.

I open the door and slip inside, begging God to let her be here. Innocently listening to the presentation. Not on a plane to the Middle East.

I scan the room, but I can't find her. My heart rate increases with each passing second. My gaze lands on her boss at the same time he spots me. He holds up a finger and quietly eases past everyone in his aisle, heading toward me.

I step back into the corridor as he reaches me. "Where's Eve?" I ask.

"She took a call and then left the room. Said she'd be right back."

"When was that?"

"Maybe ten minutes ago."

"Fuck," I mutter.

"I thought it was over. I thought you caught the guy?" He's rubbing his forehead. "What's going on?"

I'm already jogging away from her boss. "I'll explain later. Gotta find her. Parking garage?"

He points to the left. "You think she's in trouble?"

I think she's as good as dead if I don't find her.

I run toward the parking garage, praying that's where Owen or Bates would have taken her. I suspect Owen is the one who has her now. She would leave her seminar for him if he asked her. She knows him. She trusts him.

The moment I burst through the door leading to the parking garage, I hear shouting. I rush in that direction. I can't see anything yet. It's around the corner, but the words I hear make my blood boil.

"Let her go. You're cornered. There's no way out of this."

Who the hell is talking? I run harder, gun drawn now.

"He's right, Bates. Let her go. It's over. If you hurt her, you're only going to make things harder on yourself." I know that voice. It's Owen's.

I come to the corner, knowing exactly where the voices are coming from now. I don't want anyone to see me yet, so I glance around the edge of the wall to survey the situation.

"Fuck you, you pussy. And fuck you for not sticking with the plan. Are you the one who called the cops on Tony? I bet you were. Tony never should have brought you in on the deal."

"There never was a deal, Bates. I was drunk that night. I told you I didn't want anything to do with your little scheme the next morning. I can't believe you went through with this. It's over. Fucking let her go, Bates."

I have about two hundred questions, but I'll have to ask them later from whoever is left standing when this is over.

I squat down so they can't see me and inch between two cars. A man I've never seen has his gun trained on Bates. He's dressed in casual street clothes, but he's confident and seasoned. He knows what the fuck he's doing. And since he seems to be on my side, I'll figure that out later.

Owen has no weapon. He's holding his hands up in supplication.

Bates has Eve plastered to his chest, his arm around her neck. He's waving a gun erratically as he backs up, dragging Eve with him.

Her eyes are bugged out with fear. She's gripping Bates's forearm, probably because he's cutting off her air supply. She's tripping over her heels.

I don't have a clear shot of anything yet, nor would I risk

shooting at Bates with him moving around so much. I just hope her other guardian angel has the same sense.

Bates keeps backing up. Where the fuck is he going? When he grabs the handle of the SUV next to him, I realize it's his vehicle. *Shit.* He yanks the door open. Not a chance in hell I'm going to let him take Eve out of this garage, so I aim at the rear tire closest to me and shoot.

The sound of the gunshot ricochets all over the garage, forcing everyone to turn in my direction. I've ducked back out of sight though.

"Fuck," Bates shouts. "Who the fuck is shooting? Show your damn face, asshole, or she takes a bullet to the head right now."

I rise from my squatted position, gun raised, aimed at Bates. "Let her go, Bates. Owen is right. If you hurt her, you'll be in a hell of a lot more trouble."

"*You,*" he yells. "Her fucking bodyguard. Left her alone this morning, didn't you?" He laughs sardonically. "She's coming with me, so back the fuck off right now. All of you. It's your only option. If you fuck with me, she dies."

I inch forward, keeping my gun on Bates's head. If that fucker would just stand still.

"You can't get out of this," the mystery man declares. He's a big guy. Over six feet. Dark hair cut military short. Civilian clothes.

"Psst."

I glance behind me to find Davis in the spot I just vacated. His piece is in his hand too. He makes hand motions to indicate he's going around to the other side.

I nod. How the hell did Davis know to come here? I told him the threat was over last night. Another glance at the mystery man makes me suspect he's with Davis.

Owen tries to reason with Bates again. "Dude, Tony is in jail. Whatever you two were planning for today is off. Give it up. You don't want to hurt her."

Bates chuckles sardonically. "Have you tapped her, Owen? I know that cop has, but what about you? Or were you too damn polite to fuck her sexy body when you had a chance?"

I stiffen. This asshole is on my last nerve.

Suddenly, Owen plows forward, rushing headlong toward Bates.

Luckily, I'm at a different angle, so the moment Bates turns his gun from Eve to Owen, I take my shot. I'm not quite fast enough. Bates also releases a round. I see Owen go down a split second before Bates.

Eve screams as she backs away from the body at her feet.

I run toward her, noticing Davis coming from the opposite direction.

I can hear Owen moaning on the ground, but I only care about Eve.

When I reach her, she throws herself into my arms, and I flatten her face against my chest so she doesn't have to see the thick blood running out of Bates's head. I practically carry her around the end of the car to block her view.

"Is he dead? Did you check? Are you sure?" she's shouting and fighting against my hold.

As soon as it's safe to loosen my grip, I lean her back, meet her wild gaze, and cup her face. "He's dead, baby."

"But are you sure?"

I shot the fucker in the center of the forehead. I don't miss. "Yes, Eve."

Davis reaches us. The other guy hurries over to Owen. When I glance over my shoulder, I see Owen is standing now. He's holding his arm. Doesn't look life-threatening.

Eve is sobbing. "I'm sorry. I never should have left the seminar. I didn't think. I'm so sorry." She's apologizing to me?

"Baby, it's okay. I've got you. Take a deep breath for me."

She shakes her head, not getting enough oxygen.

I hold her biceps and meet her gaze. "Deep breath," I say with more demand in my voice. I don't want to dominate her here in the parking lot, but I don't want her to panic or hyperventilate either.

She draws in a breath and lets it out slowly. "You came. How did you know?"

I pull her against my chest and hug her tight again. I never want to let her go. I'm struggling to breathe myself. If anything had happened to her…

She's my life.

I don't know what the fuck I'm going to do about that, but I'm not leaving her ever.

Sirens get louder and louder a few moments before several police cars pull into the parking garage.

I see my boss first, and his brow is furrowed as he approaches me. I know he's pissed. I'm not surprised. He'll be mad at himself for not making the connection between Tony, Bates, and Owen. The self-recrimination isn't warranted. No one would have expected him to see that picture, but he'll be furious all the same.

I keep Eve against me, so she can't see what's happening around us, but I face the garage more fully now, watching as two officers approach Owen.

Davis turns toward us. "You okay, Eve?"

She nods against me, not meeting his gaze.

Davis waves the other man I don't know over. "This is Spike, Brett Pauson. He works with me at Black Blade Protection."

Brett holds out a hand and I shake it while still gripping Eve with my other. "Wondered who you were." I shift my attention to Davis. "How did you have a man here so fast?" I'd canceled with Davis last night.

Davis shrugs. "Had a hunch. Didn't like the feeling. So, I sent Brett anyway."

"Thank fuck." I glance at the group now hovering around Owen. "I have about two hundred questions."

"You and me both."

"I can tell you what little I know," Brett says. "I was in the back of the conference room when Eve looked at her phone, so I knew she'd either gotten a text or a call."

"It was a text," she muttered against me.

I rub her back. "What did it say?"

She pulls back just enough to extract her phone from her pocket and hands it to me.

My heart is overflowing over the ridiculous fact that both men in front of me are going to realize I know my woman's passcode. There's something intimate about that kind of thing.

I open her phone and read the text. It's from Owen.

I need to talk to you. It's urgent. Can you step out of your meeting for a moment?

I tip her head back. "Then what happened?"

"I glanced at the exits and saw Owen standing outside the room pacing, so I excused myself and headed that way."

"Unfortunately, it was on the opposite side of the room from where I was watching," Brett adds.

"What did Owen want?" I ask.

"I have no idea. As soon as I stepped into the hall, that other guy grabbed me, covered my mouth, and manhandled me into the stairwell."

"Which guy? The one who was holding you hostage?" I need her to clarify.

"Yes. And he seemed to know Owen." She shivers and spins around, her gaze landing on the man we are all staring at.

"Let me at least explain," Owen says.

One of the cops is crowding him, holding him by the arm —his good arm. Another cop is examining the wound.

Owen looks in our direction. "Please. Eve. Let me explain."

The four of us walk over toward Owen. I can't begin to imagine what he has to say, but we all want to hear it. My boss comes closer too. "Start talking," I tell him, my voice filled with warning.

Owen winces as the officer wraps gauze around his arm. "I guess you know about Tony," he begins.

I nod, not giving him more.

Owen looks like he's about to piss himself. He's not the firm Dom and Daddy I met last Friday. He's in a fuck-ton of trouble, so it's not surprising.

"I went to the same university as Bates and Tony. We were in the same fraternity. We hung out a lot back then. We've kept in touch over the years."

He glances at Bates and shudders. Good.

"Go on," my boss says.

"The two of them came to my bar one night out of the blue." He looks at Eve. "The night you were there."

Eve is white and looks like she might vomit.

"You were leaving as they came in, but they saw me hug you before you left and they started giving me trouble about you. They thought we were dating."

I narrow my gaze. *He wishes*.

"Get to the point," my boss says.

Owen swallows. "The guys stayed late after I closed up and we got drunk. They kept asking me questions about Eve, even though I told them she wasn't my girlfriend. Just a friend. As the night wore on, I mentioned that my bar is in the red and I thought I'd have to sell it soon."

"So, you decided you could make a buck by selling Eve?" Davis growls.

Owen shakes his head. "No. It wasn't like that. I had

nothing to do with it. The two of them decided. They said she has the look buyers are looking for. I had hoped they were joking, but they wouldn't let up. I called Tony the next morning to make sure he was kidding. He laughed at me, and I didn't like the vibe. I wasn't sure what to think, so I called the police."

My boss interjects. "You called in the tip."

Owen nods. "Yes. I didn't know what else to do. I didn't want to rat out my friends if they were kidding. Seemed ludicrous to think my friends were really in the business of human trafficking."

"Did you know Bates was following Eve?"

He shakes his head. "No. I had no idea. But when I saw you with her last Friday, I knew you were not just some random guy who came into the club. I knew you were a cop."

I hate that he picked up on that, but I say nothing.

"So, you called the second tip too?" my boss asks.

"Yes. When I left the club that night, I saw Bates lurking around outside. It freaked me out."

"Why the hell didn't you fucking tell the cops everything you knew at that point?" Davis asks.

Owen runs his hand down his face. "I didn't know what the fuck to do or what to think. I still couldn't believe they were seriously going to fucking kidnap her or sell her." His voice is raised. It should be.

"Go on," I grind out.

The man is shaking. I'm not certain he hasn't actually pissed himself by now. "I called Bates a few days later, but he blew me off. Said I was seeing things. Told me he hadn't been at the club last Friday. I called Tony too, but all I got was his voicemail. He never returned my calls, and I began to assume he was the ringleader. I wasn't sure Bates even knew for sure what Tony had planned, but I couldn't stand the stress. I haven't been able to sleep or eat all week. I kept thinking I was surely out of my mind. There had to be an explanation. But I was scared for Eve too, so I called the cops again Friday morning and told them I thought Tony was planning to kidnap her."

There are moments of silence. Eve grips my shirt at my back so tight that I can feel her little fist at the small of my back. When I glance at her, I see flames. She'd like to throttle Owen. She'll have to get in line.

"How did you end up here today?" I ask.

Owen starts fidgeting. "Bates called me earlier this morning. It went to voicemail. I didn't get the message until a while later. He sounded like a crazed lunatic, telling me about Tony being arrested, blaming me for turning them in, rambling about how I was ruining his life. But what spurred me into action was his laughter. Like a crazed lunatic. Said he was going to show me. He didn't need Tony. He could make the drop-off all by himself. He was done taking a cut from Tony. He would take over."

"Jesus," I murmur. "How did you know where Eve was."

"Bates fucking told me. You can listen to the message. I swear. He was out of his mind or something. Told me he was here at the hotel and he was going to finish the job. As soon as I heard him, I drove here as fast as I could. I figured Eve wouldn't have protection anymore since Tony had been arrested, so I wanted to warn her. I texted her to come out and talk to me."

Owen shifts his attention directly to Eve. "I swear I had no idea Bates would grab you the moment you stepped into the hallway. I had no idea he was behind me. I was trying to help. Eve, you have to believe me."

Eve stares at him.

We all do. It's a ludicrous story that we're going to need to investigate and hear ten more times, but it's also possible he's telling the truth. We'll see if it all checks out.

My boss speaks next. He sets his hands on his hips and steps into the middle of the circle. He points at Owen. "I have two thousand more questions for you. You'll be escorted to the hospital and then transferred to the station. Hope you finally got a good nights' sleep last night because you're going to have one hell of a long day."

Owen nods, his eyes wide. "Yes, sir." He glances back at Eve as they lead him away, his eyes pleading with hers.

I don't know what to think of the man right now. I'm furious with him though. He could have come forward at any point. If he knew it was serious enough that I was protecting her... Jesus.

I need to focus on Eve, not Owen or any other person. She's trembling badly, and I hold her upright with an arm around her waist. I don't give a fuck that everyone is probably looking at us. Too bad. All that matters is Eve. Not one single other person.

My captain asks her a lot of questions, which is procedure and understandable, but it gets on my nerves anyway. At some point, Davis goes inside, fills Eve's boss in on what happened, and retrieves my SUV from the other side of the hotel.

I'm grateful because now I don't have to parade Eve past anyone to get her to the car.

It's midafternoon before I finally tuck her in the passenger seat and round the hood.

My boss stops me before I open my door. His brow is furrowed.

"We need to talk," I tell him.

"I figured that was coming." He sighs.

I nod at him as I climb into the SUV.

It seems like it takes an eternity to get back to Eve's apartment, and I'm proud of her. She never fell apart. Not even while she was being grilled for information, and not now that she's in the relative safety of the car.

She doesn't fall apart when we get inside her apartment either. I'm actually a bit concerned as I take her hand and lead her directly to the master bathroom. I know the only thing that might help her center is a bath, so I turn on the water and plug the stopper in the bottom before I turn back to her.

She's smiling at me, her gaze clearer than expected. "Thank you." She cups my face.

I set my hand over hers. "For what, baby?"

"For saving my life. For being there for me. For taking care of me for two weeks. For being everything I needed. A man. A Dom. A Daddy. I'll never be able to thank you enough."

I sit on the toilet and pull her between my legs so I can hug her against me. "Any time, baby. Any time." When the tub is full, I release her to turn the water off, help her out of her clothes, and take her hand as she steps into the water. "Bubbles?"

She grins. "Yes, please."

I add her favorite bubbles and roll up a towel to set behind her neck so she can lean back. I sit on the edge of the tub and stroke her cheek while she closes her eyes. She looks almost peaceful. "You okay?" I ask, concerned.

"Yeah. I'm good."

"I'm sorry I had to take Bates out. That must have scared the hell out of you."

She blinks at me. "I'm just glad you're a good shot."

I chuckle. "One of the best. I wouldn't have taken the shot if I thought I'd miss."

"I appreciate you not missing," she jokes as she leans forward and picks up the body wash. She holds it out to me. "Will you wash me?" Her voice is dipping. Adult Eve is about to flee the apartment.

"I'd love to, baby." I pour plenty of soap in a washcloth and start with her hands, massaging her fingers and up her arms. I take my time. There's nothing I enjoy more than taking care of Eve.

As I continue, I worry about the elephant in the room. I need to talk to her about us, but I don't want to disturb her bliss, nor do I think now is the time to bring up the future. She's been through a lot. Her brain is overloaded. That's why she's turned her care over to me.

After I finish washing her, I let her sit in the tub until the water gets too cool before I pull the drain and help her out. I dry her off, wrap her in the towel, and swing her up into my arms.

She squeals. "Colton…"

I carry her to the bed, and drop her unceremoniously on top, letting her bounce, which makes her giggle. I love that sound. I strip away the towel and pull the covers up over her.

With my hand on her hip, I stare down at her. I'm the luckiest bastard alive.

"I'm not tired. I don't need to sleep right now," she tells me.

"You should be exhausted. You've been through a trauma."

"You have too. I wasn't the one who pulled the trigger. Doesn't that bother you?"

I stroke her hip through the covers. "It's not my favorite thing to do, but it happens sometimes. I've learned to manage it. I'm trained not to hesitate. When lives are on the line, I know what has to be done, and I do it."

"How many people have you had to shoot?"

"I don't think you want numbers, baby. I've killed a few people. Always when it was necessary to save other lives. Today that life was yours."

She shoves to sitting and reaches for my shirt. "Join me."

I let her pull my shirt over my head. "Are you sure?"

"Positive."

I stand and remove the rest of my clothes before climbing under the covers with her.

When she reaches for me, I pull her hands over her head and clasp her wrists in one of my palms.

She whimpers. "I always go from zero to ninety-nine when you hold me down like this."

"Just ninety-nine?" I tease.

"Out of ten," she responds, making me chuckle.

"Well, good, because I like holding you down while I torment your body." I grab her hip with my free hand and lean over to suck one of her nipples into my mouth. The moan that escapes her lips is like music in the quiet room. There's nothing sweeter than the little noises she makes when I make love to her.

I lift one leg and situate it between hers, forcing her to part her knees. This makes her arch her back, also delightful.

When I reach between her thighs, I find her soaked. Swollen. Hot. Wet. Greedy. I love it. I love everything about her.

I'm a damn lucky man.

CHAPTER 32

Evelyn

I wake up Sunday morning to the smell of bacon, and I smile. Colt is cooking. He's an amazing cook, and that's good because he's done most of the cooking in the last two weeks. He doesn't seem to mind at all that I'm nearly always little in the apartment and that means he nearly always takes care of me.

I wasn't so little last night while we made love, more than once, pausing only to eat takeout. But I feel little this morning, or maybe I just don't want to deal with the future. I don't want to think about what happens after today.

Colt is going to leave eventually. Maybe not today, but soon. Maybe he'll stay with me until he gets another undercover assignment. Maybe I can talk him into that idea. I'm sure he'll at least be on administrative leave for a while after taking out Bates.

Either way, I refuse to let the impending doom ruin the fact that I get a full day with him. Maybe even more.

I slide out from under the covers, use the bathroom, and ponder my clothing options. For the past week, I've slept either naked or in one of Colt's T-shirts. He likes it that way. Even though I spend most evenings in my little space in childish pj's or clothes, Colt removes everything when we go to bed. I get it. I think he likes to make love to my adult side.

He definitely does go out of his way to keep my little persona horny all damn day, and he can dole out amazing orgasms even when I'm little, but when it's time to actually have sex, he tends to guide me gently back to my adult self.

I open my drawers and grab a pair of pink panties and a babyish cotton nightgown. It's white with a rainbow on the front. It's so short, it barely covers my butt.

By the time I shuffle into the kitchen, I'm fully little, and Daddy turns around from the stove to smile at me. "Good morning, baby." He motions for me to come close and hugs me against his side. "Did you sleep well?"

"Yes, Daddy. Are you making pancakes?"

"I sure am." He kisses my forehead. "Why don't you have a seat? They're almost ready. I'll bring you a plate."

I skip to the table and sit. He must have suspected I would wake up little because he has set the table for my youngest self. Sippy cup. Plastic fork. Princess plate.

Daddy cuts up my pancakes like he did last time and scoots my chair closer to the table. "Davis is coming over this morning for a few minutes."

I lick the syrup off my finger and meet his gaze. "Okay. How come?"

He shrugs. "No idea. He called a bit ago and said he had something for me."

"Is he bringing Britney?"

"I don't think so. He said he was getting her a sitter."

My eyes go wide. "He gets her a babysitter when he goes out?"

I nod. “Apparently.”

“Wow, that’s hardcore. The thought never would have occurred to me.”

Daddy reaches over and tickles my side. “After everything we’ve been through since I met you, I’m not sure I’d leave you home alone either. Maybe I should get the number of his sitter when he comes by.”

I giggle as he continues to dance his fingers over my tummy. “I don’t need a babysitter, Daddy. I’m big enough to stay home alone.” The thought of him leaving me with someone else is unnerving.

He chuckles. “Oh, now I’m definitely going to find someone. I’m also going to come up with good reasons to leave the apartment so you won’t have a choice.”

I consider the implications. Since I started seeing Daddy, I haven’t craved interaction with other Daddies. I proved that last week when I couldn’t finish my scene with Owen. The idea of being left with someone else makes me pout.

Daddy chuckles. “Don’t give me a reason to spank you already this morning, baby.”

“Yes, Sir.”

We finish eating and I help Daddy clean up the table just in time for the doorbell to ring.

I glance down at my nightgown. “I’m not even dressed.”

Daddy shrugs. “I’m sure Davis doesn’t care what you’re wearing, baby. He’s also seen you naked.” He lifts a brow as he reminds me.

True.

I skip over to the door next to Daddy and wait for him to look through the peephole before opening it.

Davis smiles at me as he comes inside. “Hey, little one. Sorry to hone in on your Sunday. I won’t stay long. Britney isn’t too pleased with my absence anyway.”

"It's okay," I tell him. "Next time maybe you can bring Britney with you?"

"Sounds like a great idea."

Daddy pats my bottom. "Why don't you go find something to play with while I talk to Davis?"

"Yes, Sir." My shoulders slump though because I'd rather stay in the room and eavesdrop.

"Can I get you some coffee?" Daddy asks Davis as I head for the shelf next to the television where I keep my coloring books. I don't ask permission to stay in the room while they talk. Daddy didn't specifically tell me to leave the room. He simply told me to find something to play with. And I have. Colors.

I spread them out on the kitchen table and find the picture I want to color while Daddy makes Davis a cup of coffee. "I know you didn't come by here just to say hi. You said you have something for me?" Daddy nods toward the folder Davis is holding.

Davis lifts the folder and sets it on the counter. "Take a look."

Now, I'm beyond curious. It takes every ounce of self-restraint not to be nosy, and though I wouldn't mind having my butt spanked at some point today, I'd rather it not be for punishment.

Daddy opens the folder as he slowly slides the mug of steaming liquid toward his friend. He stares at the contents for several minutes, flipping through the pages.

I can't help but stare. It looks like there are three or four pieces of paper. I also think his hand is shaking a bit.

I'm holding my breath when he lifts his gaze to Davis. "Are you serious?"

"As a heart attack."

"Do you have any idea what this means to me?"

Davis shrugs. "I can guess."

Daddy glances at me, his face impossible to read. It almost looks like he's about to fist pump the air, but he's also hesitant. He glances back at Davis. "I haven't told Eve anything yet."

Davis nods and sips his coffee before setting it back down. "Well, I'll let you get back to your day. Take your time with that. Look it over. Discuss it with Eve. Do what you need. You know how to find us."

Us? I'm so confused.

Davis turns toward me, his face switching to full Daddy mode. "Britney would love to have you over again soon."

I glance at Daddy. "I'd like that, Sir."

"She threw a bit of a tantrum when I left her with a sitter this morning, so she's grounded for the week, but maybe next weekend. I'll set something up with your Daddy."

I shift my gaze toward Colt, my heart pounding. Will he still be here in my life next weekend?

Colt sees Davis out and then silently comes to me. He lifts me out of my chair and carries me to the couch.

I wrap my legs around him so that we're chest to chest, which means I'm straddling him when he sits. He brushes my messy hair from my face and tucks it behind my ears. I can tell he's thinking hard and I don't want to interrupt him. He'll say what he wants to say when he's ready.

"Do you have any idea how much I love you, Evelyn?"

I'm not expecting that to be his opening line, so I suck in a breath. "I love you too, Daddy."

He smiles. "I know I said there was no way we could stay together after the bad guys were caught because I would need to move to another case and be unable to see you."

I nod. There's hope in his words. I hear the hanging "but."

"I decided that wasn't going to work for me or for you or for us, so I resigned from the police department."

I gasp. My eyes go wide. That is not what I expected him to say. "What?"

He nods, grinning.

"But you love your job. You'll be unhappy."

He slides his hands down and cups my bottom, my panties the only thing between us. "I love you so much more than that job, baby."

I furrow my brow, concerned about his decision. "What does Davis have to do with it?"

He beams. "Davis just offered me a job working for his company, Black Blade Protection."

I process his words slowly. "He did?"

"Well, technically his boss did. You know his boss. Andres Phillips, though no one calls him that at work. He goes by Blade. He's a member of Surrender."

I nod. "I know Master Andres." I did not know what he did for a living or that he was Davis's boss. And now apparently Daddy's boss. I wiggle closer. "Are you sure that's what you want?"

He gives my butt cheeks a squeeze. "Positive. It's like Fate stepped in. I just sent my resignation a few hours ago while you were sleeping. It's obviously meant to be. Besides, it's the same kind of work. Protecting people and solving crimes. I'll just be working for a private agency instead of a public police force. It's perfect."

My smile spreads wide. "You're going to stay with me?"

"Forever. If you'll have me."

I close the distance between us, throwing my arms around his neck and hugging him tightly. I'm filled with relief. I can't believe how lucky I am.

Daddy's hands slide under my nightgown and rub my naked back. "How attached are you to this apartment?"

I lean back, meet his gaze, and shrug. "It's just an apartment. Why? Is yours bigger?"

He chuckles. "God, no. Mine is nothing more than a boring place where I keep my shit and sleep when I'm not on an assignment. I was thinking we should look into ditching both of them and finding a house. Someplace with a private backyard where you can play outside without anyone seeing you."

I *can* be happier. "Really?" I bounce on his lap and clap my hands together. "I'd love that. I've never gotten a house because I didn't want to take care of it alone."

"Well, you won't be alone anymore, and I'll take care of it and you." He taps my nose.

I smash myself against him again. I can't stop hugging him. "I love you, Daddy."

"I love you too, baby."

EPILOGUE

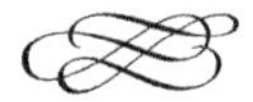

Three months later…

Evelyn

"And you have to see the backyard too," I exclaim excitedly as I grab Britney's hand and pull her from my new playroom.

She giggles as she follows me from the room. "I can't believe you don't have a bed in your room."

I shrug. "I sleep with Daddy."

"My Daddy makes me sleep alone sometimes. Plus naptime."

I had put my foot down on that subject when Colt asked me if I wanted a little-girl bed. I do not. I want to sleep in his bed. Our bed. I love the playroom. A place I can go and escape and be fully little without keeping the entire house as my little space, but I'm not sleeping alone.

I drag Britney through the house toward the back door. She hesitates when I reach up to slide the glass door open.

Davis and Colt are talking at the kitchen island, and she glances at her Daddy.

He lifts a brow. "Where do you think you're going, sweetie?"

"Eve wants to show me her backyard."

"Did you ask my permission?"

"No, Sir." She hangs her head.

"Do I normally let you go outside alone?"

"No, Sir."

I clear my throat. "I'm sorry. It's my fault. I wasn't thinking."

Davis shakes his head. "Not your fault, Eve. Britney knows the rules." He comes to her and tips her chin back.

"May I please go outside with Eve, Daddy?"

"Let's all go," Colt says. "I wanted to show Davis the shed anyway." He rounds the island and opens the door for us, but he takes my hand and pulls me against him after Davis and Britney step onto the patio. He holds my chin. "You need to be more aware of other people's rules, baby."

"Yes, Sir."

"I know I'm relatively new to age play, but if I find you using my weaknesses against me, I will tighten the reins. Understood?"

I squirm, my panties growing damp. "Yes, Sir."

"You have more freedoms than other little girls. I've learned this over the past few months. That stems mostly from my own ignorance. Do not take advantage of the holes in my knowledge or you'll find yourself over my knee before standing in a corner."

"Yes, Sir." I shift my weight from one foot to the other. I probably will test him, partly because it's in my nature, and partly because the best part of age play is when he reprimands me. "I'll be good."

He chuckles and kisses my forehead.

We've only been in this house for a week, so we're not entirely unpacked, but the backyard is my favorite part. Daddy carefully selected this house because it has a high fence with no neighbors behind us. I can be myself outside without anyone finding out about my kink. I love it, and I love him.

"Okay. Go show your friend the swing. Be sure to take turns though."

I smile at him. "Thank you, Daddy." I throw my arms around his middle and hug him tight. He's the best Daddy in the world.

AUTHOR'S NOTE

I hope you've enjoyed *Charming Colton* from my Surrender series. Please enjoy the following excerpt from *Convincing Leah,* the next book in the series.

CONVINCING LEAH

SURRENDER, BOOK NINE

"You realize he doesn't scene with anyone else, right?"

I take a sip of my tea and shrug. "That's his business," I tell my best friend Eve.

Eve chuckles. "You don't scene with other people anymore either. I'd say your relationship now falls under the umbrella of exclusive."

Luckily, the waitress picks this moment to slide our lunches onto the table and ask if we need anything else. It buys me a moment to come up with a response to Eve's unnerving observation.

Eve is staring at me with her mischievous grin as the waitress walks away.

I roll my eyes. "Craig and I aren't anything. We aren't in a relationship. We're both members of Surrender. We meet there once or twice a week and do a scene together. That's it. Nothing else."

"You have chemistry," Eve points out. "You were a favorite to watch even before Master Craig joined the club. The two of you together are magical to watch."

It doesn't escape my notice that she intentionally called

him Master Craig, probably rubbing it in that my relationship with him is more than Dom and sub if I would dare refer to him by his first name. "Thank you. I enjoy our scenes," I respond.

"Okay, let's assume for the sake of argument that you're not fooling yourself and your relationship is strictly Dom and sub a few hours a week. Why can't it be more?" Eve stabs a bite of her salad and dips just the corner of the lettuce into her salad dressing.

I decide to comment on her food habits since I'm about to lift up my burger and take a giant bite, which will have more calories than her entire plate of food. "Your eating habits are beyond fascinating. Do you need to take a picture first to prove to Colton that you got today's ten servings of vegetables at lunch?" I tease.

The unfortunate part is that it won't do me a bit of good. No matter what I eat, I remain ridiculously skinny. Some people may roll their eyes and groan, wishing they could eat anything and not gain weight, but I'd gladly trade them places for a few curves and some boobs.

She sets her fork down while chewing her bite to pull out her phone. "Good idea. Maybe he'll let me have chicken nuggets and mac and cheese for dinner if I prove I hit the rest of the food groups at lunch."

I laugh. "I don't think chicken nuggets and mac and cheese are food groups."

"If you're five they are," she points out before taking another bite.

Colton is her Daddy. They have a complicated dynamic, but their agreement with regard to food is the most fascinating. Ever since they moved in together—and now recently bought a house together—she is usually little at home. It's easiest to meet her during her lunch break when she's in full accountant business attire if I want to speak to her adult self.

Basically, Eve agrees to eat the healthiest food imaginable at lunch so she can eat like a five-year-old at dinner. She was already living this way before she met him, so nothing really changed except who's in charge.

Eve clears her throat. "You dodged my question."

"That's because you already know the answer. Craig is a Daddy through and through. He humors me by doing scenes with me at the club, but we'd never work out long-term because I don't need to remind you that I'm *not* little." I dig into my hamburger.

Eve swallows another bite. "I think you're cheating yourself out of an experience. The man is beyond interested in you. It wouldn't kill you to give his way a try just for giggles."

I shudder. "Pretending to be five is not just for giggles, Eve. It's a serious commitment. I don't mind turning over my control and submitting to someone for an hour on a Friday night, but outside of that, I prefer to be fully in charge of my life at all times." I cringe at the thought of someone dominating me in my apartment. Not gonna happen.

"It's so liberating," Eve tells me for the millionth time.

"It totally suits you. I get that. But whatever is between Craig and me isn't going there. I hope he doesn't think if he waits me out, I'll decide to give age play a try." I take another bite, but now I'm concerned.

Eve shrugs. "It's obvious to everyone that he's into you, so I'm betting more than likely he's trying to be what you need, a regular Dom."

That may be. I can see her point. The problem is that I don't need any sort of Dom, not outside the club. Not full-time. I'm a weekend kind of gal. My cravings where BDSM are concerned mostly center around getting spanked so hard that I slide into a delicious headspace that ends with a satisfying orgasm.

Secret truth—vanilla guys don't do it for me. They are too gentle. I get bored. I want more. I want to come home after a scene, slide into bed with a sore butt, and wake up the next morning still feeling the impact.

As far as sex is concerned, I've had sex with a few men at Surrender but not often. I haven't slept with Craig. I'm not opposed to the idea. In fact, I've thought about it more than once, but he hasn't asked me to. He arranges for us to play, spanks me, and gets me off with his fingers. It's amazing and fulfilling. What more do I need?

Another truth—I often grab my vibrator the moment I get home and give myself at least two more orgasms to the memory of Craig's hand on my ass. It's not difficult since my cheeks are still red hot and stinging.

Eve waves a hand in front of me and I realize I've been in my own world. "Sorry. My mind strayed."

She smiles. "I bet it did. Probably to that amazing orgasm Craig gave you Friday night. I saw. It was hot. Has he ever asked you to get together outside of Surrender?"

I take another huge bite to occupy my mouth, but she smirks the entire time. Eventually, I have to respond. "We talk."

Her brows go up. "On the phone?"

"Yeah. Or FaceTime," I admit.

"Oh. Now we're getting to the juicy parts." She leans forward, setting her fork down. "You're holding out on me. Have you met him outside of the club?"

I shake my head. "No."

"But he's asked you to and you've turned him down. Am I right?"

I squirm a bit on my chair. "What is this? An inquisition?"

She laughs. "I know I'm right. So he's an incredibly patient man who's willing to wait you out. You better not make him wait too long. Eventually, he'll give up."

She's right. I've thought of this several times. It makes me nervous because I really like him. I wish there was a way to freeze things exactly as they are now. A world in which I meet up with the perfect Dom at Surrender two nights a week, fulfill my impact-play kink, receive a fantastic orgasm, and go about my life as usual.

Committing to more than that makes my palms sweat. Eve should know this better than anyone. Until she started seeing Colton, she didn't take her kink out of the club.

Well, that isn't entirely true, I remind myself. She did take her kink home. She lived as a little at home all the time, but she didn't take a Dom or Daddy to her apartment.

What would I do if Craig decided to give up on me? It would definitely hurt, but I have to expect one day soon he'll find a little at the club who enjoys submitting to him as a Daddy. That will be the end of our relationship.

By the time lunch is over, I feel depressed.

ALSO BY BECCA JAMESON

Surrender:

Raising Lucy

Teaching Abby

Leaving Roman

Choosing Kellen

Pleasing Josie

Honoring Hudson

Nurturing Britney

Charming Colton

Convincing Leah

Surrender Box Set One

Surrender Box Set Two

Open Skies:

Layover

Redeye

Nonstop

Standby

Takeoff

Jetway

Open Skies Box Set One

Shadow SEALs:

Shadow in the Desert

Delta Team Three (Special Forces: Operation Alpha):

Destiny's Delta

Canyon Springs:

Caleb's Mate

Hunter's Mate

Corked and Tapped:

Volume One: Friday Night

Volume Two: Company Party

Volume Three: The Holidays

Project DEEP:

Reviving Emily

Reviving Trish

Reviving Dade

Reviving Zeke

Reviving Graham

Reviving Bianca

Reviving Olivia

Project DEEP Box Set One

Project DEEP Box Set Two

SEALs in Paradise:

Hot SEAL, Red Wine

Hot SEAL, Australian Nights

Hot SEAL, Cold Feet

Hot SEAL, April's Fool

Dark Falls:

Dark Nightmares

Club Zodiac:

Training Sasha

Obeying Rowen

Collaring Brooke

Mastering Rayne

Trusting Aaron

Claiming London

Sharing Charlotte

Taming Rex

Tempting Elizabeth

Club Zodiac Box Set One

Club Zodiac Box Set Two

Club Zodiac Box Set Three

The Art of Kink:

Pose

Paint

Sculpt

Arcadian Bears:

Grizzly Mountain

Grizzly Beginning

Grizzly Secret

Grizzly Promise

Grizzly Survival

Grizzly Perfection

Arcadian Bears Box Set One

Arcadian Bears Box Set Two

Sleeper SEALs:

Saving Zola

Spring Training:

Catching Zia

Catching Lily

Catching Ava

Spring Training Box Set

The Underground series:

Force

Clinch

Guard

Submit

Thrust

Torque

The Underground Box Set One

The Underground Box Set Two

Saving Sofia (Special Forces: Operations Alpha)

Wolf Masters series:

Kara's Wolves

Lindsey's Wolves

Jessica's Wolves

Alyssa's Wolves

Tessa's Wolf

Rebecca's Wolves

Melinda's Wolves

Laurie's Wolves

Amanda's Wolves

Sharon's Wolves

Wolf Masters Box Set One

Wolf Masters Box Set Two

Claiming Her series:

The Rules

The Game

The Prize

Claiming Her Box Set

Emergence series:

Bound to be Taken

Bound to be Tamed

Bound to be Tested

Bound to be Tempted

Emergence Box Set

The Fight Club series:

Come

Perv

Need

Hers

Want

Lust

The Fight Club Box Set One

The Fight Club Box Set Two

Wolf Gatherings series:

Tarnished

Dominated

Completed

Redeemed

Abandoned

Betrayed

Wolf Gatherings Box Set One

Wolf Gathering Box Set Two

Durham Wolves series:

Rescue in the Smokies

Fire in the Smokies

Freedom in the Smokies

Durham Wolves Box Set

Stand Alone Books:

Blind with Love

Guarding the Truth

Out of the Smoke

Abducting His Mate

Three's a Cruise

Wolf Trinity

Frostbitten

A Princess for Cale/A Princess for Cain

ABOUT THE AUTHOR

Becca Jameson is a USA Today best-selling author of over 100 books. She is well-known for her Wolf Masters series, her Fight Club series, and her Club Zodiac series. She currently lives in Houston, Texas, with her husband and her Goldendoodle. Two grown kids pop in every once in a while too! She is loving this journey and has dabbled in a variety of genres, including paranormal, sports romance, military, and BDSM.

A total night owl, Becca writes late at night, sequestering herself in her office with a glass of red wine and a bar of dark chocolate, her fingers flying across the keyboard as her characters weave their own stories.

During the day--which never starts before ten in the morning!--she can be found jogging, running errands, or reading in her favorite hammock chair!

...where Alphas dominate...

Becca's Newsletter Sign-up

Join my Facebook fan group, Becca's Bibliomaniacs, for the most up-to-date information, random excerpts while I work, giveaways, and fun release parties!

Facebook Fan Group:
Becca's Bibliomaniacs

Contact Becca:
www.beccajameson.com
beccajameson4@aol.com

facebook.com/becca.jameson.18
twitter.com/beccajameson
instagram.com/becca.jameson
bookbub.com/authors/becca-jameson
goodreads.com/beccajameson
amazon.com/author/beccajameson

Printed in Great Britain
by Amazon